Zoo

Danasha

Birts

✓ **W9-BYL-111**

THE CARTEL

THE CARTEL

Ashley & JaQuavis

Urban Books
1199 Straight Path
West Babylon, NY 11704

The Cartel ©copyright 2009 Ashley & JaQuavis

All rights reserved. No part of this book may be reproduced in any form or by any means without prior consent of the Publisher, excepting brief quotes used in reviews.

ISBN: 978-1-60751-738-2

Printed in the United States of America

This is a work of fiction. Any references or similarities to actual events, real people, living, or dead, or to real locales are intended to give the novel a sense of reality. Any similarity in other names, characters, places, and incidents is entirely coincidental.

THE CARTEL

Prologue

"Diamonds are forever."

—Carter Diamond

The packed courtroom was abuzz as the anticipation built, and the onlookers stared at the man who made it snow. Carter Diamond was the head of "The Cartel," an infamous crime organization, and the entire city of Miami knew it. Scattered throughout the courtroom, the entire Cartel was in attendance, all of them wearing black attire.

With a model's posture, he sat next to his defense lawyer, slowly rubbing his salt-and-pepper goatee, thinking about the weight of the verdict. Accused of racketeering and using his multimillion-dollar real estate company to launder drug money, Carter could potentially go to jail for the rest of his life. And the case had drawn a lot of heat when key witnesses began to come up missing or dead, including a politician who turned informant to save his own behind.

A slight grin spread across Carter's face as he looked at the judge and realized that the chances of a guilty verdict were between slim and next to none. Just the night before, his accountant had wired the judge one million dollars to an offshore account. And just to ensure his freedom, eight of the twelve jurors had family members missing and in the custody of Carter's henchmen. At 43 years old he was on top of the world. Fuck the mayor, Carter ran the city.

Carter glanced back at his family, his beautiful wife, daughter, and twin sons, who sat in the front row behind him. He winked at them and gave them his perfect smile.

It amazed Carter's family that he could be in the scariest of situations and still manage to make everything seem all right.

He stared into his wife's green eyes and admired her long, flowing, jet-black hair. Baby hair rested perfectly on her edges as her natural mocha skin glowed. Taryn, his wife, was a full-blooded Dominican and could have easily been mistaken for a top model. At age 38, she was just as beautiful as when she'd met Carter at 16.

Carter then glanced over to his daughter, Breeze, the spitting image of her mother and also his baby girl. At age 19, she was beautiful, intelligent, and being mixed with Black and Dominican gave her a goddess look. She had long, thick hair with green eyes, which made her every man's desire and every woman's envy. She smiled at her father, letting him know she was there to support him.

Carter looked at his two sons, Mecca and Monroe, AKA Money. They were the two oldest at 21, and although they were twins, they were completely opposite. Mecca was the wilder of the two. He wore long braids and was a shade darker than Money. His body had twenty tattoos on it, including the two on his neck, enhancing his thuggish appearance. He was the more ruthless one. Mecca, wanting so badly to follow in the footsteps of his father and become the next kingpin of Miami, was notorious throughout Dade County for his trigger-happy ways.

Money was the humbler and more reserved of the two.

His Dominican features seemed to shine through more than his twin brother's. His light skin and curly hair made him look more like a pretty boy than a gangster, but his looks were deceiving. Unlike his brother, he wore a neat low-cut and had no tattoos. Focusing more on the money aspect of the game, Money was a born hustler, and if the streets gave out degrees he would've had a doctorate. And although he wasn't as coldhearted as his brother, he wasn't to be underestimated.

It was in their blood to be gangsters. In the early eighties their Dominican grandfather ran the most lucrative drug cartel Miami had ever seen, and their father was his predecessor. Their family was "street royalty" by all means.

The media had a field day with this trial, covering it since day one. And CNN news cameras and several other stations had been broadcasting live footage of the spectacle for the last six months.

The sound of the gavel striking the sounding block echoed throughout the packed courtroom when the jurors filed into the courtroom after two hours of deliberation. The time had finally come for the verdict.

"Order in the court!" The judge looked over to the jury pool. "Has the jury come to a verdict?"

All eyes were on the juror as he paused before delivering the verdict, and all of the news cameras were pointed to Carter, trying to capture his reaction to his fate. The courtroom got so silent, you could hear a pin drop.

The head juror stood up with a small piece of paper in his hand. "Yes, Your Honor, we have. We the jury find Carter Diamond not guilty on all charges."

As the courtroom erupted with a mixture of victorious cheers and disappointing sighs, Carter nonchalantly loosened his tie and winked at the judge just before he firmly shook his lawyer's hand.

"Congratulations, Carter," the lawyer said as he gathered his files and placed them into his briefcase, the flashes from the cameras flickering nonstop.

"Thank you." Carter turned around to celebrate with his family.

When Taryn ran to him with open arms, he smoothly spun her around and kissed her passionately as if they were the only two in the room. He looked in her eyes and whispered, "I love you."

"I love you too, Carter Diamond," she replied as she hung from his neck.

Carter focused his attention on his kids. He kissed Breeze on the cheek, and she whispered in his ear, "Diamonds are forever."

"That's right, baby girl." Carter embraced her with one hand and grabbed Mecca's head with the other. He kissed him on top of the head and then did the same to Monroe.

Carter looked at all the reporters and photographers flocking in his direction and said, "Let's get out of here." With his wife and daughter under his arms, and his family around him, he made his way out of the courtroom.

News reporters tried to get a comment from him, but members of The Cartel stopped them before they could get close.

As soon as Carter exited the building, he embraced his right-hand man, Archie Pollard, AKA Polo, who was waiting outside of the courtroom, along with a wave of thugs wearing all black.

Polo leaned close to Carter's ear and whispered, "We did it, baby!"

"No doubt," Carter said. "This city is mine."

Carter stood at the top of the steps, feeling on top of the world. He pulled out a Cuban cigar and lit it, his diamond cufflinks blinging as he gave the world a view of his exclusive accessories. Looking out onto the streets, he noticed that the cops had sealed off the area to maintain traffic control. Everyone in the city was trying to get a glimpse of the "king of Miami."

Money noticed something wasn't right. As he looked at each officer and saw that they all had one thing in common. They all seemed to be of Haitian descent. By the time he realized what was happening, it was too late. One of the fake news reporters pulled out his 9 mm and pointed it at Breeze.

"Noooo!" Money screamed as he tried to warn his sister.

Polo became aware of what was about to happen and shoved the Haitian, causing him to tumble down the stairs before he could let off a shot.

All of a sudden, two dreadlocked Haitians popped out of the oversized dumpster, both with AR-15 assault rifles, and began letting off shots at The Cartel. It was complete pandemonium as shots rang out, hitting innocent bystanders, all in an effort to take out Carter Diamond.

Outnumbered, the members of The Cartel were defenseless. And Carter and his family were moving targets. As everyone scrambled for cover, Carter grabbed his daughter and wife and threw them to the ground, shielding them with his body.

A bullet ripped through Money's arm, and he fell to the ground. Mecca ran to his side, trying to protect his twin brother.

Meanwhile, Polo had pulled out his 9 mm and began to return fire. He had managed to keep the Haitians off long enough for the rest of The Cartel to come and help.

As the two crews traded bullets, many people got caught in the crossfire. The scene was a total bloodbath, with dead bodies sprawled out across the steps of the courthouse.

Carter, totally disregarding his own safety, tried his

best to cover his two favorite girls from the raining bullets.

The police officer who had escorted Carter out of the courtroom shot at the Haitians. "Come on! Follow me," he yelled. He looked at Carter and waved his hand, signaling them to follow him.

Carter hated police, but at that moment he was happy to see one. He gathered up Taryn and Breeze and followed the officer back into the courthouse.

"I parked my police car in the back. Come on! They'll be coming in here after you any second now," the cop said as he closed the courthouse door.

"Let's go, y'all," Carter yelled in a panicked voice to his wife and daughter as they followed the policeman down the stairs and into the basement.

Carter thought about his sons outside, but he knew they could hold their own. His main concern was the women. They raced through the court halls and finally made it to the exit. Just as the cop said, he had his squad car parked in the back. Carter felt relieved. They all got in, and he frantically searched his wife's and daughter's body, making sure they were okay. "Are you hit? Are you guys okay?" he asked as he continued to search their blood-stained clothes. He realized that the blood was not from them, but from all the blood flying from the other people.

"No, I'm good, Poppa," Breeze answered, tears flowing down her face, her hands shaking uncontrollably.

"I'm okay," Taryn said.

Carter hugged and kissed them both and thanked God that they were okay. His concern now was for his sons. He looked up at the cop that sat in the front seat and said, "Thanks, bruh. Look, I need you to take them to safety while I go back and—"

Boom!

Before Carter could finish his sentence, the cop put a hollow-tip through his head, his blood and brains instantly splattering all over his wife's and daughter's face as he stared with dead eyes.

In total shock, both of the women yelled, "Noooo!"

The cop pulled off his hat, and his short dreadlocks fell loosely. He pointed the gun at Carter's body and filled him with four more bullets, ensuring that the job was done. The screams of the women didn't seem to bother him as he smiled through the whole process. The man wasn't a cop at all, but a full-blooded Haitian that could pass for a regular joe, his light skin disguising his heritage.

He pointed his gun at Taryn, and she looked directly in his eyes, unafraid of death, while Breeze gripped her father and cried hysterically. The Haitian couldn't bring himself to pull the trigger and hopped out the car.

This was the beginning of a war.

Welcome to The Cartel . . . first of a trilogy

Chapter One

"Girl, females are going to hate, regardless. That's how you know you're *that* bitch."

—Taryn Diamond

Seven Years Earlier

Carter sat at the head of the table with both of his hands folded into each other. He briefly stared at each of his ten head henchmen in the face as he looked around the table, then to his right-hand man Polo, who sat to his right. As he always did, Carter took his time before speaking. He always chose his words carefully and spoke very slowly with his deep baritone voice. He poured Dom into his oversized wine cup and took a sip.

"Family, today The Cartel has expanded. The days of hand-over-fist pay is over. It's a new day, a new world, a new era. For the last ten years I have flooded the streets of Miami with the finest coke and built a monopoly. I love all of you as if you were my own blood. That's why I'm giving you the opportunity to grow. You can't hustle forever. I've recently acquired a real estate company, and this way we can turn all of this dirty money into clean money. I want all my niggas to eat with me. So, if you want to be a part of this, here is your chance." Carter took another sip and passed the cup to Polo.

Without saying a word, Polo took a sip out of the same cup, signaling his response to Carter's proposition. He passed the cup to the next man, and he did the same. Real niggas did real things, and the cup got passed around the room, and all men drank from the same cup.

Mecca and Money peeked around the corner, listening in on their father's meeting. Although they were only fourteen, they wanted so bad to be a part of The Cartel. They both noticed at an early age how much respect their father received from everyone in the streets. They would get special treatment in school from teachers and students. Some of their friends' parents would go as far as giving them presents and hinting to them to mention it to their father. They loved how real their father was. He would talk to bums on the street as if they were the president of the U.S.A. He treated every man as his equal, as long as they respected him and his family. For lack of better words, Carter was a real nigga, and both of the twins admired him greatly and wanted to be just like him . . . but for different reasons.

Monroe loved the way his father stayed fresh at all times and was a great business and family man. He observed his father's style and immediately idolized him. Carter never wore the same shirt twice and only wore the finest threads. Money also took note of and admired his father's business savvy. Every move he made was a business move, a move that would benefit him in the future.

Mecca, on the other hand, admired his father's street fame. He loved the way the street respected and feared his father. He would hear stories about his father being the man that made it snow, in a city that had never seen a winter season, or cutting off fingers if workers stole. In Mecca's eyes, Scarface didn't have shit on his father.

While other kids were worried about candy and chasing skirts, Mecca was thinking about chasing money and being the next king of Miami.

As they eavesdropped on the conference, they watched as each man took a sip out of the cup.

"Mecca and Money, come in here." Carter calmly grabbed the cup that had rotated back to him.

Since Carter's back was toward them, when he called there name, it surprised them. It was as if he had eyes in the back of his head. They slowly walked into the room. The boys stood nervously next to him, knowing that they got caught spying on him and that their father was very strict when it came to handling business. They eased up when they saw a slight grin form on his face.

Carter passed Money the cup and looked around to make sure their mother wasn't around. "Take a sip of that," he said.

Money looked at the cup as if he was scared to take a sip.

Mecca noticed his brother's uneasiness and grabbed the cup from him. He took a gigantic gulp of the liquor, and a burning sensation rushed down his throat. It took all of his willpower not to spit it out. His face twisted up as he put one hand on his chest, hoping that the burn would go away.

Polo noticed his expression and laughed loudly. "That'll put some hair on ya chest, nephew!" he said in between laughs.

Carter joined him in laughter as he watched his other son take the cup and take a moderate sip. Money's face didn't change its expression. He took the gulp like a man.

Money handed the cup back to his father and stood there with his chest out, as if he was trying to prove that he was a man. Mecca followed suit.

"Why were you two eavesdropping on Poppa?" Carter playfully hit both of his sons in the chest.

Money shrugged his shoulders as if to say, "I don't know."

Mecca looked around the table, seeing nothing but hustlers and killers. He then looked at his father, who sat at the forefront of them, and a smile spread across his face. "Poppa, I want to be just like you. I wanna be a gangster," Mecca said as he stepped in front of his brother.

One of the hustlers at the table chuckled as he looked at Mecca. "Li'l man got hustle in him. That's a gangster in the making right there," the man said.

Carter shot a look at the man that said a thousand words. If looks could kill, the man would've been circled in chalk. "No, my son will never be that. Watch ya mouth, fam," Carter stated firmly as he focused his attention back on Mecca. "Look, sons, you are better than this. This game chose us, we didn't choose the game. You got the game twisted. I do this, so you don't have to," Carter said, as a somber feeling came over him. It hurt his heart to hear Mecca say that he wanted to be a gangster like him.

"Let me show you two something," Carter said before he looked at his henchmen that sat at the long red oak table. "How many of you have lost someone close to you because of this drug game?

Slowly everyone at the table raised their hands, to help Carter prove a point.

"How many of you go to bed with a pistol under your pillow?" Carter asked. "And how many of you want to get out of the game?"

Mecca and Money looked at everyone in the room holding up their hands, and Carter's point was proven.

"Do you two understand, this game . . . is not a game?"

Mecca and Money nodded their heads, understanding

the lesson that their father had just sprinkled them with.

"Take another sip of this and head to bed." Carter smiled and handed Money the cup. After the boys took a small sip of the drink, he grabbed both of their heads at the same time and kissed them on top of it. "Don't tell your mother," he whispered to them just before they exited the conference room.

Although Carter had explained to them the cons of the street life, the allure of the game was too powerful, and Mecca and Money wanted in. They just had to wait their turn.

Breeze stood at her balcony, totally astounded by the view, and stared into the stars. Her balcony hovered over their small lake and faced their gigantic backyard. The Diamond residence was immaculate. They had just moved there, and it was a big jump from the dilapidated projects of Dade County. Breeze's 12-year-old eyes were lost in the stars as her mother stood behind her and brushed her long hair. This was a ritual they did every night, and Taryn used this time to bond with her daughter.

"Breeze, what's wrong, baby? Lately you haven't been saying much," Taryn said as she continued to stroke her daughter's hair.

Breeze took her time before she spoke. Her father had taught her to always think about what to say before saying it. "I just miss back home. I don't like it out here. None of my friends are out here. I hate it in South Beach, Mommy." Breeze's eyes got teary.

"I know it's hard to cope with the sudden change, Breeze, but your father is a very important man, and it wasn't safe for us to stay in Dade. He did what was best for the family," Taryn answered, knowing exactly how Breeze felt. She herself had been a daughter of a kingpin, so she knew what it was like to be sheltered because of a father's notoriety.

"I just don't get it. Everybody loved Poppa in the old neighborhood. Why would we have to move?"

When it came to his baby girl, Carter held back nothing. He answered any question she asked him truthfully, wanting to give her the game, so another boy couldn't game her. She knew her father was a drug dealer, but in her eyes he was the greatest man to walk the earth. She saw how he treated her mother with respect at all times. She witnessed him put his family before himself countless times and admired that. She wanted her husband to be just like her daddy.

"I know exactly how you feel. You're too young to understand right now, Breeze. Just be grateful that you have all of this. Most women will go through their whole life and never have the things you already have."

I understand. I know what's going on. I know Daddy is the dopeman. I know more than you think I know. Breeze went into her room and flopped down on her canopy-style bed. Tears rolled down her cheek as she curled up on her pillow. She missed her old home so badly. She just wanted to be a regular around-the-way girl.

Taryn, her white silk Dolce and Gabbana nightgown dragging on the floor as she went to her daughter's side, slowly entered the room and saw that the sudden change really was bothering her only daughter. She sat on the bed and began to rub Breeze's back. "I know exactly how you feel, Breeze. My father too was an important man. I remember when I was your age and was going through the same dilemma. My father, your grandfather, was an important man also. I had it much worse. It took the murder of your uncle for my father to move out the hood. Your father is just being cautious. If anything ever happened to you or your brothers, our hearts would break. He's just protecting you." Taryn reminisced about her deceased brother, who died when she was only ten. He was only 15 years old when he was kidnapped and killed while her father was in a drug war.

"I know that we have to live like this, but it's just not fair. I feel like I don't belong here. All the girls at school look at me funny because I'm mixed, and they whisper bad things about me. I try to ignore them, but it still hurts my feelings."

"Girl, females are going to hate, regardless. That's how you know you're *that* bitch." Taryn smiled and squinted her nose.

Breeze couldn't help smiling at her mother's comment. She looked at how beautiful her mother was, and her comment made her look at things differently. *Maybe they do look at me enviously*, she thought.

Before Breeze could say anything in response, Carter cleared his throat, startling them. He looked at how gorgeous the two main women in his life were. He suavely leaned against the doorway with his arms folded. "What are you guys smiling at?" He walked toward them.

"Nothing, baby." Taryn smiled and winked at Breeze. "Just girl stuff."

Carter bent over and kissed Taryn and then kissed Breeze on top of the head.

Taryn knew that Carter had come to tuck Breeze in, as he did every night, and decided to leave them alone. "I'll be in bed," she whispered to him. "Goodnight, baby," she said to Breeze as she tapped her leg. "I love you."

"I love you too, Mommy."

Taryn strolled out of the room, her stilettos clicking against the marble floor as she made her way out. Taryn would never get caught without her heels on. Nightgown and all, she always looked the part, playing her role as the queen of her husband's empire. She was wifey, there was no doubt about that.

Carter stared at his wife as she walked away and then turned his attention back to Breeze. "Hey, baby girl." He sat next to her.

"Hey, Poppa." Breeze sat up and focused on her father.

"How was school today?" Carter asked as he rubbed her hair.

"It was okay, I guess."

"Breeze, you know I know when you're lying. Tell Poppa what's going on."

"I just miss my friends. The people at my school are so funny-acting. I wish we could move back home." Breeze dropped her head.

Carter placed his finger under her chin and slowly raised her head. He looked into his daughter's green eyes and smiled. "Baby girl, don't worry about that. Everything takes time. They will come around eventually. I tell you what"—Carter stood up and smoothly put his hands in his $400 Armani slacks—"Why don't you call up some of your friends and tell them you're having a sleepover. You can invite as many of them as you want. I'll have a limo pick up each girl. Would you like that?"

Breeze eyes lit up, and she gave him the biggest smile ever. "Yes! Thank you, Poppa," she said as she leapt into her arms.

Carter had promised himself that he wouldn't let outsiders enter his new home, but he had a weak spot for Breeze. She was his only daughter, and he spoiled her more than he did his twin boys.

"What about boys?" Breeze looked at her father. "Can I invite them too?"

His smile quickly turned into a frown as he looked at Breeze like she was insane.

"Gotcha!" she said as she broke out into laughter.

"Baby, don't do that," he said, joining her in laughter. "You almost gave this old man a heart attack." Although Breeze was joking around, he knew that the day when she would be serious was soon to come. A day that he would dread.

Chapter Two

"There is strength in numbers, and we will get
through this as a family."

—Polo

Polo took a deep breath as he pulled into the South
Beach, one of the many suburbs of Miami. As he
looked around at the perfectly landscaped lawns and the
children playing carelessly in the streets, he realized why
Carter had moved his family so far away from the hood.
With its gated community and million-dollar structures, it
seemed as if it were a million miles away from the grit of
the ghetto. Carter, positive that the upscale environment
of South Beach would protect his household from the
harsh reality that the street life had to offer, had told him
that the move would be good for his family, but he was
wrong. Now Polo was forced to bury his man.

Polo and Carter had known each other since they were
young and hardheaded coming up in the trenches of Dade
County. They quickly formed a brotherly bond as they
took over the streets and inevitably entered the drug
game. *The Cartel* was what they were labeled, a notorious, criminal-minded organization that was willing to stay
on top by any means necessary. Carter and Polo had put
in work for many years and worked hard to surround

themselves with thoroughbreds that respected the hustle of the streets as much as they did. They earned money, power, and respect.

That is, until the Haitians from Little Haiti discovered the money that was being made and tried to muscle them out of town.

Carter's demise proved to Polo that the Haitians weren't to be taken lightly. He just hated that it took the death of their leader to figure that out. Nobody was untouchable. Now he had a nagging pain in his heart, and the stress of retaliation on his brain, but he knew that his hurt didn't compare to that of Carter's family.

When he pulled into the driveway to the ten-room, 7,000-square-foot home, he prepared himself for the heartache that he was about to encounter. Polo personally made sure that Carter's wife and children were taken care of. He knew that they would be okay financially, but he was determined to ensure their safety. No expense was spared when it came to the security of their family. There were about ten armed henchmen stationed outside of the house, and he acknowledged them with a nod as he passed by and walked into the Diamond home.

"Unc Po." Mecca slapped hands with his father's best friend.

Polo could tell that Carter's death was weighing heavily on his heart by the sad look in Mecca's eyes. Polo then turned to Monroe and pulled him near as well. He held them close, his arms wrapped around their shoulders. All three men had their heads down.

Polo told them, "I know it doesn't feel like it right now, but it's gon' be all right, you hear me?"

Tears formed in Money's eyes. He nodded his head, praying that his Uncle Polo was right.

Polo whispered in their ears, "You both have to be strong for your mother and Breeze. This is gon' hit them the hardest. You know how protective your father was of them. It's time to step up to the plate, twins. You got to pull your family back together."

Both boys nodded in agreement as they quickly wiped the tears from the eyes. Having been trained by their father to never show emotion, they knew that to cry was to show weakness,

"Where are your mother and sister?"

"They're still upstairs," Money stated.

Polo ascended the steps two at a time. He approached the bodyguard that he had hired to stand by Taryn's side. "Fuck you doing?" he whispered harshly.

The bodyguard quickly snapped his cell phone shut, but before he could put it safely in his pocket, Polo slapped it out of his hands.

"Do I fucking pay you to talk on your cell phone?" Polo pointed his finger in the man's face. It didn't matter that he was only 5-8, and that the bodyguard was 270 lbs of pure muscle. "How the fuck you supposed to protect anybody when you're focused on your fuckin' phone? As a matter of fact, get your ass out of here. Put somebody on this job that want to make this money, you pussy!"

The man didn't even protest as Polo lifted his Steve Madden and kicked him in the ass toward the staircase. He looked over the landing and yelled, "Mecca, show that mu'fucka the door and bring one of them niggas up that take this shit seriously." Polo fixed his clothes and wiped himself down before he knocked lightly on Taryn's door.

"Come in," she called out. "It's open."

Taryn looked as beautiful as ever standing in front of the full-length mirror in her white-on-white Dolce suit that fit nicely around her slim frame, the skirt stopping directly below her knee and hugging her womanly shape. Her neck was framed with rare black pearls that matched the pearl set that clung to her ears. Her long, layered hair was pulled back into a sophisticated bun. She spared herself of applying makeup because she knew that eventually her tears would ruin it anyway. Her natural beauty was enough to take Ms. America's crown, and her Dominican features made her look more like a mature model than a mother of three.

"Taryn, it's time to go," Polo stated as he stood in her doorway.

She nodded her head and closed her eyes as she said a silent prayer to God. *Please give me the strength to get through this for my children. They are all that I have left. Take my husband into grace and take care of him until we meet again.* "Okay, let's go," she said, trying to hide the shakiness in her voice.

She walked out of the room and down the hallway to her daughter's room. "Breeze," she said as she opened the door. "It's time."

"I don't think that I can do this," Breeze stated, tears running down her cheeks. It was obvious that she had been crying for hours, because her eyes were red and swollen. The distress from her father's murder was written all over her young face. It was almost as if her legs gave out from underneath her, because she fell onto the bed and put her head in her hands.

Taryn and Polo rushed to her side. Polo knew that Breeze would take her father's death the hardest. His only daughter, she was his pride and joy, and he had treated her like a princess since the day she was born. Breeze could do no wrong in his eyes, and they had shared a special connection all her life.

"I can't believe he's gone," Breeze stated. She felt as if the life was being squeezed out of her. "I can't do this, Uncle Po." She dreaded putting her father to rest. Never in her nineteen years had she felt a pain so great.

Taryn embraced her daughter as they sat side by side,

cheek to cheek. "I know that you can't do this, but *we* can," she stated. "There is strength in numbers, and we will get through this as a family."

Polo was speechless as Taryn's words moved him. It was then that he realized that Carter was truly a lucky man to have a woman such as her by his side. He left the room and descended the steps. He waited in the foyer with Mecca and Monroe, and when the two women came down the steps, they all walked out of the house together.

The limo ride was silent as each member of the family tried to wrap their minds around the death of their patriarch. He was the one who protected them, fed them, clothed them, loved them, made all of their decisions. He was their educator and best friend, so without him, they all felt lost.

Dear Carter,

I know that you do not know me, but I know you very well. You are my husband's son. I have thought about you countless times. If you are anything like your father, I can picture your dark chocolate skin, strong jawbone, and wide, soul-searching eyes. I wish that I could have written you under better circumstances, but I am not contacting you to deliver good news. My husband, your father, has left this earth. He was killed, and although you do not know him, I wanted to give you the chance to say your goodbyes. His funeral will be held Saturday June 3, 2008. I hope that you will join us in celebrating his life. Everyone is expected to dress in white attire. He would not want us to mourn his death, but to come together as a family and appreciate his life. I know that is how he would have wanted to go out.

Sincerely,
Taryn Diamond

Carter folded the letter up and put it in the pocket of his Armani suit jacket. He had received the letter a week ago and was debating whether or not he should actually go to his father's funeral. He had never known his father, never even heard his voice.

Why am I here? he thought in confusion as he looked at his reflection in the mirror. His designer suit was tailored specifically to his six-foot frame, and his broad, strong shoulders held the material nicely. A small gold chain hung around his neck, displaying a small gold cross.

Checking his watch, he realized that he didn't have much time to get to the church. He reached underneath the hotel bed and pulled out a duffle bag that contained pure white cocaine and two handguns. He figured he may as well drop off some dope to some of his people in Atlanta while in the Dirty South. That way, if the funeral ended up being a waste of time, he wouldn't have wasted time and money coming to town.

He pulled out his chrome .45 and tucked it in his waist. He rubbed the waves on his freshly cut Caesar and took a deep breath. He had to prepare himself for what he was about to do. He had felt resentment toward his father ever since he was a young boy. He had never understood why he had grown up never knowing the man that helped create him. Although he harbored these feelings, he still felt obligated to show his respects.

A nervous energy filled his body as he headed for the door. It was time for him to say goodbye to a man he'd never met.

As the bulletproof limousine pulled up to the church, Carter's henchmen walked up and surrounded the vehicle.

"Leave your guns in the car," Polo instructed Money and Mecca. He opened the door and prepared to step out.

Mecca told him, "The heater staying on my hip, Unc. Them dreadhead mu'fuckas deaded my father. I'll be damned if they do the same thing to me." He popped the clip into the chamber.

"First, I'm-a tell you to respect your mother, and watch your mu'fuckin' mouth, Mecca."

"Nah, Mecca's right, Uncle Po," Money said. "We need to be strapped at all times."

Polo put his foot back into the car and closed the door so that their conversation wouldn't be heard. "Okay, listen"—He looked around at the shaken Diamond family— "I know this is hard for you, but you have to trust me. Your father was like a brother to me. I love this family as if it is my own. I would never let anything happen to anyone of you. Now I promised the pastor that I wouldn't bring any weapons into his church. Your father's funeral is neither the time nor place for them. Everyone inside of that church is here to show love."

Mecca and Money reluctantly pulled their guns out of their pants and sat them on the seat in the limo.

"Everything will be fine," Polo assured them. He stepped out of the car first and held out his hand for Taryn, who graciously accepted. He put his hand on the small of her back and led her through the crowd of onlookers, and her children followed closely behind. They were all surrounded by so many bodyguards, one would have thought that Barack Obama was entering the building.

White on top of white was the only thing that could be seen when entering the sanctuary. Everyone attending the funeral was clad in their best white suits, and there were white bouquets of lilies and hydrangea flowers scattered throughout the room. The turnout was unbelievable.

Taryn immediately halted her footsteps when she saw

the titanium and black casket that sat at the front of the church. She looked around the room and observed the extravagant funeral that she had put together, making sure to take care of each arrangement personally. No one knew her husband the way that she did, and she wanted to make sure that his funeral was comparable to none. Carter Diamond was the best at everything he ever attempted, so Taryn made sure that he went out in style.

She slowly walked down the aisle. The closer she got to her husband's casket, the weaker her knees became, but she had to be strong. She couldn't let the world see her break. *My children are depending on me,* she thought.

When she finally reached the casket, her heart broke into pieces at the sight of her lifeless soul mate lying before her. She reached down, grabbed his hand, and kissed his cheek. She whispered, "I will always love you, Carter, always." She then turned with the poise of royalty and took her position on the front pew as the first lady of the streets.

Mecca's heart beat wildly in his chest. He had never imagined what he would do if something ever happened to his father. He prided himself on being strong and fearless, but there was no way that he could be strong now. And the sudden loss of Carter made him fear death.

He stepped down the aisle and gripped the sides of his father's casket when he saw his ashen face. The glow that his dark skin had once possessed was gone, and his eyes were sunk in. He felt the swell of water in his eyes cloud his vision. He closed his eyes to hinder them from falling. He picked the tiny cross necklace off his chest and kissed it. It was the chain that Carter had given all of his children the day that he'd brought them home from the hospital, 14-kt. gold crosses to hang around their necks. The chain had been changed over the years, but the cross was still the original. The children all valued their chains with their lives. Mecca walked over to his mother and sat beside her, trying to keep his emotions at bay.

Monroe stepped toward the casket next. He thought of all the times his father had spent with him. He knew that he needed to absorb all of Carter that he could, because this was the last time that he would ever see him again. He gripped his father's hand and leaned in close to his ear, as if he could still hear him, and said, "Thank you for everything, Poppa. I'll remember everything that you taught me. I'll never forget you." With those words, Money joined his brother and mother.

Breeze graced the church aisle as if it were a runway. All eyes were on her as she paused midstep. She knew that her life had been changed forever. Her Poppa, comparable to none, was the man of her dreams, and she didn't want to let him go. She stepped up to the casket as she fought to keep her pain under control. But as soon as she touched his cold skin, she lost it. Against her will, a small cry escaped her lips, and a fountain of tears cascaded down her precious face. She leaned over her father, gripping his hand, and silently prayed for God to take care of his soul. The sight of her so broken-down caused the attendees to break down as well. Her collapse signaled the collapse of the entire church, and wailing could be heard throughout.

Mecca went to her side, to get her to let go of Carter's hand. "Come on, *B*." He gently rubbed her hair and lifted her head. "Don't hold your head down. Poppa wouldn't have that." He smiled at her gorgeous face, and she gave him a weak nod of agreement as she finally left her father's casket and sat with the rest of her family.

Just as the pastor took his place at the podium, the church doors clanged open. Gasps rang out throughout the church as all eyes focused on the young man who stood in the doorway. Speculative whispers traveled throughout the pews as everyone watched the young man walk down the aisle. From his skin tone, to his confident stride and striking features, he was identical to the man they were there to bury, and one would be able to guess without reading the tattooed name on his neck that he was Carter Diamond's son. It was almost unnatural the resemblance that the two shared.

Mecca's eyes followed the man as he approached the front of the church. "Fuck is that?" he hissed.

"The nigga looks just like Poppa," Money commented in amazement.

"Mommy?" Breeze looked at her mother.

But Taryn needed no explanation. She knew exactly who the young man was. He was Carter Jones, her husband's illegitimate son.

Polo leaned into her and whispered, "Taryn, I have something to tell you. Carter didn't mean to—"

Without taking her eyes off the young man, she said, "Don't worry about it, Polo. No need for you to explain. I know who he is."

Carter felt the questioning glares of the people surrounding him. He stopped in the middle of the church and stared at the casket up front. His heartbeat was so rapid that he felt sick to his stomach. *I shouldn't be here,* he thought.

Just as he turned to leave, four men with long dreadlocks entered the room. They were the only ones wearing black. Carter frowned at their blatant disrespect. They bumped him violently as they walked past, but Carter let it ride as he turned his head and watched them continue down the aisle.

Mecca's temper immediately flared. He reached in his waistline for a pistol that wasn't there. "Fuck!" he whispered as he began to stand.

Polo grabbed his arm to halt him. "Wait a minute," he stated. "This is a part of the game." Polo didn't expect the Haitians to make their presence felt at the funeral. He had underestimated their coldness.

The church was silent as everyone waited to see how things would play out. It was no secret that the Haitians were responsible for Carter's death. The dreadheads walked up to the casket and stood silently with their heads down, as if they were in prayer.

Taryn gripped her sons' hands and let out a sigh of relief.

"See," Polo said, "they're only here to represent the Haitians. They're just showing respect for the deceased. We gon' handle that, just not here."

Before the words could reach Taryn's ears, she was in an uproar as she watched the Haitians hawk up huge gobs of spit and release them on her husband's body, defiling Carter's corpse.

"Hawk . . . twah!"

"Hawk . . . twah!"

Breeze watched in disbelief as the Haitians raised their feet and forcefully kicked the casket off the table, causing the body to roll out onto the floor. Carter's head hit the floor hard, causing a loud crack to pierce the air, and the attendees gasped in horror.

Polo, Mecca, and Monroe sprung into action, with the rest of The Cartel behind them.

"Poppa!" Breeze shouted as she rushed toward the front of the church to retrieve her father's corpse from the floor.

Taryn yelled in alarm, "Breeze!" as she watched her daughter head toward the mayhem.

Suddenly, bullets from an AK echoed throughout the church, *Tat, tat, tat, tat, tat, tat!*, little flashes of fire kissing the air, and was followed by the sound of people screaming and running for the exit.

Breeze didn't care about the gunfire. She just wanted to get to her father. But before she could reach him, one of the Haitian gunmen snatched her up.

Taryn yelled, "Breeze!"

Carter looked in horror at the front of the church. He recognized the young girl from pictures that he had been sent when he was younger. *She's my sister*, he thought as he pulled out his .45 without hesitation.

He stood up and scrambled to get between the screaming people as he aimed his gun and released one shot. His bullet hit its intended target, and the man holding Breeze dropped instantly.

Carter's clip was quickly emptied as the gun battle continued. He was clearly outnumbered, but that didn't stop him from reaching in his ankle holster and pulling out his 9 mm pistol as the three remaining Haitians shot recklessly, clearing a path to leave the church. Using his natural instinct for survival, he picked up the body of the dead Haitian and wrapped his arm around his neck, putting him in a chokehold from behind. The deadweight was heavy, but it was the only way for him to shield his body from the bullets being sent his way.

Carter yelled, "Y'all niggas wanna clap?" and shot his nine with one hand, while moving toward the Haitians, who were now headed for the door.

Carter's gun spit hollow-points toward the Haitians as the dead body in front of him absorbed his enemy's fire. *POW! POW!*

Just as he reached the exit door, one of the Haitians yelled, "Me going to kill you, muthafucka!" And the three remaining Haitians made a run for it.

Carter continued to shoot until he was sure they left

the building. Once he was positive that everyone was safe, he dropped the dead Haitian to the floor and let off his last round into his skull. "Bitch nigga!" He hawked up a huge glob and spat directly in the dead man's face, returning the favor on behalf of his dead father.

He rushed over to Breeze's side. Rocking back and forth, she was holding on to her father's dead body and crying hysterically.

"Are you okay?" he asked.

"Get the fuck away from her. We don't know you, mu'-fucka!" Mecca stated harshly as he pulled Breeze off the ground. Her head fell into his chest as he walked her away.

Polo looked around at the carnage inside of the sanctuary. A couple people had been injured, and the church was destroyed. "We've got to get the fuck out of here," Polo stated. "How did they get in?" Polo yelled in anger. He patted the Young Carter on the back. "Come on, let's go before the police show. Follow me back to your father's house."

A look of surprise crossed Carter's face.

"Yeah, I know you're his son, but right now that's the least of my worries. Just follow me back to the house. We need to talk." With those words, Polo escorted the family out of the church, and they darted inside of the limo.

The Haitians had sent a clear message—They were out for blood, and they weren't going to stop until The Cartel was out of commission.

Chapter Three

"Brother or not, next time homeboy step to me like
that, I'm-a rock his ass to sleep."

—Young Carter

The Diamond family sat in their living room along with
Polo and Young Carter. The room was quiet; no one
knew what to say. Taryn's and Breeze's eyes were puffy
because of all the crying they had been doing, the horrific
images of their loved one being kicked out of his casket
haunting their thoughts.

Mecca's Armani shoes thumped the marble floor as he
paced the room back and forth, totally enraged, two twin
Desert Eagle handguns in his hands. The Haitians had
shown the ultimate sign of disrespect and was sending a
clear message that they were trying to take over Miami. In
fact, it was Carter's decision to not cut the Haitians in on
his operation that ultimately led to his assassination.

Polo stood up and slowly walked to the window. He
looked in the front and saw henchmen, all strapped, scattered around the house to ensure their safety. With the
Haitians merciless tactics, he didn't underestimate them.
He saw the fire in Mecca's eyes and tried to calm him.

"We have to keep our heads on straight. These niggas
are going hard at us. The Cartel still runs Miami, remem-

ber that! We have to retaliate to get our backs out of the
corner." Polo removed the suit jacket that rested on his
black silk shirt.

"Fuck that! Let's get at they ass, guns blazin'! I don't
give a fuck no more!" Mecca screamed, a single tear sliding down his cheek.

Money stared into space without blinking. He was in
complete shock. The death of his father was very hard on
him. He remained silent as his twin brother let out his
frustrations. He couldn't come to grips with his father's
death.

Money snapped out of his daze and looked over at
Young Carter. It was obvious that he was his brother. He
looked so much like Carter, it was unbelievable. Young
Carter had thick, dark eyebrows just like his father, and
he even shared his tall, lean frame. His mannerisms were
even the same. He watched as Young Carter rested his
index finger on his temple while in deep thought, just as
his father used to do.

It hurt his heart that his father had an illegitimate child.
The perfect image that he had of his father was somewhat
tarnished by the news. *How could this nigga be my
brother? Daddy wouldn't step out on Momma like that*,
Money thought as he stared at Young Carter.

Taryn noticed Money staring and decided to address
the issue. She knew that there were other things to worry
about and wanted to explain the complex situation. With
tears still streaming down her face, she stood up. "I want
you guys to meet Carter Jones . . . your brother." Taryn
rested her hand on Young Carter's shoulder.

Breeze lifted her head in confusion. She looked at her
mother and then to Young Carter. "What?" she managed to
murmur. She couldn't believe what her mother was telling
them. The words were like daggers to her heart. She was

so busy grieving, she didn't even notice how closely Young Carter resembled her Poppa.

As she looked at Young Carter, she couldn't believe her eyes. She just thought that he was one of The Cartel's henchmen. He looked like a younger version of her father. *Oh my God*, she thought as she placed her hand over her mouth.

Mecca came closer to Young Carter and stared him in the face while saying harshly, "This ain't my fuckin' brother. He ain't a mu'fuckin' Diamond!" Mecca gripped his pistols tighter, refusing to believe the obvious.

Young Carter returned the cold stare at Mecca, not backing down whatsoever, but he still remained silent. Young Carter was respectful because he was aware that his presence presented a conflict to the Diamond family, but he wasn't about to back down from anyone. And the way Mecca was gripping his pistols caused Young Carter's street senses to kick in. He slowly slid his hand to his waist, where his own banger rested. He stood up so that Mecca wouldn't be standing over him. Young Carter was a bit taller than Mecca, so he looked down on him, not saying a word.

"Mecca, he is your brother! Sit down and let me explain," Taryn yelled, trying to reason. She rushed over to Mecca as the two men stared at each other intensely. "Mecca!"

"Fall back, bro," Money said as he stood up.

Mecca jumped at Young Carter as if he was about to hit him, but Young Carter didn't budge. Not even a blink. Young Carter grinned, knowing that Mecca was trying to size him up.

"That's enough!" Polo made his way over to them.

Young Carter kissed Taryn on the cheek and whispered, "Sorry if I caused any more heartache. I didn't come here for this." And before Taryn could even respond, he was headed for the door.

"Yo, wait!" Polo said as he followed Young Carter out.

"Let that bitch-ass nigga go!" Mecca yelled as he continued to pace the room.

It took all of Young Carter's willpower not to get at Mecca, but he figured that he would give him a pass for now.

Polo caught up to Young Carter just before he exited the house. "Yo, youngblood, hold up a minute."

"There's no need for me to be here. I don't know why I even came to this mu'fucka anyway," Young Carter stated, an incredulous look on his face.

"Listen"—Polo placed his hand on Carter's shoulder, trying to convince him to stay—"Mecca has a lot on his mind right now. The family really needs you."

"Look, fam, I ain't got shit to do with them. I just came to pay my respects and keep it pushing, nah mean? Brother or not, next time homeboy step to me like that, I'm-a rock his ass to sleep." Carter clenched his jaw.

Polo took a deep breath and saw that Carter was noticeably infuriated, but kept his composure out of respect. Young Carter reminded Polo of his late best friend in so many ways. Polo looked into Carter's eyes and said, "Just give me a minute to talk to—"

Carter cut him off mid-sentence, not wanting to hear any more. "Look, I'll be at the Marriott off South Beach until tomorrow night." With that, he left Polo standing there alone.

Chapter Four

"They were willing to murk women, children,
hustlers, the good, the bad, and the ugly. It didn't
matter, anybody could get it, if the price was right."

—Unknown

Carter flipped through the different denominations of
bills as he diligently counted the cash that he had just
acquired from his flip. After the drama he had experienced during his father's funeral, the business he handled
in Atlanta made the trip better for him. He would now
leave the Dirty South $180,000 richer. *This was definitely
worth the trip*, he thought to himself as he admired the
hood riches that lay scattered across the hotel bed.

He put the bills in ten-thousand-dollar stacks and wrapped rubber bands around each one, to keep the money organized. He counted the cash a second time to verify that
his money was on point. He was thorough when it came
to his paper. It was the one thing that he knew he could
depend on. Money was his first and only love. Getting
money came first in any situation, and he was determined
to keep his pockets fed.

A knock at the door interrupted his thought process,
and out of habit, he grabbed his pistol from the nightstand
and approached the door.

He had been a bit paranoid from the events that had

taken place the day before at the funeral, so he wanted to be as cautious as possible while he was in Miami. A nigga would never catch him slipping.

He looked through the peephole and eased up when he noticed the distorted image of his father's right-hand man. Sliding the chain from the hotel door, he unlocked it and allowed Polo to enter the room.

Polo shook his head as he looked at Young Carter. It was still hard for him to get over the resemblance. Young Carter looked so much like his father, it was uncanny. It was a shame that the two men never got the chance to know one another. "Can we talk?" Polo asked, both hands tucked inside of his pants pockets.

"Yeah. come on in." Carter set his pistol down. "You want a drink?"

Polo stepped inside. "Nah, I'm good." He noticed how on point Carter was and thought to himself, *like father, like son.*

Carter walked over to his bed and pulled the bedspread over the stacks of money to conceal his business. He then sat down and motioned for Polo to take a seat in the chair across from him.

"I just came to see how long you were in town for?" Polo knew that the Diamond family needed Young Carter now more than ever.

"I'm ghost tomorrow. Ain't nothing here for me."

Polo had predicted this reaction from Young Carter. He didn't expect him to feel any sense of responsibility to his family at first, but he knew that if he could convince Carter to stay around long enough, the attachment would eventually grow.

"I know this is a lot to put on your heart right now, but your family needs you."

Carter was quick in his response. "They don't even know me," he stated with disdain. "That's not my fam. I've only known one woman my whole life, and she the only family I need, nah mean?"

"Nah, I don't know what you mean, Young Carter. I saw the look in your eyes today when that Haitian mu'fucka had your baby sister at gunpoint. Only a man who had love in his heart would get at them niggas the way you did. It was instinct for you to protect her. Whether you want to admit it or not, that is your family, and they need you, especially Breeze."

"Ain't nobody tried to protect me my entire life. I've been out for self from the time I was old enough to understand the rules of the game. I don't have time to baby-sit. That's not my responsibility." Carter wanted to make it clear that he wasn't trying to get to know the Diamond family, didn't want to be around them.

Seeing their expensive house and luxury vehicles just made him resent his father even more. While he grew up in Flint, Michigan, a city that was known as the murder capital, the man that made him was taking care of the family that he had abandoned his first-born for. The pain of growing up without a father had left a bad taste in his mouth.

Polo stood and shook his head from side to side. "Everything isn't always as it seems, Young Carter. Your father had his reasons for leaving you and your mother, and it wasn't because he didn't love you."

"It really doesn't matter now. That man is in the ground, and it doesn't affect me. I just came to pay my respects. I didn't come here for nothing more or nothing less. That man has never done a damn thing for me, so I'm not gon' even hold you up and say that I feel obligated to step up and take care of his family. A better man might be able to, but that's not me."

"I understand you are frustrated Young Carter. You come here and see how happy your siblings are, and you feel cheated. I know you're asking yourself why you didn't have the same upbringing, but believe me, your father did the best he could under the circumstances," Polo stated, defending his best friend.

When Carter didn't reply he continued, "Your father—"

"I don't have a father. The nigga got my mother pregnant and then left us for dead to come play house with another bitch."

"Look, you need to watch your mouth." Polo, enraged by Young Carter's blasphemous statements, had to set the record straight. "I can't just sit here and allow you to disrespect my man like that. You don't know shit about nothing. If it wasn't for your father, you and your mother would have been dead a long time ago. He had to leave you in order to protect you."

"Fuck is you talking about?" Carter asked, hostility and anger in his tone.

Polo could see that the young man's temper was beginning to flare and then remembered that Young Carter had a valid reason to be upset. He took a deep breath and calmed himself down, to de-escalate the situation. "Look, Young Carter, I'm not here to bump heads with you. As your father's best friend, I've got nothing but respect for you. You have a misconception about the man that your pops was. I'm not saying that every decision he made regarding you and your mother was right, but he did the best that he could. Think about it, young'un. Your mother worked as a CNA since you were young. She's bringing home thirty stacks a year at the most, but you grew up in a two-hundred-thousand-dollar house in the suburbs of Flint. Who do you think purchased that house? Who paid those bills? Use your head, young fella. How many fourteen-year-old boys you know kept a thousand dollars a week in his pocket? When you graduated you were pushing a limited edition Mercedes. Who do you think copped that car for you? Let me tell you, it wasn't Mommy."

Polo's words were enough to silence Carter and make him think. His mother never told him about his father. She had never even talked about him and would explain their living situation by saying that she worked overtime, sometimes double-time, to allow them to live the way that they did. She often claimed to hit big at the casino or to have the winning lotto number. She had given her son every excuse in the book to explain the extra income. *All this time my father was sending money back home to take care of me?* Carter tried to wrap his mind around the fact that his father had never forgotten him.

"Your father never missed a beat in your life, son. You may not have gotten the chance to meet him, but he knew everything about you. It was nothing for him to fly in and out of Flint in the same day just so he could be at your Friday night football games. Remember that game you ran three hundred yards against Southwestern?"

Carter nodded his head as he placed it in his hands. "Yeah, I remember."

"Your father was there. I know he was there because he dragged my black ass with him every week. Every touchdown, every awards assembly, your graduation, he was there for all of that. When you got into that trouble with the law as a juvenile, he made sure that the case was thrown out. Fifty grand made that little mishap disappear from your record.

"Your father loved you very much, but he was a hustler too. He met your mother when she was fifteen and he was seventeen. They dated throughout his senior year in high school, and when it was time for him to go to college, he regretfully left her to better himself. Your mother was so upset with him that when he moved down here she stopped contacting him. He tried to call her, but she would never return his calls. A couple years later he met Taryn. She was beautiful, unlike any woman he had ever met, and they fell in love quickly. She is a full-blooded Dominican though, and they don't play that interracial dating shit. He had to prove himself time and time again just to be with her. If it weren't for his persistence and her refusal to leave him alone, they never would have been allowed to stay together. He knew that she was the daughter of Emilio Estes."

Carter lifted his head in surprise at the notorious drug lord's name. His eyebrows rose in speculation as he thought, *I know this nigga ain't talking bout*—

Before Carter could finish his thought, Polo said, "Yeah, I'm talking about *the* Emilio Estes."

"Damn!"

"Emilio took Carter under his wing. His coke connect allowed Carter to establish The Cartel as the most notorious and prosperous illegal enterprise Miami has ever seen. Emilio was clear in his concerns though. He told Carter that if he wanted to be with his daughter then he would have to keep up the lifestyle that she was accustomed to. Emilio told him that his family had to come first and that if he ever disgraced his daughter in any way then it would be the death of him."

"So he deserted me and my moms. He chose his family in Miami over me."

"Your father didn't even know about you until you were a young child. Your mother didn't even tell him that she was pregnant. When he found out, Taryn was pregnant with the twins, and if Emilio ever found out, you and your mother would have been put in direct danger. Knowing that he could trust his wife, he told her about you and your mother. Although she was upset at first, he explained that he had never cheated on her. She agreed to never tell her father, and they sent your mother money to support you from that day forth. It pained him that he couldn't get to know you. He wanted to be a part of your life, but his connections with the Dominican Mafia prevented that from happening. You are his first-born. You look just like him. He loved you wholeheartedly."

Confusion and anger took over Carter's body. He didn't know if he should be relieved or enraged. "It still doesn't make up for the years I spent never knowing him. I don't give a fuck what I'm facing. When I have a shorty, my seed gon' know who I am. I'm gon' be a man and take care of my family, no matter what the circumstances are. Money can't make up for the times he wasn't there. My mother couldn't teach me how to be a man. I turned to the streets for guidance. My father came to my games, but he wasn't the one who showed me how to throw the football. He never showed me how to grip a pistol. He ain't show me shit. I had to learn all that shit off humbug on my own."

"Sending you money and supporting you from afar was the only thing he could do. That cash kept you fed and a roof over your head. Your mother didn't have to worry about shit. She chose to never spend the money on herself. She never had to work another day of her life if she didn't want to. He made sure of that." Polo looked in Young Carter's eyes, trying to read him.

Carter stood up to signal that he was done with the conversation. "It still doesn't matter. This ain't home, and first thing tomorrow I'm out."

Polo stood as well, He shook his head in contempt. "A'ight, I hear you, but now you hear me. There's a war going on. Your little brothers and your baby sister need you right now. They weren't raised the way you were. They're spoiled, and they underestimate the seriousness of what's going on. This family needs your leadership, your protection. There's a lot of unfinished business that needs to be handled. Your father's seat at The Cartel is waiting to be filled."

Carter's silence was enough to let Polo know that he was considering his options. He headed for the door. Before he left the room, he said, "There's a meeting tomorrow night at the Diamond house. Your presence should be felt. If you're still in town, you should drop in. I'll be in touch."

As the door closed behind him, Carter thought of all the times he had wondered about his father. He was going crazy as he tried to recount the endless gifts his mother had given when he was growing up. He remembered growing up in the inner city up until the age of ten. At that time, his mother had mysteriously packed up all their belongings and moved them to the suburbs of Grand Blanc. *That must be around the time that Carter found out about me*, he thought to himself.

A part of him wanted to leave town and never look back, but another part of him wanted to stay. The part that had seen the beautiful face of his baby sister, the part that had witnessed the arrogant swagger of his brother Mecca, and calculating discreetness of his brother Monroe. His emotions were at an all-time high, and for the first time in his life, he was indecisive.

Unable to stay cooped up in the hotel suite, he grabbed two stacks of money and headed for the door. He needed to clear his head. He figured that the best way to do that was to visit the floating casino that sat at the end of the pier on South Beach. He didn't know that gambling ran through his veins like blood. It was a habit his father also had. What he did know was that it relaxed him, which was just what he needed at the moment.

Carter stood at a lively crap table with nothing but hundred-dollar chips in his rack. The casino was unusually packed for a Sunday night, and every table was crowded with eager participants just waiting to be taken by the house. Carter was lax from the top-shelf Rémy he was sipping on. The liquor and the intense thrill of the game had calmed him down since his earlier encounter with Polo.

"All bets set!" the dice handler yelled before maneuvering the ivory across the table and placing them in front of Young Carter. "Dice out!"

With his drink still in one hand, Carter picked up the dice with the other and tossed them toward the other end of the table with a nonchalant swagger. The dice tickled the fabric as they danced before finally landing.

"Yo! Eleven, yo!" the dealer shouted, indicating that eleven had landed on the face of the dice.

Uproarious celebration erupted around the table as everyone collected their wins and anxiously awaited Carter's next roll. He had been on a hot streak all night, hitting point after point. His luck was unbelievable. He had held the dice for forty-five minutes, which was almost impossible to do in the game of craps. He schooled the dice against the table with his head down as he watched his hands work their magic. He concentrated heavily on his technique. Every hustler had his own rhythm with the dice, and Carter was no exception.

"Excuse me, can I get in here?"

Hearing the feminine voice amongst the crowd of boisterous men caused Carter to look up. A brown-skinned girl with shoulder-length, almond-colored layers and hazel eyes squeezed into the empty rack next to him. She was so close to him that her sweet perfume played games with his senses, and he felt his manhood acknowledge her presence. He put the dice down as he watched her reach into her skintight Seven jeans and pull out a small wad of money. He waited for her to throw her cash on the table before he continued his roll.

The dealer handed her a hundred dollars worth of chips, and she put them in her rack, arranging them by denomination. He smirked at her as she made a pattern with the different color chips. It was rare that he saw a woman at the crap tables, and the one beside him had his full attention.

The men around the table grew impatient, some of them clearing their throats to signal to Carter that he should pick up the dice.

The young woman squirmed beside Carter, trying to find her place between the big men surrounding her.

"My fault, baby," Carter stated. "Here, let's do it like this." He turned sideways and allowed her to ease in comfortably at the table, giving her more room to play.

"It's all right. You good," she responded with a New York accent that immediately told him that she wasn't from Miami. She looked up at him and smiled as he stared down onto her 5-5 frame.

Captivated by her presence, he made mental notes as he admired her wide hips, thin waist, and perfectly manicured fingers and toes. His intense focus on her caused her to blush.

She lay her chips on the table. "Can I get a seventy-two-dollar six?"

Carter noticed the small tattoo on the back side of her wrist that read Murder Mama. That immediately piqued his interest. She then pointed to the dice, reminding Carter that it was his roll. Carter tossed the dice at the end of the table. "Here go your six, ma."

"Hard six!" the dealer yelled.

The girl jumped up and down and squealed with joy as if she had just won a million dollars, and Carter couldn't help but chuckle at her enthusiasm.

The man next to her was so in awe of the woman that he dropped her a twenty-five-dollar chip and winked at her, saying, "Lady luck!"

The man was so busy taking a peek at Miamor's ass that he didn't notice her lift three of his five-hundred-dollar chips out of his rack. Miamor bent over and pretended to fix the strap on her stiletto, giving the man a nice view of her assets. She did all of this in less than ten seconds. While everyone was busy collecting their money from the dealers, Miamor used the distraction to her advantage. When she stood, she gave the old man a half-smile that seemed to light up the room.

Carter shook his head with a smirk on his face as he watched the young woman's game.

"What's so funny?" she asked with laughter in her voice as she looked up at him, one hand plastered to her hip, the other reaching onto the table to collect her cash.

"Nothing, ma. I'm just happy you won." Carter licked his full lips.

"Okay," she stated playfully, as she discreetly scanning his body from head to toe. "I see you clowning me, but you need to be minding your own business and hit that six again. I still got money on the table. Everybody ain't balling like you. I see you betting with your purple chips," she said, referring to his full rack of big bills.

"I got you," he said as he prepared for his next roll. "What you drinking on, ma?"

"Hpnotiq and Goose," she replied.

The two of them stayed at the crap tables all night. They joked and laughed, flirting openly with each other. Young Carter enjoyed her company and appreciated her presence because she took his mind off his deceased father. He noticed the size of her pockets as she tried to keep up with his bets and had calculated that she had lost at least two grand trying to hang in the game.

As the crowd began to disperse, they eventually were the only two left at the table. Drunk and feeling good, they made dumb bets, Carter not caring how much he spent, but the young lady watching every dollar that the dealers trapped up.

"Seven out!" the dealer called. The enthusiasm had left his voice, and it was apparent that everyone at the table was exhausted.

"Looks like your luck has run out." The girl leaned against the table. She faced him, her head cocked to the side, her eyes low and sexy from the effects of the liquor.

"I guess so," he replied as he stepped to her, closing the space between them. "You all right. You look a little tipsy."

The girl smiled seductively and answered, "Just a little bit, but I'm good. I didn't come here alone. My girls are around here somewhere. This was fun. Thanks for the drinks."

As she began to walk away, Carter gently grabbed her forearm. "Aye, hold up," he stated softly. He reached into his Prada pockets and pulled out a wad of money. He peeled off twenty hundred-dollar bills and opened the girl's hand to put them inside.

"What are you doing?" Her eyes opened wide in surprise. "I can't take this."

"Whenever you're in my presence, everything's on me. That should make up for what you lost, even though it wasn't yours to begin with." He rubbed her hand before letting it go.

"A'ight, I see you," she replied with a laugh. She threw the money onto the dice table.

"What you doing, ma?"

She put her hands to her lips as if to shush him and then told the dealers to put it all in the field. She picked up the dice, tossed them down the table.

"Two field bet two !" the dealer yelled in excitement, amazed at the young woman's luck. "Double the payout."

Carter shook his head in disbelief. He couldn't believe that the girl had just put two stacks on such a dumb bet. The payout was lovely.

She picked up six thousand dollars from the table and handed him back three thousand. "I make my own ends, but it's nice to know that there are gentlemen still out here."

Before she could walk away, Carter said to her, "I didn't get your name, shorty."

She brought her lips close to his ear. "That's because I didn't give it to you. If you're worth getting to know me, I'll see you again," she replied with a smile as she walked away from him.

"Miamor, who da fuck is da fine-ass nigga you were kicking game to?" Aries asked as she sat in the backseat of the Honda Civic.

"Aries, shut up. Wasn't nobody kicking game to nobody. I wasn't worried about that nigga. Y'all bitches just don't know how to tail a mu'fucka without being all obvious. Our mark was at the crap table in the upstairs VIP. I just chose the table that gave me a nice view to the stairway, so I'd know who was coming and going. Dude was just a prop to make it realistic. My eye never left the prize," Miamor replied, making sure that she kept her eye on the all-black Lamborghini that was three car lengths in front of her.

"I don't know, Mia. It looked to me like you were checking for him," Robyn teased.

Miamor smacked her lips, and a guilty smile spread across her face.

"Bitch, me knew it!" Aries shouted excitedly in her Barbadian accent.

"A'ight, a'ight, I'll admit it. The nigga was a little fly. He had an A game on him. But why the fuck is we discussing that nigga? This ain't playtime. Let's get focused on this business," Miamor stated, trying to get back to the task at hand.

"Now da bitch wanna be focused," Aries stated smartly.

"I know, right?" Robyn burst into laughter.

To the average person, the three girls were rare beauties out for a night on the town. One would have never guessed that these contract killers—They called themselves "the Murder Mamas"—were responsible for sixty percent of the drug-related murders in the Dade County area. If the paper was right, they were down for the job. Nobody was an exception. They were willing to murk women, children, hustlers, the good, the bad, and the ugly. It didn't matter, anybody could get it, if the price was right.

Come on, Mia, keep up with this fucking car, Anisa thought frantically as she watched her sister's car disappear in the side mirror. Her heart began to beat rapidly as she began to think of a way to buy her friends time to catch up.

"Mecca, can we stop at this gas station up here?" she said in her sweetest tone. "All those Long Islands are making me want to pee." She rubbed her left hand on his crotch.

Mecca's dick immediately responded to her touch and began to stiffen as he looked at her fat ass, which was melting into his leather seats. "Nah, we almost there. Just hold that shit. Come put those pretty lips to work," he said with a tone of authority that didn't leave her room to object.

Anisa looked in her mirror once again. *Fuck! Mia, where are you?* She unbuckled her seatbelt and leaned into Mecca's lap. She unzipped his pants and pulled out his throbbing dick. She was immediately aroused by the sight of his long thickness, which was a shade darker than his light skin, and was the prettiest thing she'd ever seen. Her mouth watered in anticipation. The fresh smell of Sean John cologne greeted her nostrils, and she licked her lips in delight. Anisa loved a big, clean dick and figured, since she was about to kill the nigga, she might as well give him the best head job of his life before sending him to meet his Maker.

She licked the head of his length and circled her tongue seductively around his hat, and his manhood jumped from excitement.

"Ohh shit," he uttered as he kept one hand on the steering wheel and put the other on the back of her head. He entangled his fingers in her hair and gently pushed her down onto him.

Anisa took all of him into her mouth, gagging a little from his size. Her mouth was wet and warm, and Mecca was in heaven as he glanced down at the beautiful woman. She slobbered on his dick as she deep-throated him. She knew she was nice with her tongue.

Not even five minutes had passed, and she felt the swell of his rod as he neared ejaculation. He closed his eyes and almost forgot he was driving as she slid her mouth down one last time, tickling the vein underneath his shaft on her way up. It was a wrap, as she sat up and watched Mecca come into an orgasm.

"Damn, baby, let's get you up to this room. A nigga need some of that." Mecca slipped one of his fingers up her skirt, pushing her thong to the side, and massaged her swollen clit.

"Hmm," Anisa moaned as Mecca fingered her dripping pussy. He was working his fingers in and out of her like a dick, and she began to work her hips as she felt the pressure building between her legs. *If this nigga can work his fingers like this, I know he can fuck good. I might have to fuck his sexy ass before I kill him.*

Anisa squirmed in her seat and continued to check her mirrors as she enjoyed the pleasure that Mecca was providing her.

Mecca pulled into the parking lot of the Holiday Inn and hopped out of the car, leaving his car with the valet. He pulled out a hundred-dollar bill and gave it to the valet. "Take care of my car," he said. "You fuck that up, I fuck you up. Understand?"

"Yes, sir," the valet answered immediately.

Mecca walked over to the passenger side and opened the door or Anisa.

"Thanks," she stated with a smile. She grabbed his hand and walked beside him.

When they entered the hotel, Mecca checked into a regular room, using one of his many aliases.

Butterflies circled in Anisa's stomach because she was sure that her girls had gotten lost in the sauce of Miami's nightlife traffic. *It doesn't even matter because, once I slip this nigga this GHB pill, this mu'fucka gon' be out for the count anyway. It'll give me enough time to let them know where I'm at,* she thought as she reluctantly followed Mecca up to the tenth floor of the hotel.

"Where in the hell did they go?" Robyn asked in a panicked tone. "I don't see them! Can you see the car?"

"Nah, but you need to chill out. Now is not the time to start tripping. We've done this shit a thousand times. Let's just stick to the plan. Anisa knows how to handle herself. We fucked up by losing her, but she'll contact us when she can," Miamor stated confidently.

"Me don't know, Miamor. This job is on a whole 'nother level. What if she needs us?" Aries asked.

Miamor could feel the fear creeping into her team's heart. She knew that fear could easily manipulate any situation, and she was fighting to keep control. *Where are you, Nis? Let me know something,* she thought, as she too began to worry. She didn't like the fact that she had lost their mark, but she knew Anisa would be able to handle herself until they could get there.

"I just need to use the restroom. I'll be right out," Anisa said as she entered the hotel room. She quickly disappeared behind the safety of the bathroom door and locked it behind her. She sat on the toilet, her heart beating a mile a minute and pulled out her two-way. She sent the text to her crew—*I'm at the Holiday Inn on Biscayne Blvd. Room 1128*—then quickly put her phone in her purse and flushed the toilet for show. She washed her hands and walked out of the bathroom.

As soon as she opened the door, Mecca was standing there looking her in the face.

"Oh!" she exclaimed as she dropped her Chanel clutch purse onto the floor. "Shit!" she yelled out. The contents of her purse spilled out onto the floor, and she quickly squatted to retrieve the tiny packet of white powder before Mecca could see it.

"Why you so jumpy, ma?" Mecca asked, his stare penetrating her, his hand caressing the side of her face. Then he looked into the bathroom suspiciously. "I need to get in there." He walked inside and closed the door behind him.

"O-okay."

Anisa rushed over to the mini-bar and set up two glasses. She used Grey Goose because she didn't want to use dark liquor, afraid that the residue from the drug might float to the top. She used her finger to mix the powder into the glass and then removed her silver Chanel dress. She stood in her black Victoria's Secret bra and thong, and her four-inch Chanel stilettos.

When Mecca walked out, he saw her standing with two drinks in her hand. He admired the curves of her body. Her wide hips, flat stomach, and apple-shaped bottom gave him an instant hard-on. He could only imagine the treasure that she had between her thighs, and couldn't wait to taste her.

"Here, baby, I fixed us a drink. I want us to relax so that we can enjoy the night."

"I'm not drinking tonight."

Fuck you mean, you not drinking, nigga? You been drinking all fuckin' night, and now you want to change up?

Mecca could see the distress on her face. "That's a problem?"

"No, baby, I just want to make you feel good. How about we order some room service, have some drinks, and afterwards I'll let you put your dick in something warm?" She put the glass of Grey Goose in his hands and left a trail of kisses from his ear, to his chest, and continued to move south. She got to his pants and unbuckled his belt.

Just as she was about to go to work, he grabbed her hair forcefully, almost tearing it from the root. "You drink it," he stated in a menacing tone.

The look in her eyes confirmed his suspicions. When she didn't respond, he continued, "You got two choices. You can either drink it, or I'm gon' blow a hole through your top." He removed his gold-dipped Beretta 950 Jetfire and aimed it at her head.

"Mecca, what the hell is your problem?" Anisa stood to her feet. "I just want to make you feel good. You're pointing guns in my face and shit. We're supposed to be having a good time," she whined, trying to flip the situation in her favor.

"Save that shit. You think I didn't see the car that was following us, bitch? Drink up. If there's nothing going on, then you have nothing to worry about."

Anisa realized her plan wasn't working. *Where are you, Mia?* She slowly reached for the drugged drink. She knew that if she drank the liquor, she would be committing suicide. Mecca had peeped her shade, so she knew that she had to act fast. She grabbed the drink from his hands and tilted it toward her mouth.

Mecca watched intently, but just as her lips touched the glass, she violently threw the liquor in his face and darted for the door.

"Bitch!" he yelled as he cleared the wetness from his face and chased after her. She managed to open it slightly, but he was right on her ass and slammed his weight against her, causing the door to slam shut. Then he grabbed her neck and tossed her to the floor as if she were the size of a rag doll.

"Aww!"

"Bitch, you trying to poison me? You trying to set me up?" Mecca aimed his gun at her head, and before she could deny his accusation, he silenced her with two to the dome.

"There that nigga go!" Robyn pointed to Mecca as he rushed out of the parking lot.

Mia peered into his car, and immediately noticed that he was alone. It was at that instant that she felt something was horribly wrong. "Where's Nisa?" she asked, her tires screeching as she pulled up swiftly to the valet curb. She hopped out of the car and shouted to the valet, "Leave my car running. I'll be right out!"

Robyn and Aries were right behind her. They didn't wait for the elevator to make it down to the hotel lobby and darted straight for the staircase. Each girl was silent, all fearing the worst.

When they finally made it to the eleventh floor, Miamor took off for Room 1128. They were all out of breath but kept running as if their lives depended on it.

Mia noticed that the room door wasn't closed completely and pushed it open forcefully. "Nisa?" she called as she saw her sister lying in a small pool of blood. Tears immediately came to her eyes.

"Oh my God!" Robyn shouted when she saw her good friend's body on the floor.

Aries was speechless as she watched Miamor kneel by her sister's side.

"No! Nisa, wake up, baby. Don't do this, Anisa. Get up!" Mia shook her big sister's body as if she were only asleep. "Come on, help me get her up!" she yelled, looking back at Aries and Robyn for help. "Come on! She needs to get to a hospital. Help me please," she cried, her voice sounding like that of a small child.

"We've got to get out of here," Robyn whispered as she kneeled down beside Miamor.

"No! I can't leave her. Nisa, come on, get up."

"Mia, there's nothing that we can do for her now. It's too late. She's gone," Robyn said sadly. "She's gone."

Miamor nodded, her face frowned up in pain. "I know," she whispered in between sobs. She leaned over her sister's dead body and whispered in her ear, "I love you, Nis, and I'm going to kill him, I promise." She kissed her sister's cheek and then exited the room.

At first, killing the Diamond family was something that she had been paid to do. Now it was personal, something that she had to do, and no matter how long it took her, she would have her revenge.

Chapter Five

A nigga move a brick, and think he
Gotti o' somebody.

—Young Carter

The conference room in the Diamond house was in complete silence. Every hustler in the room felt awkward. It was the first time that The Cartel had held a meeting without their boss, Carter, and everyone seemed to be just staring at his empty head seat. Carter usually started the meetings with a statement or a quote, and with him not there, things were odd.

Polo noticed the uneasiness of the henchmen and stood up. He looked at Money and Mecca, who sat to the right of him, and then back at the henchmen. He took a deep breath as he unbuttoned his Armani blazer.

He walked behind Carter's former chair and rested his hands on the back. "Family, we have suffered a great loss, but business must go on. Carter would've wanted it that way. The Haitians, them mu'fuckas have no respect for the game. These niggas playin' fo' keeps, but we won't bow down to anybody, believe that. We have to let them know that The Cartel still runs Miami, point-blank!" Polo slammed his fist on the glossed oak table.

The occupants of the room included all of the head

block lieutenants from each district of Miami. They all seemed to see their paper begin to decrease and knew exactly what the reason behind it was.

Polo looked at Money, who had a law notebook in front of him. "Money, how much did we bring in this week?"

Money ran his finger down the pad and uttered reluctantly, "Two hundred fifty-three thousand."

This only added to Polo's frustrations. "What the fuck is going on, fam? Our operation does a million easy. That's barely enough to pay the runners. What the fuck!" Polo said as he focused back on the henchmen.

One of the henchmen rubbed his hand over his face and goatee. "Man, most of my workers are quitting or siding with the Haitians. They got niggas shook. Ma'tee and his crew are trying to take over the city."

"Got niggas shook? Fuck outta here. Y'all need to recruit more thoroughbreds then, real talk! We have to let the Haitians know that just because Carter is gone, it doesn't mean we're layin' down. We have to get back at them."

"That's all I been trying to hear." Mecca pulled out his twin pistols and laid them on the table. "And you know what? Them mu'fuckas tried to send some bitch at me the other day, like I wouldn't peep the shit."

"What happened?" Polo asked.

"What you mean, what happened? I left that bitch stankin' in the room." Mecca nonchalantly looked around the table.

"I told you about fuckin' with them hoodrats, Mecca. We in a war right now! You can't do that, bruh. You could have got yo'self killed," Money said, obvious aggravation in his tone.

"Bitch ain't gon' catch Mecca slippin', believe that! I knew what the bitch was on from the jump. I just wanted to get the pussy before I off'd her ass." Mecca leaned back in his chair.

The henchmen laughed at how cold Mecca's attitude was.

Polo and Money were the only ones not amused by his overconfidence. They knew how wild and careless Mecca could be. They also knew eventually his rashness, if not controlled, would lead to their downfall.

Before Polo or Money could respond, the room grew quiet. Everyone's eyes shot to the door. Some of the henchmen thought they were seeing a ghost, but it wasn't a ghost. It was Young Carter.

Polo turned around to see Young Carter standing there with an all-black hoody, and a diamond cross that hung down to his belt buckle. Polo smiled, knowing that his talk with him paid off.

Mecca sucked his teeth, letting it be known he wasn't comfortable with Young Carter's presence.

Polo waved his hand over the table. "Come in and join us."

Young Carter scanned the room slowly and looked at each man present. He then walked over to the table full of hustlers.

"Everyone, this is Carter . . . Young Carter," Polo said, introducing him.

Everyone greeted him with a simple head nod or a "What up," and Carter returned the greeting with a nod.

Money pulled the chair out that was next to him. "Have a seat."

Carter accepted the gesture and took a seat.

Young Carter and Mecca traded mean stares as he walked over to the chair, but both of them knew that it couldn't escalate, seeing they were blood brothers.

Polo cleared his throat and picked up where he left off.

Carter peeped the surroundings and realized that his father was a powerful man. The man he went his entire life hating had boss status, the same thing he was trying to achieve. He looked at the henchmen and noticed that all of them wore luxury, expensive threads and didn't look like the hustlers he was used to back home. Miami had a whole different vibe.

Young Carter stuck out like a sore thumb amongst the others. Carter was from the street, he was hood, and he couldn't help it, so he wore street clothes, knowing nothing better. While he wore Sean Jean and Timberland, the men were rocking Roberto Cavalli and Ferragamo suede shoes, and everyone wore black.

He chuckled to himself. *These niggas really believe they on some Mafia shit, fo' real. Fuck outta here. A nigga move a brick, and think he Gotti o' somebody.* He couldn't understand why they had formed this organization. Where he was from, hustlers didn't come together at any point. It was a dog-eat-dog mentality, and everyone was out for self.

In the game since he was 16, Young Carter began moving bricks by age 21. He was what you call a bona fide hustler. His mother died when he was 20, and after that, he didn't look back. He went hard on the streets. He had Flint, Michigan's coke game on lock.

Now, at the age of 25 he ran the city, hooking up with a coke connect from Atlanta and completely taking over. Young Carter didn't know it, but he was following in the footsteps of his father.

He focused his attention on what was being said in the meeting.

"We have to get at the Haitians somehow. We have to be strategic," Polo said as he sat down and began to rub his hands together. He was in deep contemplation, and for the first time, he felt the burden of not having Carter's strategic mind. Times like these, Carter was a genius at playing mental chess with the enemies.

In the middle of the discussion, Money's cell phone rang. Normally he wouldn't pick up his phone in the middle of a meeting, but he had been waiting on that particular call. He flipped open his cell. "Yo," he said in his low, raspy tone.

He remained silent for a minute, while getting the information from the other end of the phone. Then he closed the phone without saying a word.

"One of my sources thinks he knows where Ma'tee resides," Money stated, referring to the leader of the Haitian crew that had them under fire. "Maybe we need to pay him a visit."

Oversized Chloe glasses covering her eyes and Foxy Brown pumping out of the speakers, Miamor cruised down the interstate pushing 100 mph in her rented GS coupe, her long hair blowing in the wind along with the chronic weed smoke she blew out. She could afford to buy her own car, but in her profession she had to switch up whips like she did panties, to be less noticeable. She took another long drag of the kush-filled blunt and inhaled it deeply.

Throughout the last two years, her and her crew put . . . their . . . murder . . . game. . . . down. I mean, you couldn't mention *Murder Mamas*, if *homicide* wasn't in the sentence. Murder for hire was the best way to sum it up. She had done numerous hits for Ma'tee; none of them resulted in these extreme measures. The recent loss of her older sister had Miamor's mind churning. She wanted to get revenge on the man that killed her blood. But first, she needed to see Ma'tee to get more information on this guy. Only thing she knew about him was that his name was Mecca and that Ma'tee had beef with his family. When they took a job, they usually didn't ask a lot of questions. The only question they needed answered was how much money was involved.

"I swear, that nigga is dead, word to my mutha," Miamor said to herself in her strong New York accent. She pulled off the freeway and entered the town of Little Haiti, where Ma'tee lived.

After taking several back streets and dirt roads, she made it to Ma'tee's residence. Miamor looked at the elegant mansion and the 15-foot steel gate that was the entryway. She pulled the luxury car up and stuck her hand out of the window to push the intercom button. A video surveillance camera faced directly toward her from the gate.

"Wan, state cha name?" a voice sounded in a Haitian accent.

Miamor yelled loud enough so she could be heard, "Yo, it's Mia!"

"Who?"

"Miamor, mu'fucka! Open up!" she spat out of frustration.

A brief moment of silence came about just before the sound of the metal clanked, opening up for her. Miamor maneuvered the vehicle through the gate onto the long driveway leading up to the palace. She noticed that Haitians were scattered throughout the property, all holding assault rifles.

It was only the second time she had been there, but the view amazed her once again. The grass was perfectly even and greener than fresh broccoli. The driveway was filled with luxury cars and lined with beautiful flowers.

As she got closer to the front of the house, she noticed that a birthday party was going on. It was about fifty children in the front yard with noise-makers and birthday cake on their faces and hands. She saw all of the children gathered around watching the clowns making balloon animals, the kids screaming loud in excitement, and all of them having a ball.

A beautiful dark-skinned girl with long, kinky hair was front and center. She had on a princess crown and was happily being entertained by the clown as she instructed him on what balloon animal to make.

That must be Ma'tee's daughter, Miamor thought, immediately noticing the resemblance. She felt bad for intruding on an obvious family event, but she needed to speak with Ma'tee. She also saw a couple of grown women amongst the crowd, obviously the mothers of some of the children. She thought about returning another day, but she had to find out more about Mecca. She was itching to slice his throat. It was only a matter of time.

Miamor made her way to the front door, where two dreadlocked men stood guard. "I'm here to see Ma'tee," she stated as she stood before them.

Without saying a word, the guards, both with pistol in hand, stepped aside and opened the door for her.

Miamor stepped in and admired the crystal chandelier that hung from the cathedral ceiling. The glass wraparound stairs stood in the middle of the room and sat on white marble floors. The all whitewalls and furniture gave the home an immaculate look. Miamor headed to the back for the sliding glass door.

Another man stood in front of it with a pistol in his holster. Unlike the other men, he didn't wear dreads; he had a neat low cut, but was darker than all of the other guards.

Miamor looked past him, trying to spot his boss. "Where can I find Ma'tee?"

"I need to check you before you approach Ma'tee," he said, shifting his stance.

"I left the guns in the car," Miamor shot at him.

"Sorry, ma. I still have to search you." He shrugged his shoulders and crossed his arms.

Miamor let out a loud sigh, letting him know that she was irritated. She held out her hands and spread her legs. Her Seven skinny jeans hugged her large behind. Her stiletto heels made her assets seem even more enticing as she remained bent down and he began to search her from feet on up.

He felt her tiny ankles in search for a gun hostler.

"You know I can't fit a damn pistol in these tight-ass jeans."

"You never know," he said, continuing to feel her upper leg. He paused, his nose level with her crotch.

"Smells good, don't it?" Miamor said, hip to his game.

"Yeah, smells very good actually." He looked up at her and gave her a perfect smile.

"Too bad you'll never see her. I wouldn't even let you taste it. Hurry up. I ain't got all day." Miamor turned her eyes to the ceiling. She didn't even give him the respect of looking at him.

The man was obviously embarrassed as he hurried up and finished searching her. Once he was done, he opened the sliding door and pointed her toward Ma'tee, who was laid out in front of the pool, accompanied by beautiful women. There were beautiful women swimming completely nude in the pool while a shirtless Ma'tee watched in enjoyment as he sat on a beach chair, his feet crossed, and his hands behind his head. His dark skin glistened in the sun, and his muscular abs seemed to poke out of his stomach.

As Miamor slowly walked over to him, the clicking of her heels against the ground gained his attention.

He slowly sat up and looked at Miamor, admiring her shape and oversized behind. He loved the way her jeans hugged her hips, and the way she switched them when she walked. Her thighs seemed to stick out more than her waist. Ma'tee's fantasies were short-lived as he realized that Miamor was more than just a stunning woman—She was a cold-hearted killer too.

His dreads were much neater than his henchmen's, and the tips were bleached brown. He shook his head, letting them fall freely from its original ponytail. "Hello, Miamor," he said, greeting her with a smile.

"Hi, Ma'tee," she answered as she took a seat next to him. "Sorry I interrupted your daughter's birthday party, but I really needed to talk to you."

"Ey, mon, no problem. Miamor me girl, ya know," he said as he put on his shirt.

"Yeah, I know. But, listen, I need to know more about this nigga Mecca." Miamor stared in Ma'tee's eyes with deep sincerity.

Ma'tee saw the desperation in her eyes and stood up. "Why don't chu come to me office. We talk 'bout it."

Miamor nodded her head and got up to follow Ma'tee.

Just as they were about to reach the glass door, Ma'tee's daughter came running out. "Dadda, Dadda, the clown made me a giraffe, see?" She handed him the balloon animal.

"Yes, me see me baby girl's giraffe. Wonderful!" Ma'tee scooped her up in his arms.

"Dadda, when are you coming out to play with me?"

"Dadda gots to talk to me friend Miamor. Then me come back to you, okay," he said before he kissed her on the cheek.

"Okay. I have to use the bathroom now," his daughter said as she wiggled down and ran towards the wraparound stairs.

Ma'tee stared at his only child and smiled. He looked back at Miamor and said, "That's me baby girl, right dere."

Miamor smiled and continued to follow Ma'tee into his back office. She walked into the office, where Ma'tee had shelves of books. In fact with his extensive collection, the office sort of looked like a library. His shiny red oak table sat in the middle with a deluxe leather chair behind it.

Ma'tee made his way over to the chair and sat down. He waved his hand to the seat in front of him. "Sit, sit."

Miamor accepted his offer and sat down.

Ma'tee continued, "Me sorry to hear 'bout your sista. Me never meant for dat to happen, you know."

"Yeah, I know." Miamor dropped her head.

"Look, me still pay you, okay." Ma'tee pulled a briefcase from under his desk.

Miamor looked at the briefcase as Ma'tee popped it open. It was fifty stacks, ten percent of the agreed amount that they were to be paid after the job was completed. She knew that they didn't deserve the money, because they didn't finish the job, so she declined.

"No, Ma'tee, I'm good. I just want to know how to get at the mu'fucka that killed my—"

A loud scream came from upstairs. "Aghhh!" It was the voice of a little girl.

What the fuck? Miamor turned around and looked toward the door.

Ma'tee instantly recognized the voice to be his daughter's and grabbed his gun from his drawer and hurried to her aid.

Armed Haitians rushed upstairs where the girl was and what they saw devastated them. There were five bodies lying in their own blood, and Ma'tee's young daughter stood in the middle of them. She had discovered them when she went to use the restroom. The dead bodies were scattered throughout the hallway, each of them with double gunshot wounds through their heads.

Ma'tee's heart dropped when he saw his daughter

screaming in the middle of the massacre scene. He hurried over to her and scooped her in his arms.

Miamor had followed him up the stairs and was completely flabbergasted when she saw the slaughter. "Oh my God," she whispered as she put her hand over her mouth.

Young Carter drove the van down the interstate while Jay-Z's Reasonable Doubt pumped out of the factory speakers. He looked in his rearview mirror and saw Money and Mecca, both dressed in baggy clown suits and size 44 shoes, taking off their wigs and wiping off the clown face paint.

"Damn!" Mecca yelled as he forcefully snatched off his red wig. He was totally enraged that he didn't get a chance to kill Ma'tee. "I didn't see him. He was on the pool patio, and then when I snuck back in, he was gone. I should have popped him when I first saw him, but he had a guard by the door."

"He must've ducked off somewhere to smash that female that came in," Money added, noticeably discouraged also.

Carter got off on the highway and pulled into an empty parking lot, where Mecca's Lamborghini was waiting. "We'll get 'em next time," he said confidently, throwing the "clown" van in park.

Mecca peeled off the costume and jumped into his car. "If there is a next time. Because of what we just did, Ma'tee's security is going to be extra tight. We may never get that close to him again. Fuck!"

Carter and Money jumped in with him, and they pulled off on their way back home. They had just sent a clear message—The Cartel wasn't about to lie down.

Chapter Six

"In the middle of a war, there's no room for weakness."

—Young Carter

Miamor sat Indian-style next to her sister's grave, her spirit broken and feeling weak without her big sister in her life to guide her. Anisa was the reason why Miamor had been put on to the street life. She had taught her everything that she knew, and now she was lost forever at the hands of the game. Miamor had always known that the possibility of death was high, because of the lifestyle that she and her crew led. The same way that she was willing to murk a mu'fucka with no ifs, ands, or buts about it, she knew that somebody, somewhere, was willing to do the same thing to them. She just never thought that it would happen to Anisa at the tender age of 25. If she could turn back the hands of time, she would have definitely done things differently that night. It wasn't her idea to use Anisa as a pawn, but she was outvoted by the rest of the Murder Mamas, and the majority always ruled. Things are always so much clearer in hindsight, and she wished that she had convinced them to come up with a better plan to get at the notorious Cartel.

It had been weeks, and it was the first time she had been to visit Anisa's resting place. *This is all my fault,* she thought as tears formed in her eyes. She tried to fan her face to stop her tears from falling. She hated to cry, but it was no use. The tears trickled out of her eyes and stained her cheeks as she put her face in her hands, allowing her soul to release the pain.

"I'm sorry, Nisa. If I had been on point like I was supposed to be, this never would have happened," Miamor uttered out loud. She knew that wherever her sister was she could hear her.

She hadn't told anyone how she felt. Not even Aries and Robyn knew the guilt that she felt over her sister's untimely demise. She knew that the moment she lost sight of Mecca's black Lamborghini that her sister's life had been put on a countdown.

How did I let this happen? She felt the coldness from the grass that was still wet from the morning dew creep into her body. She shivered as she closed her eyes and thought of her sister's face. She bowed her head and prayed to God, feeling a closeness to Anisa that she'd never known while her sister was alive. *I'm sorry, Nis.*

Young Carter pulled his black Range Rover up to the cemetery and sat in his car for a moment to gather his thoughts. He was about to face his father for the first time. His first attempt had been interrupted by the Haitians, but now he had no excuse. It was time to make peace with the man who had created him. He got out of the car and walked up to the large monument that was his father's tombstone. He put his hand on it and leaned into the large marble, his head down. A spectrum of emotions shot through his body as he read the engraved inscription.

Carter Diamond
Beloved Husband, Leader, and Father of Four
"Diamonds are Forever"

He ran his hand over his face as he tried to contain the sorrow that took him over. He didn't know why he suddenly felt love for his father, but there was an unexpected connection between father and son that transcended even death.

"I know that you know that I'm here. I don't even know why I decided to stick around. For so long I wondered about you and why you left, why I never knew you. I understand now. I can't say that I can forget the abandonment that I experienced, growing up without a father, but I do forgive you. I swear on everything that I love that the mu'fuckas that are responsible for your death will never hurt the family." Carter began to walk away. He didn't think that there was anything left to say.

As he made his way back to his car, he stopped in his tracks when he saw the beautiful woman leaning against the passenger door. She was dressed in black Donna Karan slacks that hugged her hips and loosened at the leg, a black Donna Karan sweater, and silver Jimmy Choo stilettos. The closer he got to her, the more he recognized her face.

"Hi," she greeted as she stood with her silver clutch bag in hand.

"Damn, ma, I didn't peg you as the stalking type," he commented with a sexy smile.

A tiny dimple formed on the left side of his mouth, and that feature immediately became her favorite part of him.

"I was about to say the same thing, seeing as how I was here first," she replied, returning his smile with one of her own. "I saw you pull up just as I was leaving, so I decided to wait here for you. Who are you here for?"

"Just a family member, no one I was real close to," he responded. "I just wanted to pay my respects." He noticed that her eyes were red and swollen and there were bags underneath them. She looked tired and weak. Although she was still beautiful, there was something different about her. "You all right?" he asked.

"I'm"—She paused to think of the best way to describe her current state of mind—"surviving. My sister passed away a couple weeks ago. That's why I'm here." The woman shuffled nervously in her stance and looked at her feet.

"I'm sorry to hear about that."

"Yeah, me too." She stared off into space, and the tears returned to her eyes. She willed them away and shook her head as she looked back at Carter. "I'm Miamor," she said, offering her hand to him.

"Oh, I'm worthy of a name this time?"

Carter chuckled as he took her hand into his and shook it gently. Her name, exotic enough to complement her around-the-way features, fit her perfectly. Her brown shoulder-length layers were curled loosely and shaped her almond-colored skin. Her white teeth composed the perfect smile, and her MAC cosmetics were applied just right, not too much, but enough to make her skin glow.

"I told you, if you were worth my time, I'd see you again." She tiptoed and peeked at the tattoo that displayed his name. "Carter," she said aloud.

He noticed how she never let go of his hand as she intertwined her fingers with his own. The sound of his name rolling off her pouty lips was enticing, and he couldn't help but to be intrigued by her.

"It was nice to meet you," she stated as she walked

away. She didn't let go of his hand, until she was forced to, because of the widening distance between them.

As he watched her strut away, she waved one last time and got into a silver Nissan Maxima and pulled away. Carter shook his head from side to side, grateful for her departure. He knew that if he ever got to know Miamor, she would be his weakness. He smiled to himself as he watched her car disappear around the corner and then hopped into his own vehicle and departed. *In the middle of a war, there's no room for weakness. Love will get you killed,* he thought as he made his way back to the Diamond mansion.

Breeze stood in the dining room over the kitchen table and argued as her mother, uncle, and twin brothers ate breakfast. "Uncle Polo, I'm not going out with this big, ugly bodyguard attached to my hip! How am I supposed to chill with my girls with him following me everywhere?"

Polo told her, "It's not negotiable, Breeze. You are not to leave this house alone. One of our men will escort you wherever you need to go. If you don't like that arrangement, you better ask one of your brothers to accompany you?"

"I got plans." Mecca stated quickly.

Breeze rolled her eyes at Mecca and hoped that her other brother would come to her rescue. "Money, please?" she begged.

"Sorry *B*, no can do. Uncle Polo and Young Carter set up a meeting between me and the board of advisors at Diamond Realty. I'm going to be taking that over, and I need to sit down with the board to make sure that they understand that this is still a family business—"

"Yeah, yeah, whatever."

"Who said you were going to be the one to take over the real estate company?" Mecca inquired.

"Young Carter and I discussed it," Money replied. "We think it's best."

"And I didn't have a say in this decision?" Mecca asked in irritation.

Young Carter overheard the conversation as he walked into the room. "No, you didn't, Mecca." He gave both Breeze and Taryn kisses on the cheek, and then patted Polo on the back. "There is enough responsibility for all of us to get in on some part of the business. The real estate company is where Monroe needs to be. We need to keep one of us clean and legal, now that we are at war with the Haitians. We never know where this might lead, and the less Monroe is involved, the better." Carter slapped hands with Monroe and then sat down at the table.

Polo smiled at Young Carter's authoritative approach when dealing with his younger brothers. He knew that it was only a matter of time before the young man assumed a leadership position in The Cartel.

"Yeah, you're right," Mecca responded hesitantly as he slapped hands with his older brother. Mecca still didn't like the fact that Carter had appeared out of the blue claiming to be his father's son, but the more he got to know Young Carter, the more he respected him. There wasn't a doubt in anyone's mind regarding his bloodline, and he was slowly beginning to warm up to the idea.

"Have you eaten, Carter?" Taryn asked.

"No, I haven't."

Taryn stood to fixed him a plate and put it in front of him.

"Thank you."

Breeze whined as if she were still a child. "Uncle Polo?"

Polo sighed and pointed his fork at Young Carter. "Will you tell your sister that she doesn't need to leave the house without one of the men?"

Carter asked, "Where you need to go, Breeze? I'll take

you," "Thank you. At least one of my brothers is willing to do something for me," she stated in playful exasperation. She grabbed Carter by the hand. "Come on, let's go. We'll get something to eat later."

Carter grabbed one last forkful of eggs and put it in his mouth before Breeze pulled him out of the kitchen.

Taryn laughed out loud at the sight. "Looks like Breeze has found one more man to spoil her. That child is rotten," she stated with a smile on her face.

Carter maneuvered the Range Rover in and out of the Miami traffic as his sister sat in the passenger side, the huge Ralph Lauren sunglasses covering most of her face.

"I haven't gotten a chance to kick it with you much, with everything that's going on." Carter wanted to know how his presence in Miami affected Breeze.

"I know it seems like the only thing everyone has been worried about is The Cartel. It feels like I'm living out some old gangster movie or something. I just want things to be normal again," she replied, looking out of the window.

"So what's your take on everything that's happened?"

"You really wanna know?" Breeze pulled her glasses from her face and rested them on top of her head.

Carter nodded his head and waited for her to answer the question.

"I feel cheated because I only got to know my father for nineteen years. I loved him, and I wanted him to be there when I got married, and when I had my first child. I wanted him to be here for me. I feel like, now that he's gone, everything is going downhill. My mom is afraid every single day that the Haitians are going to harm us. Since meeting you, Mecca has become extra hard. It's almost like he's trying to prove himself to you. It's like he wants to make sure that everyone knows he is Carter Diamond's son. Monroe is the same, Uncle Po is the same—"

"And what about you?"

"Me, I'm dealing with everything the best way I know how. I cry every morning when I think of my Poppa. It's like one minute I'm upset with God for Him taking my father away, and then the next minute, I'm thanking Him for bringing you into our lives when He did. You are my brother, and I am glad that you're here, Carter. I don't know how, but you make things seem like they'll be okay."

"I'm just here to help, Breeze. At first, I wanted to say, 'Fuck Miami,' and move on with my life as if none of you ever existed, but that would be selfish. And I've never had a family, so I want to get to know you, Mecca, and Monroe."

"Well, I can tell you the way to win my heart," she said with a smile as bright as the summer Miami sun.

"How's that?"

"Everything today is on you."

"I got you, sis."

Breeze found out that she and Carter shared the same love for fashion. She took him from store to store as she shopped, picking up every designer she could find. He didn't complain or rush her in the same way her other brothers did, and he even gave honest opinions when she asked about an outfit she tried on.

"How's this?" she asked as she walked out of the dressing room in Saks Fifth with a skintight Seven jeans that fit low on her hips, almost revealing the crack of her ass, and a Fendi blouse that barely covered her breasts.

It was sexy, but definitely not something that he wanted his sister to wear. "I'm not buying that shit. As a matter of fact, you ain't wearing it even if you buy it yourself, so you might as well hang that back up." He flipped through his Apple iPhone, ignoring her.

"Come on, Carter, it's not that bad," she argued.

He didn't respond, and just continued to focus on his phone.

"You're just as strict as Poppa was," she stated with a little bit of attitude and a laugh. "I am a grown-ass woman, you know, big-head ass."

"I heard that," he stated calmly as he leaned back in the leather chair, still flipping through his phone. He shook his head once she disappeared behind the dressing room curtain. As he waited for her to come out again, he mumbled to himself, "She gon' have me fucking these little niggas up in Miami."

They went through several outfits, and he had a comment for each one.

"Nah."

"That's whack, sis."

"That shit don't match."

Breeze went in and out of the dressing rooms until she finally grew tired of his disapproval. "Okay, Carter," she said, "out of all the stuff I've tried on, you've only liked three outfits. You tell me what's hot."

Carter put his phone on the clip of his belt buckle. "A'ight, let me show you how to do this. All that hooker shit you and your girlfriends be wearing is trash."

"Excuse me, everything in my closet cost a grip," she replied, one hand on her hip.

"That doesn't mean that it's classy. I'm a man, so I know what I'm talking about." He quickly located ten different items for Breeze to try on. "You want these niggas to respect you out here, especially you. You're the only daughter of Carter Diamond. You need to dress like the princess that you are and make men come at you correct when they checking for you."

"I hear you." Breeze took the items from his grasp. She tried on the first outfit, which was a pair of cropped white Ferragamo pants that hugged her shape as if it were tailor-made just for her body. Her white shirt had a sharp collar, dipped low in the cleavage area, and fit snugly around her slim waist, her sleeves stopping short just above her elbows, and a large black fashion belt adorned her waist. She slipped her feet into a pair of black stilettos. She had to admit, the outfit was nice and made her look like a kingpin's daughter.

She walked out of the dressing room and did a full spin for her brother.

"That's more you," he stated as he stood to his feet. He checked his presidential Rolex and noticed that they had been shopping for hours. He called one of the store associates over to them. "Can you have these items boxed and bagged for us?" he asked.

The woman grabbed the items from Breeze as she changed back into her clothes.

"Let's grab something to eat before we head back," he said as they walked out of the store.

"I know just the place. It's right up the street," Breeze responded as they walked out of the store. Breeze had at least five bags in each hand as they walked the distance to the restaurant.

Carter followed her across the street and into an elegant building that was made of marble and glass. He looked up at the sign that read *Breezes*. He looked at her in confusion.

She smiled. "Poppa bought it for me on my tenth birthday."

Carter nodded, and they entered the restaurant to have a late lunch. There was a long line of patrons waiting to be served. The establishment was crowded, so they inched through the crowd until they reached the hostess.

"Hello, Ms. Diamond," the hostess greeted, obviously recognizing Breeze. "Right this way."

There were groans and complaints from the people who stood waiting, but Breeze and Carter eased right past them and into the lavish environment. The voice of Billie Holiday filled the darkened space, and all eyes seemed to be on Breeze.

As they passed the bar, Carter saw Miamor sitting on a stool with two other women and he winked at her as he passed by. When they arrived at their table, Carter pulled out the chair for his sister and then sat across from her.

Aries' eyes followed Breeze and Carter to their table. "Miamor, isn't that de guy from de Casino?"

"Yeah, that's him." Miamor's arched eyebrows frowned at the sight of him. A twinge of jealousy crept through her heart, but she knew that she had no right to be upset. She didn't even know Carter. Just because she was feeling him a little didn't mean anything.

"Damn, is that his girl?" Robyn asked.

"Must be," Miamor replied, her tone a bit more sarcastic than she intended.

"Me know you ain't green?" Aries teased.

"Hell nah!" Miamor exclaimed. "Jealous for what? I don't even know the nigga. Yo, for real, it ain't even that serious. Since when have you ever known me to be that type?"

"Whoever chick is, she's rocking them Prada shoes." Robyn nodded her head in approval.

Miamor rolled her eyes and sipped at her drink as she tried not to focus on Carter.

"What are you looking at?" Breeze asked.

"Just a friend," he replied.

Breeze turned around and stared toward the bar at the three young women that had so much of her brother's attention.

"You making friends like that already? You've only been here a couple weeks."

"It's not like that, so get your head out of the gutter."

Breeze laughed again. It was refreshing to see her smile. It was then that Carter realized that he had never seen his sister's smile, and it looked good on her. This was the first time that he'd ever seen her happy.

She peeked back at the girls one more time and then whispered, "Which one is she?"

"The one in all black," he replied as he watched Breeze look back. "Quit staring, Breeze."

"Shit, she's staring back," Breeze shot back. "She must think I'm your girlfriend or something, because her face is all twisted up." Breeze giggled. After she took a sip of water from her water goblet, she said, "You better go talk to her because she looks mad."

Carter looked past his sister's head and saw the look on Miamor's face. He stood from the table and looked down at Breeze. "I'll be right back."

Robyn turned on her bar stool. "Don't look now, but here come your boy. I think I need to use the bathroom. Come on, Aries."

"What you mean, come on? Me don't have to go with you," Aries stated with a devilish grin. She licked her lips at the sight of the dark man walking toward them.

"Aries!" Miamor whispered.

"Why me have to go with she?"

"Because she doesn't want you all in her face, bitch. Now, come on." Robyn laughed and pulled Aries away.

Miamor laughed for the first time since her sister died, and Robyn winked at her as they disappeared around the corner.

Carter slid into the seat next to Miamor. "Why is it that you're everywhere I seem to be?"

"I don't know, but if I had known that you and your girl-friend would be here, I would have gone somewhere else," she replied with an attitude.

Carter smiled at her jealousy. They barely knew each other, yet she was already staking her claim.

"Don't be like that." He scooted his stool closer to her and whispered in her ear, "I'm only interested in one woman in this room."

She smiled, but scooted her own stool away from him. "I don't want to have to fuck your girlfriend up, so don't start no shit," she said seriously.

"That flip lip you got don't suit you, ma. I'm gon' have to grow you up."

"Oh, really. I can't wait to see you try to do that because a man can't change anything that I don't want him to. I'm-a do me, regardless. I most definitely ain't changing for a nigga that already got a chick." Miamor turned to see Breeze walking toward them. "Here comes your girlfriend. You better make sure she acts right." Miamor faced the bar and sipped her strawberry daiquiri.

Carter shook his head as he watched his sister approach. He definitely wasn't impressed by Miamor's feistiness, but he liked a challenge. He knew that it wouldn't take long for her to fall in line, so he let her smart mouth slide for the moment.

"I just got a phone call from Mommy. I told her that we'd do take-out and bring dinner home," Breeze stated when she walked up.

"That's fine with me, but first I want to introduce you to a friend of mine. Breeze, this is Miamor. Miamor, this is my *sister*, Breeze," he said with a wicked smile.

Miamor, an embarrassed expression on her face, cut her eyes at Carter. He had let her sweat and show her jealousy, when all along he was with his sister. She smiled and shook the girl's hand. "Nice to meet you, Breeze."

"You too," Breeze replied.

Carter stood to leave and didn't say a word as he walked away from Miamor and headed for the door.

No, this nigga didn't. Miamor watched his back as he made his way through the crowd.

Carter stopped at the hostess' desk and wrote a note to Miamor. He asked the hostess, "Can you hand this to the young lady at the bar?" handed her a twenty-dollar tip, and then left out behind Breeze.

The hostess tapped Miamor's shoulder. "Excuse me, miss."

"Yes?"

"The gentleman that just left asked me to give you this." The hostess dropped the folded piece of paper on the bar.

"Thank you," she replied as she eagerly opened it.

Meet me at the end of the South Pier tonight at midnight. Don't front like you ain't coming, ma. Do yourself a favor and be there. I want to get to know you, Miamor.

Carter

PS: Dinner is on me

Miamor smiled as her friends reappeared at the table.

"What did he say?" Robyn asked.

"Nigga didn't say nothing," Miamor said. "He came over here to tell me that chick is his sister, that's all."

The friends resumed their conversation, and Miamor threw in an occasional comment to make them think that she was paying attention, but her mind was on Carter. She was definitely going to the pier that night. She checked her cell phone to see what time it was and immediately started counting down the minutes until she saw Carter again.

Chapter Seven

Only God can judge me.

—Miamor

Miamor stood nervously at the end of the pier. Goose-bumps covered her arms as the mist from the turbu-lent ocean blew onto the pier and sprinkled her with light kisses. Looking out on the water, she watched the waves as they washed up onto the shore. The white foam that they created was the only color she saw as she stared out into the black night.

"What are you thinking about?" Carter asked.

The sound of his baritone voice caused her to jump slightly, and she turned around to greet him. "You," she replied as she looked up at him.

Carter took in her feminine essence as his eyes scan-ned her body. She wore a mocha-colored wrap dress that stopped mid-thigh. It fit snugly around her voluptuous frame, revealing one shoulder and her toned upper back. Her thick thighs and lean legs glistened under the moon-light, and her hair was swooped to the side in an elegant bun.

"You look nice."

"Thank you," she blushed as she wrapped her arm in

his, and they began to walk toward his car. "So tell me where we are going tonight?" she asked.

"You'll see," he replied as he led her down the steps of the pier.

She followed him, but before stepping her feet into the sand, she removed her Louis Vuitton stilettos and placed them in her hands.

He chuckled at her as he watched her shrink before him.

"Shut up." She hit him softly on the arm. "These are a three-hundred-dollar pair of shoes. Where are we going anyway?"

"You'll see," he replied as he led her to a secluded area on the beach.

Miamor followed him behind a row of huge boulders that sectioned off a small piece of sand and smiled when she saw the intimate midnight picnic that Carter had set up.

"What is all this?" she asked in delight as she sat down on the blanket. There were fruits, champagne, melted chocolate, and white rose petals everywhere. Carter had even gotten jarred candles and set them up around the sight. No man had ever gone through so much trouble to impress her, and she was taken aback by Carter's effort. He was definitely a different type of man, and she looked forward to the night ahead.

"I want to get to know you. I don't want there to be people around, or for you to feel like you got to put up an act in front of me," he replied. "I see your tough-girl demeanor, but I'm not buying it."

Carter pulled the champagne out of the ice bucket and poured two flutes. He handed one to her, and she gratefully accepted the drink as she lifted the flute to her lips.

"Why is it so hard for you to believe that this is me?"

"Because I see through you," Carter replied. "I'm trying to get to know the real Miamor."

"Okay, so tell me what you want to know?" Miamor folded her legs behind her and grabbed some grapes.

"Whatever you want to tell me."

"There isn't a whole lot to tell. What you see is really what you get." Miamor didn't really know what Carter wanted to hear. How could she sum her entire existence up in a couple words?

"No offense, ma, but I don't see a whole lot," Carter stated.

Miamor cut her eyes at him and stood to her feet. *I don't know who the fuck this nigga think he is.* "Then what the fuck am I here for?"

She began to walk away. She didn't know why, but tears came to her eyes as she stormed off. It wasn't that she cared about what Carter thought of her. He wasn't the be-all and end-all , but she was offended by the fact that she appeared shallow at first glance.

This nigga don't know shit about me. He doesn't know that I caught my first body when I was just ten years old. It wasn't because I'm a killer or murderer, but because I mistakenly shot him while he was on top of my sister raping her. He doesn't know that after that Anisa and I were on our own because my mother was so enraged by the fact that we killed the man who kept a roof over our head. He sitting over there talking about he don't see much. Fuck him! She cursed him silently as she wiped her eyes and fled down the sandy beach.

Miamor was pissed off that Carter felt that he could pass judgment on her. *Only God can judge me*, she thought. She was so upset that her anger turned to sadness and regret as she thought about all of the negative things that she had been through. The average chick couldn't have survived her life's circumstances, but under pressure Miamor was forced to evolve into a woman who never wore her heart on her sleeve. She had become just as conniving, manipulative, and hardened as any man in the streets. *He really don't know who I am. He got me all the way fucked up.*

"Aye, hold up." Carter grabbed her arm.

"Let me go!" she yelled as she snatched her arm away from him and continued to walk away.

Carter could see that his words had hurt her, and he immediately regretted being so forward with her. He grabbed her again, and hugged her tightly from behind as she fought to free herself from his hold. She was crying and visibly upset.

Carter felt like an asshole, but he had no clue that her tears were from the many demons that she had battled throughout the years. Her sudden breakdown had nothing to do with him. She had learned to suppress her emotions well. In her area of expertise there was no room for feelings. Allowing herself to feel anything clouded her vision, and she always had to stay focused. Distraction meant death for her, and she'd learned that the hard way with Anisa. She hated herself for letting Carter see her so weak, which was why she fought so hard to get away from him.

"Whoa! Miamor, calm down," Carter stated.

"Get the fuck off of me!"

"I apologize. I was out of line," he said as he continued to hold her tightly.

Miamor's knees gave out underneath her as her sister's death hit her harder than ever before. It had been so long since she'd cried that, now that she had started, she couldn't stop herself. All the pain that she had suppressed over the past thirteen years was pouring out of her.

"Shh," Carter whispered in her ear as his arms comforted her. "Let it out, ma. This is what I was talking about. Now I see you. This is the girl I want to get to know," he told her.

Carter let her collapse onto the sand, but his arms never left her body. He sat with her as she cried her eyes out, and eventually she stopped fighting him and found a comfortable space within his embrace.

After the tears stopped, they sat there silently, yet content with the intimate moment that was unfolding, Carter holding her in his arms and Miamor listening to his strong heartbeat as she felt safe for the first time in her life.

"I'm sorry for popping off on you earlier," she finally whispered in a low tone.

"It's all right, Mia. I apologize for coming at you wrong. I didn't want to hurt your feelings. I just want to get to know the real you. The woman that I just saw break down is the one that I'm trying to know. You think you can make that happen?"

"Yeah, I can do that," she said with a half-smile.

"One day I want to know what made you cry like that. I want to learn everything about you. I want to know what makes you cry, what makes you laugh, what you want out of life, what your dreams are. I want to know you, ma."

Tears came to her eyes again as she stared into his brown, trusting eyes. She looked at the small scar that seemed to fit so perfectly with the features on his face. She was at a loss for words as she listened to him speak.

Miamor couldn't help herself as she looked at the handsome man before her. His words were getting to her. She didn't know if it was game or not, but if it was, she concluded that it was one that she would let herself believe. She felt compelled to kiss the lips that were saying all the right things. She leaned in and kissed him softly. His lips were soft and big. His masculine hands lightly massaged the back of her neck, causing her heart rate to increase. The fresh scent of Issey Miyake filled her nose, and she inhaled deeply, enjoying the scent. She had the first-kiss jitters as butterflies fluttered in her stomach.

Carter picked her up without ever breaking their kiss and carried her back to their picnic site. Setting her down gently, he watched her as she leaned back on her elbows and looked up at him. The lust and passion that burned in her eyes signaled what time it was.

Miamor couldn't contain the fire that was ablaze between her legs. She had to have him, opening and closing her legs seductively while he gazed down at her.

Carter could see her neatly trimmed pussy hairs, and his excitement heightened when he noticed that she wasn't wearing any panties, her skin blending with the color of the sand perfectly. Her body exuded sexiness. Carter licked his lips as he pulled his shirt over his head.

Miamor put one finger in her mouth and sucked it erotically as she enjoyed the chiseled view in front of her. She took the moisture from her mouth and circled it on her clitoris. Her love button throbbed intensely as she rolled it between her fingers.

"You like what you see?" Miamor asked as she inserted two fingers inside herself. Miamor was so sure of herself. She wasn't shy and was comfortable in her own skin, so she continued to please herself for a minute or two. Her pussy was soaking wet, and she began to grind her hips to her own beat. She closed her eyes as her other hand massaged her now stiff nipples. The feeling caused a low moan to escape her lips.

Carter kept looking down at her and felt his dick get hard. His manhood was urging him to get in the game, but he contained himself, trying to savor the moment, not wanting to be too eager.

When Miamor took her finger out of her pussy to taste her own juices, Carter could no longer contain himself. The print of his eleven inches was bulging in his jeans, and he quickly stepped out of them and positioned himself on top of her. He grabbed one of the strawberries and put it in her mouth as she nibbled on it sexily. His mouth found hers, and their tongues intertwined. He could taste the sweet fruit on her tongue along with the sweet taste of pussy as his rock-hard erection rubbed against her thigh.

Carter stuck his finger in the melted chocolate and rubbed it on her nipples as he feasted on them, tugging at them gently with his lips and tongue.

"Mmm," Mia moaned, her back arched from the tingling pleasure that was shooting through her back.

Her body was like a buffet, Carter pouring champagne on top of her and licking it clean, never leaving a trace behind. He made his way down to her womanly opening and lifted one leg in the air, which she rested on his broad shoulders as her eyes rolled back in her head. Carter then introduced his tongue to her clitoris, licking it gently as if he were tongue-kissing her mouth instead of her pussy.

Miamor began to shake uncontrollably. No man had ever done her body so good. Carter definitely knew what he was doing. His head game was out of this world. Most men rushed and only went downtown to benefit themselves by getting the pussy more wet, but Carter took his time, inserting two fingers as she grinded on his face.

"Oh my God," she moaned as her hands found the back of his head. "Wait," she whined. Carter was eating her pussy so well that Miamor couldn't wait to return the favor.

She sat up on her elbows and attempted to get up, but Carter pulled her back underneath him as she lay back and watched his swell glisten in the moonlight, pre-cum resting on the tip. He rubbed her clit with his hat, and the warmth from his body temperature made her hot, sizzling against her honey pot.

It had been a long time since she had been intimate with someone, and it wasn't until now that she realized how much she missed a man's touch. "I want to feel you inside of me," she whispered as she wrapped her arms around his back and slid her hands down until they reached his toned behind.

"Wait, I don't have a condom," he whispered. He silently cursed himself for not being prepared.

Miamor looked him dead in his eyes. "Then don't make a baby, if you don't want one." She pulled him into her, and he immediately filled the space between her legs, his thick hardness throbbing inside of her as her walls contracted around his large shaft.

"Shit, you feel so good," he told her as he rocked in and out of her with a slow, passionate rhythm.

Miamor was silent as she stared into his eyes. She had never been with a man that looked at her the way Carter did at that moment. Their gaze expressed more than any words could ever do. They had a sexual chemistry that was out of this world, and he was making her body hurt in a pleasing way. A tear slipped from her eyes, and he kissed it away as it rolled down her cheek.

Miamor moved her wide hips in unison and matched him pump for pump, and Carter put his hands underneath her rear and lifted her hips, allowing him to dig deeper into her.

"Carter!" she called out in ecstasy as he explored depths in her that she didn't even know existed. "Carter," she repeated as he sped up and pounded into her a little harder.

She was about to cum, and from the low grunts that

came out of his mouth, she could tell that he was about to nut at any moment. "Make me cum, Carter," she whispered.

He pumped into her harder at the sound of her voice.

"Ohh shit, daddy, make me cum," she begged.

He stroked her faster. "I'm-a make you cum, Miamor. Oh shit, your pussy is so good, ma."

She grabbed his ass and rotated her hips into him as she felt her body reach its peak. "Oh my . . . aww!" she screamed, as her toes curling and her body tensing up from the intensity of her orgasm.

"Damn, ma," Carter said, pulling out and nutting against her flat stomach.

Miamor snuggled underneath Carter as they lay naked on the empty beach. He reached out and grabbed the blanket from their picnic and covered their bodies with it as they sat together and looked out on the ocean.

Carter was silent, and Miamor instantly began to regret having sex with him. *Damn, I know this nigga probably thinking I'm a ho. I shouldn't have fucked him this soon,* she thought. Miamor had only been with one other person in her entire life, and she didn't know why she had let Carter have her body so easily. There was something about him that she trusted, and he had her open.

"Carter, I don't want you to think—"

"I don't, so don't worry about it," he replied before she could even finish her sentence. He already knew what she was thinking, but he wasn't shallow enough to worry about anything that happened before him. They were both grown as hell, and he didn't want her to feel awkward for allowing him to enjoy her physically.

He turned her face toward his. "As long as you act like a lady, I'll never think anything less of you, understand?"

She nodded her head. "Will I get to see you again?"

"I want to spend some time with you, but I need to take care of some business back home first."

"Back home? You're not from Miami?" Miamor realized she didn't know a damn thing about this man.

"Naw, I'm from Michigan, from Flint." Carter played with her fingers. He brought her hand to his mouth and kissed it.

"How long will you be gone?"

Carter smiled. He could hear the disappointment in her voice. He knew he had to be careful with this woman. He could see that Miamor played tough on the outside, but on the inside, she was hurt and neglected from her past, which made her susceptible to heartbreak. Her vulnerability pleased him, and he was willing to become her protector, if she played her cards right.

"Not long. I just need to tie up some loose ends. It looks like I'm gon' be moving down here for a minute. Don't worry, Miamor, I'll make sure I check for you when I get back."

She sat with her back to his chest and turned her neck to kiss him on the lips. "I better get going," she said as she grabbed her dress and stepped into it.

Carter stood and slipped back into his clothing as well.

Miamor retrieved her clutch bag and pulled out a pen to write her number down. She grabbed his hand and wrote it on his skin and then wrote his number down as well.

"Call me when you come back in town," she said as she looked up at him with a smile.

Carter grabbed the back of her neck and brought her body close to his as he leaned down to kiss her lips. "Be safe."

Miamor stepped out of his arms and walked away. She smiled and waved before walking down the beach, toward the pier.

Carter shook his head as he watched her stroll away.

Her hair was a mess, and sand stuck to her legs as her hips swayed from side to side, but she had his attention. Her swagger was intriguing. He rubbed his goatee, and a sly smile graced his lips. "I'm gon' definitely check for you, Miamor, believe that," he said to himself as she disappeared into the darkness.

Chapter Eight

"Welcome home."

—Unknown

Breeze hugged Carter goodbye. "Are you really coming back?"

"Yeah, *B*, I'll be back. I've got to get some things together in Flint, but as soon as that's taken care of, I'll be on the first flight down." Carter could see the doubt in his sister's eyes. "I promise."

Money and Carter slapped hands and embraced. "Be safe, fam," Money told him.

"No doubt, baby."

Mecca walked by and nodded his head, but didn't acknowledge Carter's departure with words, and Taryn hugged him gently.

"We better get out of here before you miss your flight." Polo patted Carter's shoulder, and they hopped into the black limousine and pulled away from the estate.

Ma'tee noticed the black limo pulling away from the Diamond estate and halted his driver. "Wait," Ma'tee instructed as he sat a block down from his intended destina-

tion, "me will sit here for a second and watch." He checked
the 9 mm Desert Eagle that was holstered in his waistline
to ensure that it was locked and loaded before he nodded
his head at his driver. "Tell de guard dat Mr. Diamond forgot something," Ma'tee said, hoping that the guards would
not want to check the inside of the car as they pulled up
to the gated entrance. He wanted them to think that his
limo was the same limo that had just left the estate fifteen
minutes earlier.

His driver followed his instructions to the tee, and just
as Ma'tee had expected, they were given access to the
household without suspicion. The guards were clueless to
the fact that their enemies were the true passengers behind the dark limo tint.

Ma'tee looked to his full-blooded Haitian soldiers that
sat around him, all armed with semi-automatic pistols and
ready for whatever. When the limo stopped in front of the
house, he exited the limo calmly and rang the doorbell,
his goons positioned behind him.

Breeze answered the door, and her smile quickly faded
when she noticed the Haitian men at her doorstep.
"Aghh!" she screamed.

"No need to scream, Diamond princess," Ma'tee stated
calmly, realizing that he was standing in front of the only
daughter of his sworn enemy, Carter Diamond. "Me come
peacefully to talk with de head of de Cartel."

At that moment, Taryn came gliding into the room.
"What are you screaming about, Breeze? Who is . . ." Her
words trailed off, and her eyes turned cold as she stared
into the eyes of Ma'tee, the man who had murdered her
husband in cold blood.

"How dare you!" Taryn screamed as tears filled her
eyes. She smacked Ma'tee across the face with all her
might. Her rage was apparent, and she stood her ground,
even though fear gripped her heart.

Ma'tee's soldiers tensed up at her reaction, but again Ma'tee instructed them to stand down.

"Go and get your brothers." Taryn spoke calmly but sternly, yet her eyes never left those of the enemy. She didn't want to give them the pleasure of seeing her intimidated.

Breeze ran out of the room to get her brothers.

"Me come in peace," Ma'tee repeated when Mecca and Monroe appeared.

"Fuck mu'fuckas coming to the estate!" Mecca screamed. He immediately pulled two .45's from his waistline and trained them on Ma'tee.

"We need to talk," Ma'tee stated. "As chu can see, chu family is not untouchable, young Mecca. If me wanted to bring malice to chu door, chu sista and mutha would be dead right now. Me come to call a truce."

"Only after you murdered my father and we put the heat on your ass. You're here because of what happened at your daughter's birthday party. *You* are not untouchable, Ma'tee. If we wanted to bring malice to your door. then you would've buried your fucking daughter last week," Monroe stated calmly. He pulled his own 9 mm from his waistline and rested it in his palm at his side.

"Me understand. Bloodshed came to close to me home wit' me baby girl. Me will stand down if de Cartel will."

Mecca yelled, "I'm-a murder your fucking daughter, mu'fucka. Fuck a truce, bitch. You took my father, I take her—Fair exchange ain't no robbery!"

"Yuh kill me daughter, ah kill you sister, then what, young soldier? De Cartel has nothing to lose by calling a truce. Yuh keep yuh territory and we all gain peace of mind."

Monroe knew that a truce made sense, but was reluctant to make a deal with the devil. "How do we know you will keep up your end?"

"Me a man. Me will keep me word. Me word is all me have." Ma'tee held out his hand.

Monroe stared contemptuously at Ma'tee's hand, rage burning in his heart from the fresh wound of his dead father. He knew that the truce was a wise decision, at least for the time being. He shook Ma'tee's hand firmly, staring him in the eye. Monroe's gaze was nothing short of menacing, and it held an underlying message. One that said he had not forgotten what Ma'tee had done to his father.

"We have an understanding. Now see yourself off of our property," Monroe stated. He watched as the Haitians retreated and the limo disappeared beyond the security gates. Money turned to Mecca and said, "Go handle that stupid mu'fucka at the gates. Dead his ass. They should've never made it to the door."

Mecca stormed out of the house and walked across the large manicured lawn while Ma'tee and his limo approached the steel gate. They reached the exit at the same time, and Ma'tee rolled down his window.

The guard posted at the gate looked at Mecca approaching and then shifted his gaze back to Ma'tee.

"I just thought you should know why you're about to die," Ma'tee said as he lit a cigar and rolled his window back up.

At that exact moment Mecca reached the guard and removed his chrome 9 mm Ruger.

"Me-Mecca, I didn't know that was—"

BOOM!

Mecca didn't hesitate to pull the trigger. The guard's life was ended instantly as the hollow-point bullet ripped through his skull. Mecca then hit the button to open the gate for Ma'tee's limo, and ice grilled the car as it rolled away toward safety.

Truce or no truce, I'm going to avenge Poppa's murder. Niggas got me fucked up.

* * *

Carter was finally home after being in Miami for the past couple of weeks. He walked into his spacious two-bedroom that sat in a suburban area just outside Flint, Michigan. Carter took a deep breath as he realized how good it felt to be there. His condo was small but comfortable. He had just purchased it a year earlier. He always said, when his money got right, he would move out of the hood, and that's exactly what he did.

The brick walls were ornamented with various Afrocentric paintings. A large picture of Bob Marley smoking a joint and playing his guitar hung above the fireplace. The place was definitely a bachelor's pad, but Carter had decorated it pretty well. He tossed the duffle bag full of money onto his brown sectional sofa and pulled his gun from his waist and placed it on the bar-style kitchen countertop.

Carter was getting money in Flint, and it wasn't a secret. For every getting-money dope man, there were a hundred broke niggas, so Carter knew that he was a target for the local stick-up kids in his old neighborhood. Moving out of the hood was not an option after Carter began to become a heavyweight in the streets.

Just as he was about to walk to the refrigerator and toss out some of the food he had left there, he heard a noise coming from the back. *What the fuck was that?* Carter scooped up his gun and listened closer. He heard commotion coming from his back room and knew that someone was trying to find his stash. His street instincts immediately kicked in. He switched his banger off safety and began to creep to the back.

As he got closer, he saw that his guest bedroom was where the noises were coming from. His door was closed, so he crept up and kicked it open, his gun drawn.

The big-butt Latino woman screamed, "Oh, daddy! Fuck me, *papi!*" as Ace beat it from the back.

The sounds of Ace's balls smacking against the woman's genitalia filled the air, and his chain jingled on his bare chest as he continued to sex the girl, while Carter pointed his gun at him. Carter smiled and lowered his gun as he chuckled to himself. He was laughing at how crazy his best friend was. He didn't even stop pumping when he saw Carter bust in. The girl was so busy getting her back blew out, she didn't even notice Carter come in.

Ace looked at his best friend and threw his head up, greeting him while still pleasing himself.

Carter walked out shaking his head from side to side. He knew it wasn't a good idea to leave an extra set of keys with Ace. He'd told Ace to come in and check on his spot periodically, not bring his jump-offs there. "That nigga is wildin'," Carter said in irritation as he walked to his living room and tossed his gun on the couch.

Ace and Carter had been best friends since third grade and were more like brothers than anything else. Carter didn't like the fact that Ace had a chick up in his spot, but didn't say anything. He didn't want to cock-block his man, but he was surely going to express his discomfort later.

Carter took a seat on his couch and felt his cell phone vibrate on his hip. He looked at the caller ID and smiled. It was Miamor calling. *I got to stay focused. I'm going to get at her later,* he thought to himself as a small grin spread across his face.

Carter wanted to pick up for her, but he wanted to stay focused on his brief return home. He was planning to move to Miami and get on his hustle. He figured Miami was a good place for him to take over and join the family business. He saw more money in the three weeks in Miami than in a year hustling in Flint. The move was a must for him.

Just as Carter finished his thought, Ace came from the back, buttoning up his Sean John jeans.

"Fam, what's good? I thought you weren't coming back for a week or so?" Ace walked over to the bar and rested his hands on the counter.

Carter remained silent and just looked at him with a piercing stare.

Ace knew that his right-hand man was upset with him, so he tried to make light of the situation. "Did you see that ass on that broad?" He nodded his head in the direction of the back room.

Just before Carter could tell Ace about himself, the naked Latino woman came walking out, and all eyes were on her. She walked out without a care in the world, as if she wasn't butt naked. Her behind was so big, you could literally sit a cup on top of it and it wouldn't move. The only thing she wore was red pumps, and her plump, voluptuous ass cheeks shifted sides with every stride. The nonstop jiggling had the two men in a trance.

"Hello, *papi*," she said as she looked over at Carter on the sofa. She then turned to Ace and gave him a passionate kiss before walking over to the refrigerator and grabbing some orange juice.

"Ace, you didn't tell me you were having company." She put her hand on her hip and cocked her head to the side.

Carter couldn't believe his ears. His man Ace was stunting for a ho, pretending that it was his condo, rather than Carter's.

Ace looked at him and read his mind. He grinned and shrugged his shoulders as if to say, "How could I not stunt for an ass like that?"

Carter shook his head and headed out the door. He motioned for Ace to follow him. Once they reached the door and out of earshot of the woman, Carter told him, "Have that trick out of my shit in an hour. You owe me a stack

for fucking in my bed too, nigga. You buying me some new
sheets and all." Carter's face was expressing his anger at
that point. He peeked around the corner to get another
look at the horse ass the woman was toting and then
looked back at Ace. "Shorty got a fat ass, though," he said
as he smiled and stuck out his hand.

Ace returned the smile and shook his man's hand. He
was relieved and surprised by Carter's reaction. He was
sure he was going to spazz out for him having a girl up in
his house and pretending it was his own. He and Carter
were like brothers and Carter wouldn't front his man out
like that, but Ace surely was going to pay out of his pockets for his little fun.

"I got you, Carter. My fault about this little situation.
You know my baby mama be popping up at my crib acting
a fool. Anyway, I'm glad you back home, my nigga. Shit
been crazy since you left. After I drop her off, I'll meet you
at the spot. I need to pick up anyway."

"Look, I'll pick up the cash from the spot. You just get
her out of here and meet me there when you finish up,"
Carter said as he opened the door and headed out. Just
before he closed the door, he turned around and looked at
Ace sternly. "Don't ever bring a bitch to my house, Ace.
We got to stay smart, all right?"

"All right," Ace said just before he closed the door.

Carter drove his black-on-black 2008 Impala down I-75,
bobbing his head to rapper T.I.'s CD. He was on his way to
visit his candy shop. Having been away for weeks, he
knew he had a nice piece of change waiting for him in the
hood. Before he left, he had hit all his four head soldiers
with a half kilo on consignment. That meant around
$40,000 altogether was owed to him.

For years Carter had been dealing with straight blow—

raw cocaine—but after he was exposed to Miami's heroin trade, he wanted in. Monroe and Polo had offered him a position in the business, and the offer was too good to refuse. He told them that he had to return home to handle some business and would return to join The Cartel.

Carter's soldiers didn't know, but he was going to refuse the consignment money and give it to them as a farewell gift. He was ready to leave the murder capital that he called home.

Carter pulled onto the block of North Saginaw and Harriet and saw his goons standing on the corner trying to make pay. He crept up the street behind his limo tint and parked on the curb in front of the candy shop.

As soon as Carter stepped out, he shut down the block. It was scorching hot at 96 degrees, and the sun seemed to bounce off his iced-out Jesus piece. Shirtless, his chain hung down to his belt buckle, and all of the tattoos on his ripped body were on display. He wore a Detroit fitted cap pulled low over his eyes, crisp jeans, and butter Timberland, to top it off.

Everyone had their eyes on him, and the hood threw him an onslaught of greetings. Even the small kids playing in the streets stopped and admired him.

Carter proceeded to walk into the candy shop.

"Carter! What's good?"

"Yo, Carter, glad you home."

"What up, boy."

Carter released a small smile and a peace sign as he headed into the apartment projects where the coke was manufactured. He walked up to the fifth floor of the projects. He knocked on the door in a pattern only he and his workers knew and gained entry. When he walked in, the smell of cooked dope filled his nostrils. It was business as usual with topless women cutting up the cooked coke on the round wood table, and naked women with a doctor's mask scattered over the room, doing their assigned job in the drug operation.

Carter smiled, knowing that his small operation was still running smoothly during his absence. He'd left Ace in charge while he was away, and just as he expected, everything was butter, making the offer that Polo had made him even more tempting.

Carter walked through the house and greeted his workers and henchmen as he made his way to the back where the money was held. He walked into the room and saw one of his head lieutenants, Zyir, a blunt hanging out of his mouth, running money through the money machine.

Zyir was a little nigga. Only 18, he was a smooth-faced, fast-talking hustler at the top of his game. He had been working for Carter since he was 14 and was the one who ran that particular spot. Zyir reminded Carter of himself, and Carter knew that he was the future. He had a certain swagger about himself that typified gangster.

Zyir was so busy staring at the money, he didn't even see Carter enter the room.

"Family, family, what's good?" Carter asked as he walked toward the table.

"Oh shit! My nigga. What's good?" Zyir got up and embraced Carter. "When you get back?"

"I came in last night. How's business?"

"Up and down. Yo, I got that for you, plus interest," Zyir said, referring to the weight that Carter had hit him with before he left.

"Yeah, that's what I'm came to talk to you about." Carter took a seat. "That's on you, fam. You don't owe me anything."

"You serious?"

"Yeah, you good. I'm outta here for good this weekend. Take it as a gift, nah mean? From now on, you can get the coke from Ace. He got the same connect, and the prices are going to remain the same." Carter held out his hand.

Zyir shook Carter's hand. He was happy to hear that he didn't owe Carter any money, but sad to hear that his man was leaving the city for good. He knew that Flint was losing a thorough dude. Honestly, he didn't like the idea of buying coke from Ace because he knew how hotheaded he could be at times.

Zyir couldn't believe that Carter would give up his successful cocaine operation. "Yo, are you really leaving for good?"

"Yeah, fam, I'm done." Carter knew that the paper he was making in Flint was remedial, compared to the opportunity that awaited him in Miami with The Cartel. He was about to follow in his father's notorious footsteps. Carter turned to leave, but before he left, he took off his 3-ct. pinky ring and tossed it to Zyir.

Carter loaded his Range Rover with his luggage with the help of Ace and Zyir, as he prepared to leave for Miami. Once the car was loaded up, Carter slapped hands with his crew and told them that he would send for them, once he got comfortable in Miami. Anxious to get back to Miami, he got in the car and pulled off. He tried to convince himself that he was looking forward to getting money there, but seeing Miamor again was definitely a factor in his decision.

Chapter Nine

"We don't die, bitch!"

—Mecca

When Monroe stepped into the conference room, he was shining like new money. The nervous energy in his stomach quickly subsided as he shook hands with the group of men who had invested in Diamond Realty. His Oleg Cassini designer suit and Steve Madden shoes solidified his position as the new head of his father's company. He walked, talked, and dressed the part, but he was aware of the skepticism and larceny in the hearts of his business peers. His father's business partners were not too keen at the thought of him heading the business.

Diamond Realty had been founded from drug money and private investments from the board members. In its seven years of being in business, the commercial and high-end residential real estate company had acquired some of the most sought-after properties in Florida and was worth well over a hundred million dollars in equity alone. The company's worth was growing by the day, and the board members felt that Carter's position should have been given to someone more qualified than his son.

"Monroe, it's good to have you on board," Harper Spokes greeted as he and Monroe shook hands.

"It's good to be on board, Harper," Monroe responded.

Harper took a seat at the head of the conference table, sat back comfortably in the chair, and loosened his necktie a bit. "I know that it's going to take some time for you to get used to the way we do things here. Getting into the swing of things is going to take some time, but I'm willing to teach you everything I know. A little training from me, and you'll be a pro," Harper stated confidently. He figured that if he played the role of mentor, it would be easy for him to call the shots from behind the scenes.

Monroe walked behind Harper and put his hands on his shoulders as he looked out at the rest of the board members. "That won't be necessary, Harper, although it was a gracious offer. The way we do things are about to change, indeed." Monroe patted the back of Harper's chair, signaling him to arise from his seat. He then tightened Harper's necktie and looked him sternly in the eye. "I'm the boss," he stressed. "The way that we do business will revolutionize so that I am familiar and comfortable with the daily operations and you all are the ones in training. You all will be the ones adjusting, because you have to learn the way that I conduct business."

Monroe pulled out a chair in the middle of the conference table. "Have a seat, Harper." He gave the man time to sit down before he continued. "Now I can assure you that it is very similar to the way that my father did things, but I will not allow myself to be at a disadvantage in my own company. New leadership brings about new policy. If any of you think that it is time for you to move on to new ventures, I completely understand. I will accommodate you with severance pay, but I can guarantee that if you stay on board we will all see a substantial rise in profits. The way that I am going to expand Diamond Realty is going to be nothing short of remarkable, and I would love to have each of you on my team. What do you say?"

Silence filled the room. Monroe wasn't naïve and was sure that there were members who doubted him and even some that wanted to get up and leave, but they were cowards and would never speak up. He took their silence for submission and was satisfied with their fear of him. It was the same type of respect that his father had demanded, and the torch had just been passed down. He nodded his head, hung his suit jacket on the back of his chair, and then took his seat. "Since there are no objections, let's get down to business."

"Are you almost done? This is taking all damn day."

Mecca looked over at the dark-skinned beauty sitting beside him. Her long legs glistened as she positioned them on his dashboard while painting her toe nails.

"Look, Leena, don't start popping that bullshit. I told you what I was doing today. You the one thought I was going to fuck with a bitch, so you tried to bring your happy ass with me. You know what time of the month it is, so just sit back and chill," Mecca stated with a smirk as he eyed the woman beside him.

Leena sucked her teeth and rolled her eyes, but remained quiet. She folded her arms across her chest and, out of habit, began to pout.

Mecca shook his head. He reached over to grab her hand. He knew that he was the one who had spoiled her, so he couldn't be too upset with her. He had been in an on-again, off-again relationship with Leena since they were young teenagers. She had witnessed his transformation from boy to man and knew of his involvement in his family's business.

"I'll take you shopping after this, a'ight."

"Yeah, okay," she replied as she tried to keep the smile from spreading across her face.

In truth he would do anything to keep a smile on her face. Leena was the only woman to capture his heart, and he loved her more than she knew.

Mecca drove up the avenue in his apple red F-150 pickup with chrome rims. He cruised slowly up the block so that his presence could be felt. It was the first of the month, which signified payday for The Cartel, and he was riding around like a landlord, collecting his rent. It was the first pickup since his father had died, and so far two of their many block lieutenants had come short, causing Mecca to have a short fuse.

These mu'fuckas coming short on my money. It's about to be a problem. Not a dime was missing when Poppa was alive. Now these fuck-ass niggas wanna step outta line. Mecca maneuvered his way to the two-story colonial-style house on the end of the block. He put his truck into park and pulled out his cell phone to call his worker inside the trap house.

"I'm outside. I'm about to send a bitch to the back door. Give my money to her."

Leena looked at Mecca like he was crazy and shook her head no. "Nigga, you got me fucked up. I ain't going up in there, and I don't know who the fuck you calling a bitch," she whispered more to herself than to him.

Mecca ignored her and continued to speak into the phone. "Is my money right?" he paused again to let his worker respond and then hung up. "It better be," he stated to himself. He then turned to Leena and said, "What the fuck I tell you about talking shit while I'm on the phone? Go get my shit, and don't look in the bag either, with your nosy ass."

"Whatever, Mecca. I'm not new to money. I don't have to take shit from you." Leena hopped out of the truck and walked across the lawn.

Mecca knew she wasn't lying. She had the type of beauty that made niggas want to wife her. She was sophisticated, and her superior attitude made her appealing to most men. If she wasn't on Mecca's arm, there would be many men willing to extend theirs, and she knew it. She turned many heads as her voluptuous behind shook with each step she took.

Out of respect for Mecca, the hustlers on the block didn't try to get at her, but Mecca shook his head and laughed to himself as he watched them drool at the mouth.

Thirsty-ass niggas, he thought as he watched Leena disappear down the long driveway. *They'll never get a taste of that. That's all me.*

"Hey, Mecca," a random hoodrat called out. She stepped close to his truck, while sucking on a red Blow Pop. In fact all of the groupie broads had come out of hiding as soon as they'd heard the beat from Mecca's subwoofers turn onto the block. The old saying, out of sight, out of mind, must have been true because as soon as Leena stepped out of sight, the hot girls on the block flocked to him.

Mecca looked up and down at the girl. She was attractive in a ghetto kind of way. Her skintight booty shorts left nothing to the imagination, and her sleeveless tube top hugged her ample breasts. What really got his attention was the way her tongue was pulling on that red sucker. It made his dick jump slightly. He scanned her quickly from top to bottom and was turned off by the re-washed Reebok classics that adorned her feet. Mecca knew his status and would never be caught dead entertaining a chick like the one before him. *Every nigga this side of*

Dade done probably dug this bitch out, he thought in disgust. He even grew irritated that she had thought herself worthy of even stepping to him.

"Come here," he stated as he prepared to put the girl in her place.

Her lips spread into a seductive smile as she sashayed across the street. She stepped close to his window, but Mecca frowned at the fact that her focus seemed to be behind him. He instantly noticed that her eyes seemed to look past him to his passenger window. He could almost smell the .380 pistol that was creeping up on him.

Instinctively, Mecca's sixth sense kicked in, and he pulled his twin Desert Eagles from underneath his seats. With one gun in each hand he reached out on both sides of him and fired hollow-points—*Boom! Boom!*—dropping the girl and the gunman at his passenger window instantly.

Just then, a shotgun shell crashed through Mecca's rear windshield. Glass flew everywhere as the deafening sound vibrated through the vehicle.

Mecca ducked low as he reached for his door handle and scrambled out of the truck. *What the fuck?* He sent hollow-points flying across his truck hood in an attempt to keep the shooter on the other side at bay.

Mecca stayed low against his car door to avoid the gunfire of his attacker. He could hear people screaming as they ran to get out of the crossfire. He looked underneath the car and put bullets into the legs of the gunman.

"Aghh!"

Once Mecca saw the gunman go down, he sprang into action and rushed to the other side of the car. "Nigga trying to murk me!" he yelled furiously as he kicked the shotgun out of the fallen soldier's reach. He aimed his gun at the dude's head.

"Please, man, please don't kill me," the dude pleaded.

Mecca snatched the ski mask off the gunman's face. He had expected to see a dreadhead, due to The Cartel's ongoing beef with the Haitians. To his surprise, it was one of his very own soldiers lying at his feet. *What the fuck? My own camp plotting on me now?* Mecca was astounded and didn't know what to think.

"Don't bitch up now, mu'fucka! You had the balls to get at me!" Mecca screamed as he pistol-whipped the man. "Who sent you, huh?" Mecca's brought the cold steel down across the man's face with brutal force, causing blood to splatter onto his white t-shirt. "You trying to kill me?" He hit the man once again, baffled that he had to prove that he was the king of Miami's concrete jungle.

Leena came running out of the house with a duffle bag full of money in her hands. "Mecca!" she screamed in fright at the sight before her.

"Go back in the house!" Mecca yelled at her without even looking her way.

The man groaned in pain as he bled on the hot pavement. Mecca pressed the gun to the middle of his forehead.

"Nah, man! Nobody sent us, I swear. We were just gon' rob you. My brother and his girlfriend, that's it, man. We just wanted the money. Please don't kill me."

"Niggas really think we slippin' out here!" Mecca yelled as he stood up and addressed the crowd of hustlers and courageous spectators. "Y'all niggas really think we touchable now, huh?" Mecca was like a pit bull as he stood above the dude and looked every hood nigga in his eye, while they watched on in horror. "We don't die, bitch! Diamonds are forever, mu'fuckas." Seething through a clenched jaw, Mecca unloaded the rest of his clip into the man's dome and then hopped into his truck, speeding away recklessly.

* * *

Mecca steadied his driving and eased off the gas pedal when he saw the Miami police cruisers coming his way. He hit the steering wheel repeatedly as he tried to gain composure of himself. His adrenaline was uncontrollable as he thought about what had just occurred. The song "Many Men" filled the interior of the truck as his cell phone continued to ring. He looked down at his caller ID and noticed that it was Leena. "Fuck!" he yelled aloud, realizing that he had left her there with a duffle bag full of drug money.

"Hello?" he answered.

"What the fuck you mean, hello? Mecca! You left me here! Why would you just pull off on me like that?" Leena screamed.

Mecca could tell that she was crying, and guilt immediately plagued him. He hadn't even thought to retrieve her from the house when he pulled off. The only thing that was on his mind was fleeing the scene before the cops arrived.

"Mecca!" Leena cried.

"Leena, listen to me, all right. Calm down. You know I wouldn't leave you for dead. You couldn't ride with me, baby girl. You saw how I left that nigga leaking. I didn't want you tied up in no murder, so I just pulled off. I'm gon' send somebody through to pick you up, a'ight."

"Mecca, oh my God, the police just pulled up. Please come and get me," Leena whispered, her tears flowing.

"Leena, I'm-a send somebody through for you. Just sit tight. You didn't see shit, and you don't know shit, understand?"

"Yeah, baby, I understand."

Mecca told her, "Hurry up and put Sheed on the phone." When his block lieutenant came on, Mecca instructed him to hide the cash.

"What you want me to do about ol' girl?" Sheed asked.

"Just let her stay there for an hour or so. I'll send some-body to pick her and the money up when shit die down."

"Mr. Diamond, your brother Mecca is here to see you," the receptionist called out over the interoffice intercom.

Monroe hit the reply button on the intercom and picked up the phone so that the other members of the board couldn't hear both ends of the conversation. "Porscha, can you tell him that I'm in a meeting right now."

"I know, sir. I'm sorry for interrupting, but Mecca says it's an emergency."

"I'll be right out." Monroe turned to his business associates. "If you all will excuse me for a couple minutes . . . I have some business to tend to." Monroe quickly exited the room, and his eyes widened in shock when he saw his brother covered in blood.

"Umm, Porscha, can you tell the board members that this meeting is adjourned and find a time that works with them so that we can reschedule. Hold all calls too please." Monroe nodded for Mecca to follow him.

"Fuck happened to you?" Money asked as they entered another conference room.

"I just bodied a nigga in front of Sheed spot."

"In front of Sheed's spot? What were you thinking, bro? You supposed to be handling the street business and you making shit hot on one of our most lucrative blocks?"

"I know but—"

At that moment Money's cell phone rang, interrupting Mecca. He checked his BlackBerry and noticed that it was Carter. He immediately picked up and put Young Carter on speakerphone.

"What's good, fam?" Carter greeted.

"Man, we got problems this way." Money knew that

Carter could give them good advice on how to fix Mecca's mess.

"What up?" Carter asked.

"Mecca caught a body."

"What?"

"Man, Young Carter, it ain't even how Money making it sound. I wasn't on no hot shit or nothing. I send Leena into one of the spots to collect the cash, and these mu'-fuckas run up with they pistols blazing and shit, trying to rob ya boy."

"You had your bitch with you while you were picking up the money?" Carter asked.

"I told yo' ass about having Leena riding with you during business," Money stated sternly in disbelief. "You need to keep her out of harm's way, bro. Today is the perfect example."

"Look, the police came, so I hopped in the truck and sped off, but everything happened so fast, fam. I left Leena there with the money."

"You left her there?" Money askd.

"With the money?"

"Yeah, mu'fuckas, damn! I left her there with the money."

"That's your brother," Carter stated in amusement.

"That's *your* brother," Money told him.

"But on a serious note, Mecca, fall back for a couple days, just to let things settle, a'ight, fam."

"Yeah, I hear you," Mecca replied hesitantly. He hated taking orders from his older brother, and still wasn't used to there being more than Money, Breeze, and himself, but inside he knew that Carter was right.

"A'ight, fam, I'll be back in town in a couple days. I'll be in touch," Carter said before hanging up.

Mecca pulled his bloody t-shirt over his head and slapped hands with his twin brother.

"Go sit your ass down somewhere, bro. I'll go pick up the cash and drop Leena off at home." Money headed toward the door.

"Yo, Money!" Mecca shouted.

Money stopped and turned around to listen, raising his eyebrows to let his brother know that he had his attention.

"I love her, fam. Make sure she's okay for me, a'ight."

Money nodded and left the room.

Money pulled up to Sheed's spot. Sheed was one of their best workers, so he was positive that his street lieutenant would be able to handle the police. There were no squad cars in sight, but the block was live with residents sitting around discussing the events that had happened that day. Money stepped out of the car and all eyes seemed to be on him. He was slightly irritated at how much attention Mecca had brought to their block, but he understood that Mecca had to react. It was either kill or be killed, and Money knew that Mecca had made the best decision that he could have made under the circumstances.

He knocked on the front door, and it opened instantly.

"Fam, the police was asking everybody questions. I didn't see shit, nah mean?" Sheed allowed Monroe to enter his living room.

"You got that?" Money asked.

Sheed pulled the duffle bag out of his coat closet and tossed it to Money. Opening the bag to make sure it was all there, Money tried to inventory the cash quickly by sight.

"Come on, fam, don't insult me," Sheed said. "You know I'm one hunnid."

Money gave Sheed a look that spoke volumes. Sheed took the hint and shut up, while Money continued to thumb through the bag. Once he was satisfied, he took out five stacks and set it on Sheed's table. "Thanks for keep-ing things quiet and looking out for Mecca's chick. Where is she?"

"She's in the den. She's been tripping ever since she saw dude body on the lawn. She's spazzing, yo."

"Don't worry about it," Money said as he walked to-ward Sheed's den. "I'll take care of it." He walked into the room and saw Leena sitting on the couch, her face in her hands. "You all right?"

His voice startled her, and she looked up in surprise. "Money? Where's Mecca?" she asked, tears in her eyes. "He just left me here for dead. The least he could've done was come back for me."

"Come on, Lee, let's get out of here." Money reached for her arm and pulled her from the couch.

Money helped Leena into his 2009 pearl white Cadillac STS before getting into the car himself and speeding away. Leena was quiet, and it wasn't until they arrived at her luxury ocean view apartment that she did speak.

"There was blood everywhere," Leena whispered. "You didn't see it, Money. It was horrible." She walked over to her window and looked out onto the ocean below her. "How can a city so beautiful harbor so many secrets?"

Money didn't know how to respond, so he remained silent. He knew that she would be shook up after witness-ing Mecca kill someone. It was natural.

"You know Mecca would never let anything happen to you, right?"

Leena laughed lightly and shook her head. "I don't even want to think about him right now," she stated, still upset with Mecca for leaving her at the murder scene.

Money walked toward her as she continued to stand in front of the window. He stood behind her, wrapping his arms around her waist and whispered in her ear. "You know I would never let anything happen to you, ma."

Money's touch sent shivers down her spine, and she closed her eyes and reveled in the moment.

"I love you, Monroe," she stated, guilt in her voice.

Leena had never meant to fall for both brothers, but over the years as she dated Mecca, she began to see that Monroe possessed everything he was lacking. Mecca had cheated on her, whereas Monroe was faithful, even though she wasn't rightfully his. Mecca had a temper, whereas Monroe was calm and always in control. Mecca loved the limelight, whereas Monroe played the back. Mecca was a hothead, spur-of-the-moment type of man, whereas Monroe was strategic and calculating. They were completely opposite, but Leena loved them both. But Money was the one that she wanted to be with.

Leena turned around to face Money. "When are you going to tell Mecca about us?"

Money released her from his embrace and sat down on her oversized couch. "I don't know," he stated honestly.

"I can't keep doing this, Money. The more I'm around Mecca, the more I see that he's not the man for me. He isn't even ready to stop fucking around on me. I want to be with you. We shouldn't have to sneak around like this. Messing around with both of you has me feeling cheap and dirty. I'm not one of these little groupie chicks out here, Money. I feel like you want it to stay like this forever. What? You don't love me? You don't want to be with me? Is this thing we're doing just a game to you?"

"You know I care for you, Lee."

"But you don't love me?" she questioned with a slight attitude, nodding her head up and down as if she was starting to see things clearly.

"Yes, I love you, but he's my brother. He loves you too. You don't see it, but I hear the way he talks about you, Leena. He may not be ready to commit to you, but he loves you. No matter how much I try to justify this, he met you first. And I'm fucking you behind his back. You don't belong to me!" Monroe shouted vehemently as he stood and began to pace the room back and forth.

His words brought tears to Leena's eyes. "Oh, so is that all I am to you—a good fuck? A piece of property? Just to let you know, Money, I don't belong to anybody. I'm a grown-ass woman that deserves to be happy, and I'm not happy with Mecca." She shook her head at him in disgust. "I can't fuckin' believe you! Is that really all I am to you? Another bitch you fucking?"

"No!" Money yelled in frustration. He caught the volume of his voice and toned it down before he continued, "I love you, Leena. Don't act like you don't know, ma," he said as he wiped a tear from her face.

His lips touched hers gently, and the soft texture of her full mouth instantly aroused him. Monroe's hands moved with the experience of a Casanova as he slid her shirt smoothly over her head, revealing a purple satin bra. His kisses went from her lips, to her neck. He traced her collarbone with his tongue and moved south until his mouth met her large brown nipples. They were sensitive to the warm sensation of his tongue, and the more he licked and tugged at them with his lips, the harder they became.

"Hmm," she moaned as she inhaled deeply. Her fingers began to unbutton Money's designer shirt, and she ran her hands across his broad, well-defined chest.

Money paid attention to every single erotic spot on her body. He was in no rush to get between her legs. He knew that foreplay was the key to a woman's sexuality, and the more he explored Leena's body, the wetter she became. No spot on her body went untouched. He caressed, and his mouth became intimate with, some of her most delicate places.

He picked her up, scooping her into his arms and carried her into the lavish bathroom. He sat down on the edge of the large Jacuzzi-style bathtub while she sat in his lap. Their lips seemed to be glued together as Money reached for the brass knobs that turned on the water. He finished undressing Leena and then placed her inside of the water. She looked up at him seductively as she watched him remove the rest of his clothes.

His dick grew another two inches when he saw her fingers slip into her womanhood as her thumb massaged her clitoris. Joining her in the steaming water, he took her foot into his hands and rubbed them softly. A low moan escaped her lips as he kneaded her calf tenderly. Money kissed the bottom of her foot and then sucked on her big toe. The sensation that shot up her back caused her to cum instantly.

A sexy smirk crossed Monroe's face when he felt her body shudder. His hands moved up her leg, and he parted her thighs as he slid in between them, Leena reaching down and massaging his length.

He stood from the water, bubbles now dripping from his six pack. His eight inches were average, but the thickness of it was astounding. Leena's eyes beamed in anticipation because she knew that he would stretch her pussy walls to their limit, as he had done so many times before. Pre-cum began to ooze out of the tip, and it looked too tempting not to taste, so she got on her knees and took him into her mouth.

Monroe's jaw hit his chest as he looked down at the beauty beneath him, one of her hands wrapped around his pole, masturbating his length as she sucked it, the other hand tickling his balls. A grunt fell from his lips as he grabbed the top of Leena's head, tussling his fingers through her hair as he grinded slowly. He could feel his nut building, and he had to force himself to ease out of her mouth.

Her head game was superb, but her pussy was even better. It was wet, and warm, and tight. He pulled her to her
feet and without words turned her around to bend her
over. With the flexibility of a dancer, she bent over and
clapped her ass cheeks together. Monroe slapped her big,
dark behind and ran his dick up and down her dripping
wet slit.

Damn, he thought to himself as he looked at the juices
dripping down Leena's thigh.

Money inserted himself slowly and immediately went
to work on her, his rhythm slow and his thrusts powerful,
his light-skinned, muscular ass cheeks flexing as he moved
in and out of her. Leena enjoyed the view as she admired
his toned back and behind in the mirror that showed his
reflection. The sight of him moving in and out of her,
mixed with the fact that he had reached around her and
was now fingering her clit, caused her body to shake.

She bucked her ass wildly. Each time she backed it up,
their skin slapped together loudly. He was hitting it so
good and making her so wet that her pussy began to fart.

Slap, slap, slap—fart . . . slap, slap, slap—fart . . .

The music that their bodies were making could be
heard throughout her apartment.

"Money," she whined as she played with her own nipples, "I'm cumming."

"Tell me you love me," he whispered in her ear as he
went into her as deep as he could go. Once he was all
the way inside of her, he pulled her hips down quickly and
with force over and over.

"Aghh . . . I love you, daddy!" she screamed.

"Whose pussy is this? This my pussy?" he asked as he
hit her with long, slow strokes, kissing the back of her
neck each time he stroked her deep.

"Yes, baby, it's yours," she whispered as tears clouded
her vision. "I'm cumming!"

She popped her pussy back so good that Money came with her, while he was deep inside her warmth, and they both collapsed back into the warm water in satisfaction.

They each washed and rinsed themselves quickly. They stepped out and Money wrapped a towel around his waist before wrapping her in a large red towel. He pulled her close and kissed her lips. "Never ever doubt my love for you, understand?" he said seriously as he stared Leena in the eyes.

Leena nodded her head. "Promise me that you'll tell Mecca soon. I can't continue to share myself with both of you. I love you too much. I only want to be yours." She reached up and took his face in her hands and kissed him lightly on the lips. "Promise me," she repeated.

Money sighed deeply. The last thing that he wanted to do was hurt his brother, but he couldn't share Leena with Mecca for too much longer. Every time Mecca and Leena were together, it ate him up inside. He knew that he couldn't put off the inevitable any longer. "I promise," he replied as he pulled her close and kissed her forehead. "I promise."

Chapter Ten

"Real bitches do real shit."

—Miamor

Miamor, Aries, and Robyn sat at Applebee's dining and having drinks. They were there to discuss their new hit.

Miamor couldn't stop thinking about Carter. Their sexual episode lingered in her mind for days, and every time she thought about it, her clitoris tingled. It was hands down the best sex she'd ever experienced, and he had her mind blown. Her profession didn't allow her to fall for men, but the way Carter handled her and made love to her had her thinking about him in a different light than other men.

As she sat across from her girls, she thought, *I can't wait to see him again. It's something different about him, but I can't put my finger on it.*

"So how much is this nigga trying to pay?" Robyn asked Miamor as she took a sip of her Long Island Iced Tea.

"The job pays the usual eighty stacks. That's twenty"— Miamor stopped mid-sentence and remembered that the caper wasn't going to be split four ways anymore.

A brief moment of silence arose as the girls realized that this was their first hit since Anisa's death.

Miamor, wanting to be strong for her crew, continued. "Remember Black from South Beach?" she asked in a low voice as she clasped her hands and leaned into the table to be more discreet.

"Yeah, I remember him. He had us take care of that snitchin'-ass nigga a couple years back, right?" Robyn responded.

"Yeah, that's him. He wants us to take care of a nigga named Fabian. Black has a younger brother doing life in the pen for drug trafficking. From what he told me, his brother weighs like a buck twenty soaking wet. The story is that Fabian was violating Black's little brother in jail, doing him real dirty, you know, raping him and shit. Fabian got released from the joint about six months ago and 'posed to be moving major weight around his area. Black wants us to get at his ass. But there's a catch"— Miamor quickly glanced around to make sure no one was in her mouth.

"What's that?' Robyn asked.

"He wants us to cut off the nigga's dick off before we kill him." Miamor released a small smirk.

Aries and Robyn burst into laughter simultaneously. They knew Miamor had to be playing. The request was too outlandish to be taken seriously.

"Get da fuck out of here, bitch!" Aries said in between her laughter. But when she saw that Miamor's smirk had faded away, she knew that she was dead serious.

Robyn began to shake her head, not believing what was being asked of them. "You have to be fucking kidding me?"

"I know the shit sound crazy, but the nigga we supposed to hit was raping Black's brother in the joint. He wants him to feel violated the same way his brother did. He is offering us an extra twenty stacks if we do it his way."

"Twenty thousand?" Aries and Robyn asked at the same time.

"Twenty thousand dollars." Miamor nodded her head.

"Ooh, big daddy, you working with an anaconda," Robyn lied as she stroked Fabian's dick with her hand. As she prolonged her extended hand-job on Fabian, she thought, *Where the fuck are these bitches at? This dirty-dick nigga gon' want me to put my mouth on him in a minute.* Robyn had been getting in good with him for the past week and finally convinced him to go to a motel room without one of his goons tailing him for security.

"Show me what that head game like, ma." Fabian placed his hands behind his head and lay back on the bed.

Robyn was enraged on the inside. Miamor had told her that they would enter the room five minutes after they were in. Now fifteen minutes had gone by since they'd entered the motel room. *Where these bitches at? Fuck!*

She tried to figure out a way to buy a couple of minutes. Normally she would do whatever she had to do to get the job done, but in this case she had to reconsider. The thought of putting a homosexual's pipe in her mouth made her almost gag.

She stood up and improvised to stall time. "I'm-a dance for you, daddy. Just sit back and watch," she said as she began to do the belly roll and move her mid-section in circles. She raised her skirt and exposed her neatly trimmed vagina. She put her finger in her mouth and then began to rub her clitoris slow and hard.

Fabian was going crazy thinking about going inside of her pretty, pink love box. He smiled while stroking his hard dick. He was so hard, veins were sticking out of his dick as the tip of his joint pulsated.

It wasn't Robyn's intention to get aroused, but the width of Fabian's big black rod made her dripping wet. *If the nigga wasn't a homo, I might've gave his fruity ass some. That's what wrong with these bitch-ass niggas now—All the brothers either down-low booty chasers or just don't got no act right.* She let her finger slide into her vagina. She was so wet, she felt her juices drip onto her inner thigh.

At that point Fabian couldn't take it any longer. He jumped up and swiftly grabbed Robyn under her butt cheeks, quickly lifting her so that she was face level. During his stint in the penitentiary, he had worked out extensively, and his bulky, muscular physique confirmed that. It was nothing for him to lift Robyn's entire body with ease.

"Oh shit!" Robyn yelled, caught by the element of surprise. Her legs swung freely as her crotch sat dead in the middle of Fabian's face.

Fabian knew all the moves to get Robyn to nut. He began to work his tongue like a tornado on Robyn's clitoris. She couldn't believe the position that she was in and had only read about shit like that in books.

This nigga sho' can eat a pussy. Robyn gripped his bald head and ground her hips against his face. The top of her head kept hitting the ceiling, but she didn't mind, it was well worth it.

She kept looking at the door, expecting her girls to bust in at any moment. She had paid for the hotel suite earlier that day and gave Miamor the extra room key. Actually, she was hoping that they didn't come in at that moment because she didn't want Fabian to drop her while she was so high. She tried to get a couple more face thrusts in before it was over.

"Let me down!"

Fabian slowly let Robyn down and began to take off her clothes. He lay on the bed and sat up on his elbows as he stared at her drenched pussy.

Robyn knew that she had to think quickly because she

wasn't about to give him a shot at her goods. *He ain't sticking that mu'fucka up in me, that's for damn sure.* "Turn around on your stomach," she instructed as she sucked her own nipples.

"What?" Fabian asked in confusion.

"Turn around, nigga. I want to lick yo' ass," she lied seductively.

"What? Don't nothing go by my ass, ma. Come get on this dick and stop playing."

Robyn knew what the deal was. She knew that he liked what she was proposing, him being gay and all. She just had to play it right. "It will feel good, I promise."

Fabian lit up inside when Robyn first told him to turn around. He just didn't want her to know his little secret. Her request was music to his ears. He hadn't got a rim job since leaving prison. Fabian looked in Robyn's eyes and saw that she was serious and quickly flipped his muscular ass around.

Just then, Robyn saw Miamor and Aries slide through the door quietly, both with pistols in their hands. Fabian was so busy smiling and anticipating getting his back slurped, he didn't even see them coming.

"What took y'all bitches so long?" Robyn shouted as she began to put on her clothes.

"What?" Fabian asked as he turned around. But he didn't see what he was expecting to see. He was staring down the barrel of Miamor's 9 mm.

Before he could even react, Miamor went across his nose with her gun, causing it to split and swell up instantly. "Tie this mu'fucka up," she instructed calmly and reached into her bag to pull out the butcher knife.

Fabian instantly began to plead for his life as Aries tied him up to the bedposts. "Look, I will give y'all bitches anything you want," he pleaded as Aries finished tying him up.

Aries hit him in the eye with the butt of her pistol. "Watch chu mouth!" she said as she watched him grimace in agony.

"Let's hurry up and get this shit over with," Robyn said as she finished putting her clothes back on.

"Okay, here." Miamor handed Robyn the butcher knife.

Robyn shook her head from side to side. "I ain't cutting that nigga dick off!"

"Oh shit! Oh fuck! Please don't cut my joint off. Please! What the fuck did I do to deserve this foul shit?" Fabian bucked against his restraints, and tears began to form in his eyes.

"Stop crying like a little bitch!" Miamor yelled. "Put a sock in that nigga's mouth."

Aries grabbed one of his socks off the floor and forced it down his throat.

Miamor handed Aries the knife. "Aries, you do it."

"You got Aries fucked up. Me ain't touching he dick, bitch." Aries stepped back from Miamor.

"Y'all bitches soft!" Miamor yelled. "I got to do everything myself! Real bitches do real shit." She grabbed Fabian's dick and gave it one good hack. The knife only went halfway through, so she whacked it again, this time cutting it clean off.

Fabian squirmed in pain, his muffled scream like a lion's roar, and his eyes flew open in excruciation, while his body writhed violently.

Miamor didn't know if it was more painful for Fabian to feel the knife or to see his soldier lying next to him, totally detached from his body. Blood began to cover the sheets and Miamor hoped off of him.

"I get the twenty stacks for that, straight up!" Miamor yelled as she grabbed a towel to clean her hands and the knife.

Robyn turned her head to avoid seeing the bloody scene and yelled, "Fuck that! We splitting that shit."

"Yeah. We split that!" Aries added.

"You bitches didn't wanna help, so why should I split it up?" Miamor contested.

"I . . ." Robyn paused. The stench in the air almost made her gag. She pulled Miamor into the bathroom, so she could tell her about herself.

Aries followed quickly, not wanting to miss anything, and the three girls huddled in the bathroom like sardines in a can.

"Yo, why you bugging, Mia? You know the rules. We always split the take evenly," Robyn said with attitude.

"Why do I have to do the dirty work and split it? Straight the fuck up! You two were scared to cut, but now you want a cut. Fuck that!" Miamor snapped her head to the side.

Robyn scowled. "Miamor, what's gotten into you? You are tripping. You ain't acting the same lately."

"It's de nigga she giving she pussy to. He got she head fucked up."

"Look, this ain't the right time to be talking about this, so step the fuck off."

"Yeah, she's right. Let's handle this nigga, and we will finish this later." Robyn opened the bathroom door and squeezed out.

"Oh shit!" Robyn yelled as soon as she saw what had happened.

"What's wrong?" Miamor shouted as she hurried out of the bathroom. Miamor looked at the bloody bed and saw that it was empty and the door was wide open. "The nigga got away! Fuck!"

They all rushed to the door and saw the man running butt naked across the parking lot. Aries lifted her gun to shoot at him, but it was too late. He was already out of range.

"Fuck! Fuck!" Miamor yelled as she put both of her hands on her head. She knew that they had just fucked up big time, and now wasn't nobody getting paid.

Chapter Eleven

"Oooh, Carter, we got to stop, but this dick so good."

—Miamor

Miamor couldn't get Carter out of her head. Even while she was on a job, he was constantly entering her thoughts, and she hated herself for feeling him so much. It had been two weeks since their steamy encounter on the beach and she was open. *Why hasn't he called me?* she thought to herself. *I knew I shouldn't have fucked him so quick. He probably thinking I'm one of these sack-chasing busto bitches.*

Miamor shook the thought of Carter out of her mind as she reluctantly crawled out of her three-thousand-dollar cherrywood canopy bed and stretched her arms high above her head. She tiptoed as her body extended in relaxation toward the sky, causing her to shriek in delight. She looked at herself in the mirror and wiped the sleep out of her eyes. She pulled her hair up in a raggedy ponytail and noticed the slight bags that were beginning to form under her eyes. *I've got to get some rest*, she thought. *I look like shit.*

Her eyes drifted down to the picture of her and her

friends that sat on the dresser. She picked it up, and a smile slowly spread across her face as she looked at herself, Aries, Robyn, and, most importantly, Anisa. It had been taken over a year ago at a Fourth of July party. She reminisced how they used to step into the club. They were forever fly and were always led through the crowd by Anisa. Mad niggas lusted after their crew, and they got a lot of attention wherever they went. They were always the belles of the ball and the center of attention. Anisa had been the ringleader of their clique, the one to teach Miamor all of her murdering and hustling ways. Her big sister was truly her best friend, and now that she was gone, Miamor felt a strange hole in her heart.

A solitary tear leaked out of her eye, and she quickly brushed it off her face. She set the picture back on her dresser, turning it face down as she walked out of her bedroom. Every time she looked at something that reminded her of Anisa, she broke down. No matter how much Miamor's girls tried to convince her otherwise, she continued to blame herself for her sister's death.

She stopped in her hallway and looked down at her sister's bedroom door. It was closed. She hadn't stepped foot inside it since Anisa had been killed. She just couldn't bring herself to look at her sister's things. She quickly turned and made her way into her kitchen. She opened her cabinets and pulled out some pancake batter. Tears came to her eyes as she slammed the box of batter on the counter. She leaned onto the countertop and wept as she thought of her sister. Every Friday morning, she and Anisa would cook pancakes together. It was a silly tradition that they had shared since their pre-teen years, but it was something that she cherished. Miamor knew that she would never share another intimate moment with her sister, and it hurt her to the depths of her soul.

"Ughh!" she screamed in frustration. She hated feeling

so weak. She had never been the emotional type, but her sister's death brought out years of harbored emotions.

Miamor looked around her condominium, and everything about it reminded her of Anisa. Anisa picked out the furniture, the scent of the candles, even the food in the refrigerator, all of which served as a constant reminder of her failure to protect the ones around her.

She poured the pancake mix out of the box and turned on the faucet to rinse it down the sink. "I can't stay here. This shit is gon' drive me crazy," she said out loud to herself. She opened up her kitchen drawers and searched until she found the card of the realtor that had sold her the condo. It was time for her to sell her place. *I have to find a new spot. I can't even breathe in here.* She grabbed her cell phone and quickly punched in the numbers.

"Harper Spokes, please."

Carter looked at all of the possessions he had brought back to Miami from Flint. There was no way he could continue to live out of a hotel. He had made the move South, now he needed to find his own spot. He picked up his cell and called Monroe.

"Money, this is Carter," he stated when his younger brother answered the phone.

"What's good, bro?"

"Aye, I just brought all of my stuff down here from Up Top. Now I need a place to put it," he replied, laughter in his voice. "Do you have time to show me a few properties today?"

"My schedule's pretty full today, fam, but I can get one of the board associates to take you around. You looking to rent or buy?"

Carter replied, "Come on, fam, do I look like one of these rent-a-center-ass niggas? You know I ain't living up in no shit I don't own."

"Yeah, I hear you. Well, come on down to the office when you're ready."

"A'ight, I'll be down there in about an hour."

Carter dressed simply in an all-white, short-sleeve Sean John button-up with a crisp, white t-shirt underneath, his light jeans and Prada sneakers completing his hookup. Then he put on a 10-kt. necklace that had three tight rows of colorless diamonds.

After hanging his iPhone from his hip and tucking his .45 in his waistline, he was ready to go. Carter hopped in his Range, tucked his gun away in a hidden compartment behind his custom stereo, and then headed toward Diamond Realty.

When he walked into the office, he brought an instant smile to the face of the attractive receptionist sitting behind the desk.

"Hi, is there something that I can do for you?" Her eyes roamed suggestively over Carter's muscular build.

Her come-on was obvious, and he gave her a polite smirk in response. "I'm here to see my brother, Monroe Diamond."

The receptionist licked her lips and stated, "You can go right back to his office."

Carter nodded and then headed down the hall.

Before he was out of sight, the receptionist called out, "And if you need *anything*, don't hesitate to ask."

Carter smiled but didn't reply. He simply continued on his way until he came to an office that read *Diamond* on the door. He knocked lightly on the door.

"Come in," Monroe called out.

Carter entered the office and slapped hands with Monroe. They pulled each other close for a brief second before sitting down.

"Carter, this is Harper Spokes. Harper, this is my older brother, Carter."

Harper shook hands with the young man beside him and said, "You resemble your father."

"So I've heard," Carter answered.

"He was a good friend of mine. I'm sorry for your loss," Harper said.

"Thank you."

Money cleared his throat. "Harper tells me that we have a couple properties for you to view today."

Harper pulled out a portfolio with available properties inside, and Carter chose three that he was interested in purchasing.

"How quickly are you looking to move in?" Harper asked.

"As soon as possible."

"You *are* aware that Diamond Realty only deals in high-end properties. Do you need financing? How do you plan on paying for the property?" Harper asked, causing Money to look up from the stack of papers on his desk.

Money, a bit offended at Harper's question, replied bluntly before Carter could answer, "In cash."

Carter, offended as well, said, "What other way is there?"

"Just like your father . . . you work in cash. That's how I like it," Harper stated.

"I bet you do," said Carter in a sarcastic tone.

Although Miamor never kept a dirty house, she cleaned it from top to bottom to ensure that it was presentable for her prospective buyer. The only room that she hadn't touched was Anisa's.

She loved her realtor. As soon as she called him and told him she wanted to sell her place, he was on top of things. Within a few hours he had called her back and told her he had found a potential purchaser. The day slowly crept by as she waited for her realtor to arrive. It was five o'clock in the afternoon when she finally heard the knock on the door.

Miamor opened her door, and her jaw hit the floor when she saw Carter standing beside her realtor.

"Ms. Matthews, this is Carter Jones," Harper stated. "Carter Jones, Miamor Matthews."

Carter was just as surprised to see Miamor standing before him. She didn't seem too happy to see him but, for business purposes, held out her hand for him to shake it.

"Mr. Jones," she said.

Carter smirked at her act, but played along, giving off the perception that they had just met.

"Well, if you don't mind, we'll just take a look around," Harper stated.

Miamor shook her head in protest. "Oh no, Harper. Please allow me to show him around. You can make yourself comfortable here in the living room," she stated.

Miamor walked down the hallway, and Carter followed her into her bedroom. He closed the door behind him. Turning to face her, he noticed that she was standing with her arms folded across her chest. "Come here," he stated in a low voice.

Not one to hold her tongue, she asked, "Why didn't you call me?"

"I was out of town. You knew that." Carter stepped closer to Miamor and pulled her near him.

She rolled her eyes, but allowed herself to step into his personal space. "You still could have called. You had me here feeling all fucked-up about sleeping with you. Don't lie to me, Carter. You can tell me if you ain't checking for me like that."

Carter ran his finger across her breast until he felt her nipple swell under her silk dress.

Miamor's breaths became shallow as she reached up

and pulled his head near hers. His tongue probed the inside of her mouth. It was thick, and his kiss was sensual. She immediately became wet as she thought of another place she would like him to lick with his juicy tongue. *There is something about this man that I can't resist*, she thought as she reached down and gripped his throbbing manhood. She was so hot and bothered that she considered taking his tool out and fucking him on the spot, but she had a white man sitting in her living room.

"Wait!" she whispered as she continued to kiss him. "We can't do this right now." Miamor had spoken the words, but she made no effort to stop Carter from slipping his finger up her White House designer skirt. She wore no panties, so his fingers were instantly drenched in her feminine juices. "You didn't even call me," she moaned.

"I'm sorry, ma. It's all about you," he answered as she reached for his belt buckle.

"Don't lie to me," she whispered in lust.

"I don't lie, Miamor." He lifted her shirt and bent down to kiss her stomach gently.

The two were in pure lust for one another as they attacked each other.

"What do I got to do to get some of this, ma?" he asked charmingly. He'd wanted to call her and had every intention of doing so, but his mind had been preoccupied with business.

"Do what you feel," she stated frankly, staring at him in a challenging way, massaging his hardness through his Calvin Klein boxers.

Grunting lustfully, Carter picked her up by her waist as she wrapped her long legs around his body, grinding her hips into him with a fuck-me passion. The friction alone had her ready to climax. The heat between the two of them burned recklessly as Carter carried her to the over-

sized cherry wood dresser that sat against the wall,
sweeping everything off of it in one motion, causing a
loud crash to erupt through the condominium.

"Shh!" she whispered as she sucked on his neck.
"Harper is going to hear us."

Carter ignored her and sat her onto the dresser. He
opened her legs, while she unbuttoned his pants and slid
them down. He entered her without hesitation, moving
with a slow rhythm, holding both of her thighs open as
wide as they would go. He looked down at his dick as it
moved in and out of her. The sight of her massaging her
swollen clitoris made his manhood swell even more, and
he pounded into her relentlessly.

Knock, knock, knock!

"Is everything all right in there?"

Miamor's eyes grew wide in alarm at the sound of
Harper's voice. Carter was fucking her so good that she
couldn't stop the moans from slipping off her tongue. She
looked at Carter.

"He heard us," she whispered.

Carter continued to fuck her as he whispered, "Then
you better stop all of that moaning, ma."

In and out, in and out . . .

Miamor groaned in pleasure, "Uh-uh, I can't," as she
thrust her hips at him in a slow grind. Until now she'd
never had a nigga who had a big dick and knew exactly
how to use it. She was losing her mind. "Oooh, Carter, we
got to stop, but this dick so good," she moaned as she
made the lower half of her body roll in circles.

"Excuse me, guys, is everything okay?" Harper asked
again.

Miamor began to reply, "Everything is—ooh shit!"

But Carter hit her with the death stroke, hitting her
G-spot and silencing her.

In and out, in and out, round and round.

"Oh shit! Oh shit!" she screamed as the mirror to her dresser began to hit the wall it was leaning against. "Carter! Oh my God, baby, yes!"

Knock, knock, knock!

"Harper, we're fine! Everything is—Yes, Carter, right there! Carter, don't stop!" she moaned.

Carter was making her body explode in ways she had never experienced, and her legs began to shake uncontrollably.

"I'm cumming!" she announced. "Oh my, oh!" she screamed one last time before her body went limp in Carter's arms.

Seconds later, Carter climaxed as well and kissed her sweaty forehead before releasing her.

"Get rid of Harper," she said as she pushed him gently off of her. "And when you do come back to me, I'll be waiting in my bed."

Miamor removed the rest of her clothing and then got underneath her luxury comforter as Carter pulled up his pants and backpedaled out of the room, eyeing every curve on her body. Harper stood checking his watch as Carter walked into the living room, adjusting his jeans.

When Harper looked up and saw Carter walking toward him with his shirt off, his mouth hit the floor in surprise. "Umm-I-I . . ." Harper didn't know what to say as he adjusted his glasses nervously. He had certainly heard what had taken place in the bedroom. The small hard-on that showed through his business slacks and the red embarrassing flush of his face indicated that he had heard everything.

"I'll take the first place we viewed. You'll have your money tomorrow." Carter opened the front door for Harper.

Astonished, Harper headed for the door. "Okay, I-I—"

Before he could say another word, Carter closed the door in his face.

He made his way back to Miamor and picked up where they had left off, pleasing her in every sexual way over and over again until she was so tired that she could no longer cum.

Miamor lay cuddled up to Carter. She was so comfortable in his embrace. *I could get used to this*, she thought.

"Why are you selling your spot?" he asked her out of the blue.

"I can't stay here. I shared this place with my sister, and ever since she died, it just doesn't feel like home. Everything in here reminds me of her. I miss her."

"There's nothing wrong with missing her, Miamor. Selling your crib won't erase that feeling."

"I don't want to talk about that," she whispered. "I just want to enjoy my time with you. Ain't no telling how long you'll be around. I have to appreciate you while you're here," she said half-jokingly.

"I'm here as long as you want me to be." Carter pulled her on top of his body. She lay directly on top of him and rested her head against his chest as he stroked the top of her head. Carter looked down at the beautiful young woman and felt connected to her.

Carter didn't know it yet, but she loved everything about him. She loved the way he was rubbing her head. She loved the way he dressed, the confident swagger that he possessed, and the dimple on the side of his face was an added plus. She definitely loved how he had put his thing down on her. Both times they had slept together she had been completely satisfied. She was checking for him in the worst way.

They lay there together for hours, and eventually

Carter slipped into a comfortable sleep. Miamor heard his deep breathing and eased her body off of him. She made sure that he was undisturbed as she tiptoed away from the bed.

It had been so long since she had seen a man in her bed, and she couldn't believe that she had allowed Carter to seduce her once again. She didn't regret it though. Everything in her wanted to get to know the man that lay in her bed, and she was grateful for his presence. She picked up his button-up shirt and put in on. The shirt swallowed her, but she wore it anyway.

She went into the kitchen and opened her refrigerator to see what she had to cook. There wasn't much of anything. She and Anisa ate out most of the time, so besides breakfast food and bottled water, there wasn't much inside.

She grabbed the phone book and ordered a gourmet dinner from a five-star restaurant that was close to her home. She went out to pick up the food, and when she came back, she set up her dining room and arranged the table. She also brought out a bottle of vintage Merlot from her wine rack and lit two apricot-scented candles, setting the mood for the perfect evening.

Miamor didn't want to wake Carter before she showered, so she handled her business and then dressed in a seductive Victoria's Secret camisole and panty set. The gold fabric looked good on her brown skin. She then put soft curls in her hair and went into her room and climbed on top of Carter.

"Wake up," she called out.

Carter opened his eyes when he felt her nudge him. He pulled her down onto him playfully. He enjoyed the way she felt in his arms.

"I have a surprise for you."

"Oh yeah, show me what you got."

Miamor grabbed his hand and pulled him up. She dragged him into the dining room where a full-course dinner consisting of New York strip steak, steamed vegetables, garlic potatoes, and Caesar salad awaited him.

"You made all this?"

"Yeah, I can do a little something in the kitchen," she replied, telling a little white lie. She wanted to hook this man, and allowing him to think that she could cook was a part of her plan. *I'll buy this nigga breakfast, lunch, and dinner for the rest of his life if I have to.*

Carter looked at her with a "quit bullshitting" expression on his face, but was flattered by her attempt to impress him. He took a seat at the table, and they enjoyed the food and drank an entire bottle of champagne together.

They laughed and chatted like old friends, getting to know each other better, both of them hiding secrets that they couldn't tell if they wanted to.

After they ate, Carter removed her plate from in front of her and took it into the kitchen along with his own. "Yo, Mia, where your garbage?" he yelled.

"It's in the kitchen closet!" she yelled back. As soon as the words left her mouth, she hopped up out of her seat. "Wait!" As soon as she walked into her kitchen, she saw Carter standing with the food delivery bags in his hands and a smile on his face.

"Homemade, huh?"

"I never said *homemade.* Those were not my exact words," she defended playfully, knowing she had just been busted.

Carter put the bags down and wrapped his arms around her waist. "That's okay. You don't have to know how to cook, ma. We'll hire a chef."

Miamor laughed sweetly as she hid her face in his chest from embarrassment.

He lifted her face and kissed her lips gently. "I had a good time with you. I haven't been this comfortable with a woman in a long time."

"Good." She tiptoed and kissed his lips again. She could feel the night coming to an end and wished she could turn back the hands of time and relive the last few hours again.

"I've got to go," he stated. He noticed her eyes go from happy to sad in a split second.

Miamor nodded. "Don't make me wait another two weeks before you show your face again." She looked him in the eye seriously.

"Don't worry, ma, I won't," he replied as he walked into the room and gathered his clothes.

Miamor walked him to the door, and although she hated to see him go, she didn't protest. She didn't want to seem desperate, and she definitely didn't want to scare him off by being to clingy. She stood hugging her door as he walked out.

Carter kissed her forehead and said, "Close this door and lock it behind me."

"I will." Miamor waved one last time. She closed the door and locked it just as he had instructed then she leaned up against it, sighing deeply.

Carter. Carter Jones. He had a hood swagger, a gentlemen's finesse, and a businessman's savvy. He had her attention, and she couldn't wait to see him again.

The next morning, Miamor awoke to the sound of someone knocking at her door. No one beside her friends and now Carter knew where she lay her head, so she figured that it had to be one of those people. She looked at the clock on her bedroom wall. *Damn it! It's only 9:00 in the morning. Who the fuck is this banging at my shit like they fucking crazy?*

She pulled herself out of her bed and went to answer it. Looking out of the peephole, she saw three people standing at her door. *What the fuck is going on?* She snatched the door open in irritation. "Can I help you?" she asked.

Miamor noticed that the woman before her held a white chef's hat in her hand, and she frowned in confusion.

"A Mr. Carter Jones has requested our services. He has contracted us to be at your service whenever you call," the woman explained.

Miamor couldn't help but smile. "So you are my personal chef?"

"Yes. We'll make you whatever you want at any time of the day. All you have to do is call," the woman stated with a friendly smile.

Miamor shook her head in disbelief and then stepped to the side as she let the woman and her two-man team into her place. *This nigga is too much*, she thought.

"I'm Rachel, by the way," the woman said as she extended her hand.

"Miamor," she responded as she shook the friendly woman's hand. As soon as she opened her mouth to speak, her cell phone rang. She rummaged through her Hermes bag until she located it. "Hello."

"I just wanted to see if I could stop by for breakfast."

The sound of Carter's baritone brought a smile to her face. "I don't know. I'm not that great of a cook."

"I thought I took care of that problem."

"Well, I'm not really dressed. I don't like to have company over when I'm looking a mess," she replied, playing hard-to-get. Miamor heard her doorbell ring again and rolled her eyes to the ceiling because of the interruption.

"You see, considering how you got up out the bed last night to shower and do your hair before you woke me up, I figured you were high maintenance."

Miamor smiled and replied, "Just a little bit," as she made her way to the door. She was so into her conversation that she opened her door without looking out of the peephole.

Carter stood before her leaning against her doorframe, his cell phone in one hand and a black designer garment bag in the other. "Now you don't have an excuse." He handed her the bag and hung up his cell phone. "Go get dressed. I'll be waiting for you when you get out."

Miamor was ecstatic. She had never been courted in such an upscale manner. Half the time she didn't even have time to seriously entertain a man, but she was going to make time for Carter. She took the bag from his hand with a bashful smile and unzipped it, revealing a Marc Jacobs original. She had heard that the popular designer was coming out with a new high-end line of clothing, but it wasn't due out until early 2010. Here Carter was standing in front of her with a dress that hadn't even hit stores yet.

How the hell did he get his hands on this dress? Bitches about to hate. "Make yourself comfortable. I'll be out in about an hour," she said, blushing graciously.

Miamor hopped into the shower and applied her MAC cosmetics before attempting to put on the dress. She wore her hair in a bone-straight wrap, with Chinese bangs cut in a slant across her forehead. Spraying Donna Karan's latest fragrance all over her body, she found herself hoping that Carter would like the scent. It was odd for her to care about what a nigga thought of her, but she had to admit that she wanted Carter to feel her as much as she was feeling him.

Miamor admired her strapless pale yellow dress that fit her body loosely and ended just below her knee. The silk fabric wrapped around her slim waist and lay seductively around the curves of her body, giving the ensemble an edgy look, while the simplicity of the rest of the dress had an old Hollywood glamor. It was sophisticated and much different than her normal style, but she liked the change. And she had the perfect Manolo stilettos to go with it.

Looking at herself in the full-length mirror, she had to smile. She was the shit and she knew it. She emerged from the bathroom an hour later and walked back into the living room, where Carter sat waiting patiently for her.

He looked up at her, and the look on his face told her all that she needed to know. He was pleased with her appearance. She had accomplished her goal.

"Thank you for the dress," she said. "I love it."

"Thank you for wearing it. I love it too." Carter grabbed her hand and led her over to her dining room, where Rachel, her chef, presented them with breakfast.

"You are too much. You know that, right? I've never met a nigga like you." Miamor laughed. Carter was on point in every way.

"There ain't another nigga like me," Carter replied with a smirk.

Normally conceit appalled Miamor. There was nothing worse than a stunting-ass nigga who couldn't back up all the shit that he talked, but Carter's confidence was attractive, and he had already proved that he didn't make empty promises. She knew that he was an entirely new breed. His game was different than the Down South men she had encountered, and she appreciated his refreshing Flint swagger.

"You got a passport?" he asked out of the blue.

"Yeah, I got one. Why?"

"I want you to come away with me this weekend to Costa Rica." Carter said it in a nonchalant manner, as if he was merely asking her to go out on a casual date.

"I can do that," she replied with a breathtaking smile.

Carter knew that she was trying to keep her cool, because the infectious smile she displayed gave away her excitement.

They ate their breakfast together, chatting like old friends, and then spent the entire day together. They shopped arm in arm as they hit the designer stores, and although she was prepared to pay for her own items, Carter covered every expense. She couldn't believe how perfect he seemed to be. He was the one thing that her life had been missing.

For so long, everything had been negative in her life. She was all about her business—murder, murder, murder, kill, kill, kill—and had forgotten how good it felt to just live. She had cut off her emotions, because allowing herself to feel anything was a sure way to get herself killed. Carter, however, was becoming the exception to her rule, and she only hoped and prayed that he was worth the risk.

Chapter Twelve

"All I need in this life of sin is me and my girlfriend."

—Tupac Shakur

Miamor and Carter, both with an oversized martini cup in their hand, sat on the secluded shores of Costa Rica, enjoying the scenery. The sun began to set, illuminating an orange hue onto the ocean as they sat at the edge of the water.

Miamor glanced over at Carter and smiled. She was definitely impressed. Carter's body was intact, and she loved it when a man took care of his body by being in shape. She glanced at his six-pack, and then she looked at the noticeable bulge in his white linen shorts. She smirked, remembering how he'd laid the pipe down the previous night. Carter's sex game was on point. He never left her disappointed and made sure that she got hers every time.

Carter noticed her staring and playfully asked, "What you looking at, ma?"

"You," Miamor answered sexily, leaning over to kiss his lips.

Carter examined Miamor's body and loved the way her one-piece Chanel swimsuit hugged her frame. The fabric could barely hold in her voluptuous ass cheeks, and Carter loved every minute of it. He watched as Miamor reached into her matching Chanel bag and pulled out a Dutch and a bag of Miami's finest. She licked and split the Dutch like a pro and filled it with the goods.

"You on this wit' me?" she asked, knowing Carter didn't smoke.

Carter shook his head no and watched as she lit up the "la." Carter loved the fact that Miamor was so street, so hood, but yet so classy all at the same time. And her Brooklyn accent turned him on. When he was with her, he felt like he was with his partner, because they could relate on so many levels. He knew that either, one, Miamor's father was a real street cat, or two, she had a serious relationship with a street nigga. Either way, he knew that she had been taught well.

What Carter didn't know was that neither Miamor's father nor any of her exes had been in the streets. She was a street bitch in her own right.

Carter decided that he wanted to know all about Miamor and thought now would be the perfect time to ask. "So what's your story?" he asked as he took a sip of his drink.

Miamor slowly blew the smoke out. "What do you mean?"

"What do you do? I noticed that you wear the best clothes, and that expensive condo you trying to sell ain't cheap. How do you get your money? You got a nigga back home cashing you out?"

"No, ain't no nigga breaking me off. I make my own money."

Miamor hit the la, to buy herself more time to think of her lie. *I can't tell him that I kill niggas for a living, and that my crew and I have caught over forty bodies over the years. What am I supposed to say—'Yo, I'm a Murda Mama'?* "My father left me a nice piece of change before he died." She looked into Carter's eyes, trying to sense if he bought the lie or not. "And he had a lot of properties back home in New York that I own now."

Carter looked in Miamor's pretty hazel eyes and instantly knew that she wasn't telling him something, but he was determined to find out more about his beautiful mystery woman. His stare was so deep that he made Miamor nervous.

"Thank you for bringing me here," she said, desperately trying to change the subject.

"I enjoy your company. No need to thank me. I needed to get away."

"From what?"

Carter sat up in his chair and looked her directly in her eyes. He had encountered many women in his life, but none compared to the one before him. She seemed to have the complete package. He had seen prettier chicks, even some with better bodies, but Miamor was different. A bit rough around the edges, he was confident that she could be trained.

While every other woman he had ever courted tried to become wifey, Miamor just went with the flow and was comfortable with her status in his life, whatever it may be. There was no pressure with her, and he appreciated the fact that she didn't sweat him.

"Take a walk with me," he said as he stood and reached down to help her up from her seat.

Miamor lifted her designer shades off her face and placed them on top of her head as she looked up at Carter. "Where we going? You know I'm tipsy, nigga. We've been sipping on mai tais all day." She laughed. "I probably can't even stand."

"I got you." Carter licked his lips.

Miamor stood and held his hand, clinging to his arm as

she steadied herself. It felt so good for her to just be able to relax.

They walked through the sand of the darkening beach, the horizon a phenomenal mixture of exotic oranges and reds, setting the perfect atmosphere for an intimate walk on the beach.

In the States, she could never let her guard down, so to be so far from home was like heaven to her. *Me and Nis used to always dream of traveling*, she thought. She looked down at her feet as thoughts of her murdered sibling crossed her mind.

Carter noticed the sad expression take over her striking features. "What's wrong?"

"Nothing. I was just thinking about my sister. I'm sorry. I didn't mean to ruin the mood," she said with a weak smile.

"You didn't. Tell me about her."

"She was the most perfect person ever," she whispered.

A wind gusted up to shore from the ocean, and Miamor wrapped her arms around herself. "She always wanted to travel. She would be so jealous that I'm here right now if she was alive." She laughed, thinking of how Anisa would've cussed her out if she hadn't invited her. "She taught me everything I know, and she saved me from living my life in fear and in pain."

"In fear of what?"

Miamor stopped walking and put her head down as memories of her childhood came rushing back to her. Carter lifted her chin with the tip of his finger and noticed the look of rage going through her eyes.

A single tear trailed her cheek. "My mother abandoned us for a boyfriend who liked to molest little girls. One night he came into my room to touch me, and my sister told him to take her instead. I remember the first time it happened. I heard her screaming for him to stop, and I laid in my bed the entire night listening to him violate her. He threatened to kill us if we ever told our mother." Miamor had tears streaming out of her face as she stared out into the ocean, the dark arms of the night enveloping her and Carter on the deserted beach. "Anisa got pregnant. She was only twelve and was walking around with a baby in her stomach because of him. We were afraid to tell our mother, so she came up with a plan to lose the baby. She purposefully started a fight with these girls in our neighborhood and told me not to jump in, no matter what. They beat her until her body miscarried the baby. There was so much blood, and she was in so much pain, but we got through it . . . together. I remember being so scared. I thought my sister was dying. That same night, our mother's boyfriend was back in our room. He pulled Anisa into his bed. She was crying and screaming, and I couldn't take it anymore. I knew that she was in pain. I grabbed a gun that my mother used to keep hidden in the coat closet and I killed him. I shot him in the head. I saved her then, but I wasn't around to save her this time. I was supposed to be, but I wasn't, and now she's gone. The one time that she needed me most, I let her down."

Carter didn't know what to say. He knew that no words would heal the old wounds that she'd just reopened. He pulled her close, and she wrapped her arms around him as she wept in his arms. No words were spoken, but a bond was established between the two of them.

"I'm scared, Carter. I didn't use to fear shit, because I had Anisa behind me. Now it's just me, you know?" Miamor exhaled.

"You don't have to be afraid of nothing, ma, not with me. I got you. Understand? All I ask is that you keep it real with me."

Now that he knew her history, he had a much better understanding of the woman she was today. He knew what made her tick. He felt the walls that she had built around her heart, but he was willing to be patient as he knocked them down one by one. She had let him in. That was the first step.

Carter and Miamor stood on the beach for what seemed like hours just engrossed in each other's embrace. It wasn't until the tropical rain began to fall that they retreated to their five-star resort room.

When they showered together, Miamor ran her hand all over Carter's soapy physique as her honey pot heated up.

"Uh-uh." He removed her hands before she caused him to get an erection.

After learning of Miamor's past, he was even more intrigued by her. She wasn't just another chick that he wanted to fuck. He knew that she played tough on the outside, but was really a fragile soul on the inside. Carter told himself that he would be careful with her heart. He didn't want to be the one responsible for breaking it.

"I already know your body, Miamor. On this trip I want to get to know your mind and your heart." He kissed the nape of her neck, rinsed his body, and stepped out of the shower while she followed close behind.

His words touched her, and she realized that she had never been treated with as much respect as Carter had just given her. The way he was spending money, wining and dining her on this trip, she planned on paying him back as soon as they hit the sheets.

Carter read her thoughts and said, "You don't owe me shit. I'm feeling you, ma, but if you gon' be my bitch, you got to be my nigga too. I have to trust you with everything I am. There are some things that you don't know about me."

Miamor's eyebrows rose in disapproval.

"It ain't about no other chick or nothing. But there are

some things that I just can't trust with everybody, nah mean? I'm trying to build a friendship with you so that *if* we decide to take this to a serious level, the relationship will have legs to stand on."

Carter didn't know it, but his logic and the way that he spoke it made Miamor trust him more than anyone she had ever known. He was literally blowing her mind. Miamor kissed his neck and nibbled on his ear as she whispered. "I hear you, Carter, but I already trust you." She took his fingers and placed them between her slit. "And I don't want you for a friend. I have enough friends. I want you as my man." She kissed a trail down to his rising manhood and took him into her mouth.

"Ooh, shit," he moaned as he grabbed the back of her head.

Miamor looked Carter directly in his eyes as she gave him the best head he'd ever received in his life.

The club was jammed packed as Rick Ross blared out of the speakers, and the entire Cartel was in attendance at Club Moon, a club that Polo was a silent partner in. It had been months since they went out and partied because of the war with the Haitians, but Polo thought it would be a good tool to get everybody's mind off the current turmoil.

Mecca, Money, Breeze, and Leena were in the middle VIP section popping bottles of Rosé, celebrating Breeze's birthday, while other members of The Cartel were scattered over the room, their hands close to their bangers, ready for whatever if something popped off.

Mecca had two bottles of champagne in his hand. He said to Breeze, "It's jumping in this mu'fucka!"

Money held a single wineglass in his hand and had been sipping on the same glass all night. He wanted to be on point at all times, and by the way Mecca was downing the drinks, he knew that he had to be extra cautious. "Yeah, it's popping tonight, bro." Money took a small sip. He looked over at Breeze who was dancing with Leena and waving her hands in the air and yelled, while holding his glass in the air, "Happy birthday, *B*!"

"Thanks, baby!" she yelled as she began to dance on two guys that approached her.

One of the guys turned around and began to dance with Leena as the DJ switched to a slow R. Kelly song. Money smiled as he saw that everyone was having a good time and laughing. It had been so long since he had seen Breeze smile and she looked like her old self again.

Mecca walked over to Money, almost tripping over himself. It was obvious that he was drunk. "Bro, I need another bottle of"—He paused mid-sentence as he noticed the man dancing on his woman. His anger began to set in when he saw the man rubbing all over Leena's ass while she danced seductively on him. Mecca's eyes were glued on them as the liquor made the innocent dancing rendezvous seem more sexual than it actually was.

Money knew his brother too well and saw that he was getting ready to flip. "Yo, Mecca, fall back. They're just dancing, nigga. Goddamn!" Money laughed lightly and nodded his head to the song.

Mecca took another gulp of the champagne, menacingly staring at the guy who was feeling up his woman. "Do he know who the fuck I am?" Mecca asked himself as he continued to down the drink.

Money brought his ear closer to Mecca. "What?"

Before Money could stop him, Mecca jumped up and walked over to Leena and the guy. Without warning, he broke the champagne bottle over the guy's head, causing him to drop instantly.

The guy's friend, who was dancing with Breeze, ran up on Mecca, but before he could touch Mecca, he was staring down the barrel of a pearl-handled 9 mm handgun.

"What, nigga? What!" Mecca screamed as the DJ stopped the music.

"Mecca! Stop!" Leena yelled as she grabbed his arm. "We were just dancing, baby!" She looked at the man holding the back of his bloody head.

Mecca wasn't trying to hear that. "Bitch, you my woman! This nigga was grabbing yo' ass like y'all was fuckin' or something!" he yelled.

The vision of another man groping his woman was too much to bear, and jealousy took over. Mecca pointed the gun to the man's leg and let off a round, causing a loud thud to echo throughout the spacious VIP room.

"Aghhh!" the man yelled in agony as he gripped his bloody leg. The entire room was in complete pandemonium as people ran for cover, afraid of getting hit by a stray bullet.

Money got up and grabbed his drunken brother. "Yo, Mecca, that's enough!" He signaled for one of his henchmen to come over to them. Money leaned in the henchman's ear and told him to call their family doctor to fix the man up and instructed him to give the man twenty-five thousand dollars as hush money.

Money was noticeably frustrated with his Mecca's recklessness, since it wasn't the first time he had to clean up his mess. He forcefully grabbed him and took him out the back exit, where their cars were parked.

Leena and Breeze followed them out, not believing what had just happened.

"Mecca, you always fuckin' shit up. Damn!" Breeze shook her head from side to side.

As Money, Mecca, Breeze, and Leena exited the club through the back, all you could hear was Breeze arguing with Mecca. "You always go and do some crazy shit. Damn, Mecca! We can't even have a good time without you popping off! You're nothing like Poppa. You need to learn how to control your emotions!"

"Breeze, I'm sorry, sis, but the nigga was tryin' to disrespect me. You know I ain't having that shit. This city is mine," he said in a drunken slur as he stumbled to his car.

"Whatever!" Breeze said before she got into Money's Escalade.

Money was giving Mecca a look of disappointment and shaking his head from side to side. He knew his brother was getting out of hand and that his rashness could eventually lead to his own demise. "Bro, you can't move like that. That shit was straight-up stupid. Shooting a nigga don't make you no gangster. That ain't what we about, family. Now, if the nigga went against the grain, I would've been right there with you, but what you did was wrong and simple-minded. You have to think first and then react," Money said, quoting his deceased father. Carter Sr. had always told hotheaded Mecca, "Think first and then react."

Guilt began to set in with Mecca, so naturally he began to put it off on someone else. He didn't respond to Money and looked over to Leena, who was leaning on his car and crying in her palms.

He stormed over to her and grabbed her by the shoulders forcefully. "It's all yo' mu'fuckin' fault! If yo' ass wasn't flirtin' with the nigga, this wouldn't have happened. You were inviting that nigga to touch all on you."

Leena yelled, "Mecca, stop! You're drunk, and you're hurting me!" She tried to break loose from his grasp.

Mecca's mixture of intoxication and anger caused him to backhand Leena, and she fell to the ground. Mecca quickly grew remorseful as he saw his woman hit the concrete.

Money rushed over and pulled Mecca away. "What the

fuck is wrong with you?" he yelled. "Hitting a female?" He helped Leena up and examined her face and bloody lip. "Are you okay?" Money whispered, as he wiped the blood away from her lip.

Leena looked in the eyes of the man she was desperately in love with. "Yeah, I'm okay." She wanted to be with Money rather than Mecca so badly. Even though Mecca and Money were twins, they were the exact opposite, and Leena felt like she was with the wrong sibling.

"Get in the car, okay. I'll take you home." Money focused back on his drunken brother. "What the fuck is yo' problem, Mecca? You are getting out of hand." He gripped Mecca up by his collar, pulling him close to him so that he could be the only one about to hear what he had to say. "If you ever hit a woman again, I'll"—Money was so enraged by his brother's actions, he couldn't finish his sentence. He just pushed Mecca toward his car and pointed his finger at him and shook his head in disappointment.

Mecca remained silent, knowing he was dead wrong.

Money looked at Breeze, who was in the passenger side of his car, and yelled to her, "Take this drunken fool home! I'll take Leena home and meet you at the house." He walked over to Mecca's car and opened the passenger door for Leena.

Mecca was overwhelmed with guilt as he tried repeatedly to apologize to Leena, but the pleas fell on deaf ears.

"Come on, Mecca." Breeze grabbed his hand and helped him into the car.

Mecca dropped his head in shame as he realized that he had overreacted, and the guilt began to sink in.

Carter drove Mecca's Lamborghini down the highway toward Leena's home.

Money hated driving Mecca's cars. In his eyes, they were way too flashy and drew too much attention. He glanced over at Leena, who was crying quietly, wishing she had never come out that night.

Money wanted so badly to be with Leena, but he couldn't betray his brother in that way. He gently ran his hand over her cheek and wiped away her teary eyes, trying to comfort her. "Mecca doesn't mean any harm. He does love you. He just has a fucked-up temper, nah mean?"

"He sure has a fucked-up way of showing me he loves me," Leena said, tears streaming down her face. She kissed Money's hand as he rubbed her cheek.

Money thought Leena was crying because of what Mecca had just done to her, but that was the farthest thing from her mind at that point. The tears were coming from the thought of her knowing that she and Money could never be.

Leena placed her hand on her stomach as she melted in Money's hand. She had found out that morning that she was three weeks pregnant with his child. She knew it was Money's, because she hadn't been intimate with Mecca in months. He had been too busy to satisfy her lately. She decided to have an abortion and take her secret to her grave, but the pressure was too much to handle by herself. She had to tell Money.

"Money, I'm pregnant," Leena said almost in a whisper.

"What?" Money asked as he swerved in traffic, not believing what he had just heard.

"I said I'm pregnant, Money. It's your baby."

"What are you talking about? How do you know it's mine? It ain't mine. I strapped up every time."

"I know it's yours because you are the only person I have been with. Mecca and I haven't done anything in months. I know it's yours. Remember that night, after them niggas tried to rob Mecca?" Leena asked, referring to the last time they'd made love without using protection.

Money kicked himself inside, knowing the time she

was talking about. He was so caught up in the moment, he'd slid up in her raw. "Fuck!" He hit the steering wheel out of frustration. The guilt began to set in as Money thought about how he had betrayed his best friend and twin brother.

"I love you, Leena," Mecca whispered just before he lowered his face to his table to inhale the line of cocaine.

As soon as Breeze had dropped him off, his conscience began eating at him. He felt bad for putting his hands on the only woman he'd ever truly loved. His long hair was wild and unbraided, which made him look like a mad man as he used his nose as a suction vacuum for his preferred drug. Mecca threw his head back and held it up to prevent his nose from running. Mecca was high out of his mind. He had snorted five grams of coke within twenty minutes, and the effects of the drugs were kicking in.

He grabbed the bottle of Rémy Martin and took a large swallow of it. He distantly heard a Tupac song pump out of his home stereo and recognized the tunes. He stood up almost stumbling and went over to turn the music up.

All I need in this life of sin is me and my girlfriend

Down to ride to the very end, just me and my girlfriend.

Mecca held the bottle of Rémy in his grasp and drunkenly rapped along, thinking about his love, Leena. He couldn't take it anymore. He had to go over to her and make things right. Although he treated her bad at times, he really was in love with her, and she was the only woman he had truly ever loved.

Mecca staggered over to the keys to his Benz and snatched them off the counter. He was about to confess his love for Leena. "Leena, I love you, baby. I'm sorry," he said as he stumbled out the door and into his Benz to go see his woman.

* * *

"I don't know what to do, Money. I'm in love with a man I can't have," Leena said as tears streamed from her eyes. She sat on her sofa across from Money expressing how she felt about him.

Money was speechless as he looked into Leena's eyes and realized the feeling was mutual. He began to slowly shake his head, knowing that what they had done was wrong. His father had taught him that family always came first and that loyalty was the single most important thing a man can have for his family. Money's father's teachings were embedded in his brain as his heart and mind played tug of war. On one hand, he knew that betraying his brother was wrong, but on the flip side, not taking responsibility for what he had created would eat at him. His father had also told him that abortion was wrong and that a real man takes care of his family by any means necessary. Money was lost.

"Leena, this ain't right. This ain't right," Money mumbled as he buried his face in his palms. All he could think about was his twin brother.

Money had no other choice but to force an abortion upon Leena. He wasn't willing to let a woman come between him and his sibling. *That's my flesh and blood, my brother. Blood in, blood out, I can't let her have that baby*, Money thought as he looked at Leena crying her eyes out.

He sat next to her so that he could console her. He ran his fingers through her hair and gently put his finger under her chin and made her look at him in the eyes. "Leena, we are going to get through this . . . together." He returned the deep stare at Leena. "We can't have this baby, though. It's wrong."

"I never wanted it to be like this," Leena told him, heartbroken.

"Everything is going to be okay. But this between us has to stop." Money gently kissed Leena on the lips. Money's lips were magic to Leena. Just by his touch, he drove Leena wild. She felt her friend in between her legs begin to thump, and before she knew it, her hands were in his pants looking for his rod. She gently began to stroke it, to make it grow.

Money promised himself this would be the last time he would have sex with his forbidden love.

"*All I need in this world of sin . . .*" Mecca sung drunkenly as he approached Leena's house. He was going to apologize to his woman and make things right.

When he pulled up, he noticed his Lamborghini parked in her driveway. "Money still here?" he asked himself as he pulled two houses down from Leena's house. He threw the car in park, grabbed the half-empty bottle of Rémy, and hopped out.

Mecca staggered to Leena's house and noticed that the front light was on. He walked in front of the house, and what he saw through the front glass made his heart drop. Mecca dropped the Rémy bottle, causing it to shatter into pieces on the sidewalk. He saw his twin brother passionately kissing his woman. He watched as Money pulled out one of Leena's big brown breasts and began to suck on it. Mecca was in complete shock as he watched Leena straddle his brother. His eyes bugged out as he saw his brother rub on Leena's behind with one hand, while removing her thong with the other.

"What da fuck!" Mecca walked closer to the front glass and witnessed the treachery happening.

Money and Leena were so into one another that they didn't notice Mecca staring at them through the large front glass. And Leena's moans could be heard from the outside as she rode Monroe with more passion than she had ever ridden Mecca.

Mecca's sadness instantly turned into rage as he reached for his gun and headed for the front door. Seconds later, bullets from his .40 caliber pistol was ripping through the wood of the front door.

Leena scrambled to the corner of the room out of fear. She didn't know what was going on, and Money grabbed his pistol from his waist and pointed it at the door. Then he saw Mecca burst through the front door, tears in his eyes.

"Mecca!" Leena yelled as she saw the look in his eyes. She knew that their secret was out of the bag.

Mecca pointed his gun at Leena. He screamed, "I can't believe you, bitch!"

Money put away his gun and tried to calm down his brother. "Mecca, put the gun down. It's not what it looked like," he tried to explain.

"It's not what it looked like? Nigga, fuck you!" Mecca pointed his gun at his brother. The two people he thought he could trust were the very ones deceiving him. He pulled the hammer back on his gun and aimed it at his brother's head.

Money put both of his hands up and tried to reason with him. He knew his brother very well, and when he looked in Mecca's eyes, it was obvious that he was high as a kite. "Bro, listen, put the mu'fuckin' gun down. You high. Now stop, before you do something you gon' regret."

"The only thing I regret is fuckin' with this stankin' ho!" Mecca pointed his gun back at Leena. The thought of her being intimate with his brother sent him over the edge. "I hate you!" Mecca screamed as he put both of his hands on his head, and his tears began to fall freely. "I loved you,"

Mecca whispered just before he pointed the gun at Leena and let off two rounds. He watched as the bullets ripped through her chest, and she fought for air.

"Noooo!" Money yelled as he rushed over to Leena and cradled her in his arms. "Breathe, Leena, breathe!" he instructed her as blood oozed out of her mouth.

Leena fought for her dear life as she gripped Money's hands and looked into his eyes.

"Breathe, Leena!" Money screamed as he tried to keep her from slipping away. "Call an ambulance!" He looked back at Mecca, who was pacing the room with both of his hands on his head.

Mecca whispered, "Oh my God! What have I done?" He frantically continued to pace the room. He looked over at his brother and Leena, and what he saw and heard broke his heart.

Leena was taking her last breath, but before she slipped away, she looked Money in the eyes and whispered, "I love you, Monroe Carter," just before she stared into space, leaving this earth.

A single tear slid down Money's face, and he felt Leena's grip suddenly loosen. He knew that she was gone.

A tear fell from Mecca's eye also, but it wasn't one of sorrow, but a tear of rage. He'd just witnessed the woman he loved tell his brother that she loved him. "Her last words were that she loved you, not me," he whispered as he slowly raised his gun and pointed at Money.

Money ran his hand over Leena's eyelids to close them, and then he gently kissed her forehead before he turned his attention on his brother. "Mecca, put the gun down." Money put his hands in front of him. He knew his brother was unstable.

"You always thought you were better than me, nigga. You could've had any woman you wanted, but you had to take mines. Now look at you. Look what you made me do.

Look! Poppa and Ma always favored you over me." Mecca's tears fell freely down his face, and his hand began to shake. He remembered what his parents used to say when he would get in trouble and began to mimic them. "You need to be more like Monroe. Monroe wouldn't act like that," he said, his voice shaky.

As all of his emotions boiled over, Mecca looked Money in the eyes and let off a single shot that entered the left side of his chest where his heart resided.

Monroe heard the gunshot, but didn't believe his own flesh and blood had shot him. As the burning sensation in his chest settled in, he fell to the ground, and his life slowly slipped away.

High out of his mind, Mecca watched as his brother lay dying in a puddle of his own blood.

"Unc Po!" Mecca yelled into the phone as he held his twin brother's corpse in his arms, "They killed Money. Oh my God! They killed my brother!" He instantly regretted what he had done, and remorse quickly brought his cocaine high down.

"Mecca, what are you talking about? Calm down! What's going on?" Polo didn't want to believe what he'd just heard.

"Them Haitian mu'fuckas, they killed Money!" Mecca responded as he cried like a baby.

"No, no, no." Polo dropped to his knees. The news of his godson's death was too much for him to bear.

"They killed Leena too. Come and get me, Unc. They killed Money. They killed my brother," Mecca stated as he wept uncontrollably. He hung up the phone and put his own gun to his head. "I love you, bro. I'm sorry. I'm so sorry," Mecca whispered right before he pulled the trigger, but fortunately for him, the gun jammed.

* * *

A knock at the door awakened Carter and Miamor, and he sleepily arose to answer it.

"Mr. Jones, I have an urgent message from your uncle." The concierge held out the piece of folded paper.

Carter opened it and read the words:

> *Money was killed last night. Come home immedi-*
> *ately. It's an emergency.*
> *Polo*

"Fuck!" Carter screamed as he punched the wall nearest him and balled the tiny note up in his palm. He rested his head against the doorframe and let out a roar of pain that caused a shiver to run down the concierge's spine.

Miamor rushed to his side. "Oh my God! Carter, what's wrong?"

"We've got to go. Pack your things. I have an emergency back home," he said through tear-filled eyes.

Chapter Thirteen

"Bitch, you's a Murder Mama! . . . We don't give a
fuck where the coroner bag 'em."

—Robyn

"**B**itch, are you paying attention to me?" Robyn threw
a pillow in Miamor's face, snapping her out of her
trance.

"Yeah, I'm listening. I hear you, damn," Miamor replied
with a slight attitude as she tossed the pillow back.

"Whatever. You didn't hear nothing me just said," Aries
teased. "Bring your head out de clouds, Miamor. We got a
chance to get back at The Cartel and get at that mu'fucka
that killed your sister. This is important."

The three girls sat comfortably on Miamor's bed while
they plotted their revenge. Miamor was trying her hardest
to concentrate, but she couldn't. Every time she closed
her eyes, Carter crept into her thoughts. Her time in Costa
Rica was like a fantasy. He had showed her a side of life
that she had never experienced before and had opened up
the heart that she thought had been forever closed by
lock and key.

Miamor shook her head, sat up against her headboard,
and looked at both of her friends. They were her sisters,
her partners in crimes, and she knew that her distraction

could put them in jeopardy. *I have to get focused*, she thought.

"What did that nigga do to you over on that island?" Robyn asked with an insinuating tone. "I know you ain't stressing him like that. Not Miamor, not the one who said niggas ain't good for shit, but a broken heart."

"He's not like that," Miamor stated in Carter's defense.

"I know I did not just hear she say that." Aries put her hand on Miamor's forehead. "Are you sick or something? 'Cuz this ain't de same bitch I sent over to that island."

Miamor had to laugh as she knocked Aries' hand away. "I'm serious. Yo, he's not like that. I don't know, there's something about him that has me stuck. He's . . . he's . . ."

"You fucked him, didn't you?" Robyn asked.

The smile that spread across Miamor's face revealed the answer before she could even speak.

"Ohh. She fucked him! Was he good? 'Cuz he could get it any day from me." Aries stood up and bounced her voluptuous behind up and down doing a freaky dance. "I would put it on him."

Miamor laughed as she pulled a .45 from the shoulder holster she was wearing. She removed the clip and popped the single bullet from the chamber then pointed the pistol at her friend. "Bitch, I'm-a put this on you if you keep talking like that."

Aries ignored Miamor's idle threats as she continued to pop her ass and hips. "Whatever. I would have that fine mu'fucka all up in me. Them bullets don't stop no show."

Miamor and Robyn were laughing so hard that tears were coming to their eyes.

"Okay, okay, can ya'll bitches concentrate for a hot little minute while we discuss this business?" Robyn asked.

Aries stopped dancing and sat back down on the bed, while Robyn pulled the daily newspaper from her Hermes bag and spread it across the bed.

"You think Ma'tee still want the Cartel job done?" Robyn asked.

"I don't know. There was a truce or something established between them, so now I'm not so sure." Miamor shook her head.

"Well, you need to call and see, because we gon' get at the boy Mecca, regardless. We might as well get paid in the process. You feel me?" Robyn asked.

Miamor nodded and flipped up her cell phone to dial Mat'ee.

Ma'tee greeted her as soon as he answered the phone, "Miamor? Me ain't hear from yuh? How yuh doin'?"

He knew exactly who was calling him due to his high-tech security. When he received a call, he knew your first and last name along with your current location, so she wasn't surprised. He was always on point.

"I'm well. Thanks for asking," she hesitated but was urged on when she noticed Aries waiting in anticipation. "Look, I'm calling regarding that unfinished business we had with each other. You still need that job done?" she asked, getting straight to the point.

"Unfortunately, me have to put that on hold. After what happened at me little angel's party, me hand was forced to call a truce. Me a man of honor. Me word is all me have. Me will not break de truce. The only way me will put the contract back up is if de Cartel break de agreement first. Then and only then will me pay yuh for de bounty."

"I hear you. Look, if you change your mind, we're ready. Just say the word, and we'll make it happen. Is the ticket still the same on that?" she asked.

Ma'tee let out a small chuckle. "If they do not hold up their end, then me will pay one point five for it."

"Well, like I said, Ma'tee, I'm trying to see that, so let me know," she said before hanging up.

"What did he say?" Robyn asked eagerly.

"Bounty's not good unless The Cartel breaks the truce first. Otherwise, he is going to keep his word. He's willing to pay a mill five, if they do show shade."

"Then we have to make sure the Cartel breaks de truce, so we can see that cash and kill de kid Mecca," Aries replied.

"I don't know, y'all. Y'all talking about initiating a war between two sides that have agreed to lay low. With everything that happened with Nis, my head is all over the place. Emotions throw my judgment off. Everything I've been going through with her death has me all fucked up. I don't know if I'm ready to get at them again."

"It's hard on all of us, Mia. We loved Anisa too, and it's not just about the money anymore. They made it personal when the nigga Mecca killed her," Robyn said.

"I haven't forgotten, Robyn. He's gon' get it, believe that," Miamor said, venom in her voice and tears in her eyes.

"Well, we think we found a way to get at him and bring down the Cartel too." Robyn pointed her finger at the newspaper on the bed, causing Miamor to pay attention to it.

"Is this Mecca's obituary?" Miamor picked up the paper and studied the face closely. Confusion swept over her face, and her forehead dropped in a deep frown. "Somebody got to him before we did?"

"Not Mecca, his twin brother Monroe," Aries stated smugly.

Robyn added, "The funeral's tomorrow, Mia. You know Mecca and the rest of The Cartel will be there. It's our chance to catch 'em while they're weak,"

Miamor lifted her eyes from the newspaper to meet Robyn's gaze. "At his brother's funeral?" she said with doubt. "I don't know."

"Bitch, you's a Murder Mama! Ain't nothing to think about. We don't give a fuck where the coroner bag 'em. The nigga disrespected—" Robyn yelled.

"So he got to get it," Aries chimed in, finishing her friend's sentence. "Fuck them, Mia. Let's get at these niggas."

Miamor nodded her head in agreement, and in an instant the coldness in her heart settled back in. Fuck The Cartel. Fuck Mecca, his world, and everyone in it. Miamor was about to avenge her sister's death and make Mecca's mother feel what she had felt when she buried her sister. "I'm in."

Mecca sat in the family room of the Diamond house. His insides were hollow, and he cried to himself, tears falling uncontrollably from his eyes. *What did I do? Money, my baby, my blood, what the fuck did I do?* he thought silently. His conscience was eating him alive. He had murdered his twin brother. They had come out of the womb together, and now that Money was gone, Mecca didn't feel whole. He couldn't believe that his rage had blinded him to this point, and he knew that if he hadn't been so intoxicated from the drugs and booze that his temper would've never taken him so far. *I'm so sorry, bro. I love you, baby. I love you, man.* His mind was spinning, and his heart ached. "This is all my fault," he cried.

"Mecca, this is not on you. Those Haitians are to blame for this, not you. Nobody saw this coming," Polo stated as he paced back and forth.

Mecca knew that the lie he'd told would hold up. It was a convenient story that pointed the blame toward their beef with Ma'tee, but seeing the anguish that he had caused his family was more than he could take.

"Why is this happening to us?" Breeze asked. "First

Poppa, now Money. They are tearing our family apart."
Her eyes were red and swollen as if she hadn't gotten
sleep for days. She looked to her mother for answers.

But Taryn was stricken beyond belief and couldn't open
her mouth to answer. She knew that if she spoke then, her
tears would leak from their confinement. She couldn't
allow that to happen. Just as she had been the foundation
that held her family up during her husband's funeral, she
had to be strong now and perform what was once her husband's role and be the glue that held her family together.

The sound of the doorbell interrupted them, and Mecca
went to answer it. When he opened the door, Carter stood
before him. They slapped hands, and when Carter pulled
him close, they fell into a hug as Mecca cried. Young
Carter was the only brother he had left. The only other
male in the Diamond family he could call on. He was family, and all they had was each other. "I'm sorry, fam,"
Mecca sobbed.

Holding his brother and hearing him break down
caused tears to come to Carter's eyes. "It's all right, fam.
Let it out, baby, let it out," Carter whispered as he pulled
Mecca's head into his chest as if he was his lil' nigga.

Mecca was always so boisterous, so hard; now his
spirit was half gone. He was getting ready to bury a part of
himself, and he knew that when Money's casket hit the
dirt, his heart would too. His twin brother was gone, and
Carter had no idea that Monroe's death had been at the
hands of Mecca himself.

Polo stepped into the foyer, but when he witnessed the
two men united as brothers he paused. He didn't want to
interrupt their moment.

"He was my brother, man. My baby," Mecca sobbed.

Carter and Mecca released one another. They stood
there face to face, and for the first time there wasn't even
the slightest bit of animosity between them.

When Polo cleared his throat, they turned around to face him. "We need to talk. In the kitchen," he said.

They followed Polo to the kitchen and took a seat at the table.

Carter stared at Polo. "How the fuck did this happen?"

"It's my fault, man. Money took Leena home because of me. We had a fight, and he was doing me a favor. Once I cooled down, I decided to go over there to check on her. When I got there, I saw two dread mu'fuckas running out of her crib. I rushed in to see about Leena, and they both were laid out in there, fam." Mecca dropped his head, unable to hold his brother's stare. He couldn't tell them what he had done. It was something that he would take to his grave.

"We've got to get a handle on this," Polo stated.

"What the fuck happened to the truce? We kept our end up. What triggered this?" Carter asked.

"We don't know, but we've got to retaliate," Polo replied.

"Right now we just need to make it through today. I don't think it's too smart for us to keep fanning the flames. It's obvious that we're touchable right now. They've killed two of our soldiers, our leaders, and we've only knocked out their henchmen. We need to think before we attack," Carter said.

"I agree," Polo stated.

Taryn walked into the room. "The limo is here," she announced, her voice barely audible.

Carter arose from his seat and hugged her tightly. "I'm sorry," he told her as they embraced.

"You have to fix this, Carter," Taryn told him. "I need you to save my family . . . our family. Keep Breeze and Mecca safe. I don't know how much more of this I can take."

Carter nodded. "I will, I promise."

Polo escorted Taryn to the car, and Breeze held onto Carter's arm for dear life as they followed behind. She cried softly. It was almost time for the funeral to begin.

"Look, when we walk in this mu'fucka, we go straight to the front of the church. Mecca will be sitting on the front pew, so that's the easiest way to hit him. Act like we're going to view the body and then start blazing on 'em. There will be members of their entourage all over the church, so make sure you spray anybody that's standing in the way. There are three of us going in here, so I want there to be three of us leaving out," Miamor stated.

The girls wore knee-length H & M raincoats with knee-high boots. Inside their coats they held "street sweepers." They weren't fools. They knew that they were outnumbered in bodies, but in bullets and ammunition, they were equal to anything that The Cartel could throw at them.

They exited their vehicle and walked into the church. There were hundreds of people inside the place as the girls made their way down the aisle, but they noticed that security was on point.

Miamor's hand gripped the steel inside her coat, and she could hear her heartbeat in her ears. She could see the backs of the family's heads as she walked. Mecca sat on the end. She knew it was him because of his long braids, and a slight smirk crossed her face. She could already taste his blood in her mouth as she bit down on the inside of her cheek, something she always did when she saw her unsuspecting prey. She was indeed a calculating killer.

Miamor stepped to the casket and looked down at Monroe. Robyn and Aries stood by her side. They all waited for her signal.

Miamor stood silently, and a single tear slid down her

cheek. Monroe looked so peaceful, so gentle. He looked to be the exact opposite of his murderous twin brother Mecca. She exhaled and jumped slightly when she felt someone grip her arm. She turned around, ready to bust off on the first face she saw, but the man before her caused her to take a step back.

"Oh my God," she whispered.

Her girls looked at her in confusion.

"What are you doing here?" Carter asked her.

Miamor's eyes gazed over at Mecca. His face was in his hands. She scanned the entire pew and took in the faces of the Diamond family. Her eyes stopped when she noticed Breeze. *Breeze is Carter's sister. Breeze is Mecca's sister. Carter is Mecca's brother. He's a part of the Cartel*, she thought. The room felt like it was spinning as she looked up at Carter. *This was the emergency*, she thought, putting two and two together slowly in her head.

"I didn't know you knew my brother."

"I-I-" Miamor was at a loss for words, and her mind was unable to formulate a lie.

Robyn stepped up and said, "She doesn't, I do. We were friends, and I'm just coming to pay my respects. I'm sorry for your loss."

"Thank you." Carter peered at Miamor. "You okay?"

She nodded, still unable to speak.

"Look, I've got to get back to my family, but I'll call you, ma." He leaned in and kissed her on the cheek before walking away.

Miamor turned to her friends. "I have to get out of here," she whispered.

"Mia, what about the plan?" Robyn asked.

"Fall back. I can't do this right now."

"But, Miamor—" Aries interjected.

"I said fall the fuck back." Miamor walked out of the

church and almost ran to her car. When she got inside, her head fell to the steering wheel in defeat. "He's his brother," she said aloud. "He's a part of The Cartel."

Robyn and Aries exchanged glances. They knew that Miamor was feeling Carter. She had broken her number one rule and gotten emotionally involved.

"Miamor, fuck him. He's one of them. Let's go back in there and do what we came here to do," Robyn stated.

Aries looked sympathetically at her friend, but kept quiet.

"I can't, Robyn. It's not that simple."

"It is that simple. You gon' choose him over Anisa? Somebody has to pay for what Mecca did to her."

"Robyn, shut de fuck up, okay. That's she sister you're talking about," Aries said in Miamor's defense.

"I thought she forgot," Robyn said smartly, her arms folded across her chest.

"Bitch, shut the fuck up talking! That's your fucking problem—you talk too fucking much. I can't even hear myself think. I know what the fuck I have to do. I was there, Robyn. I know, okay. I just can't do this right now," Miamor said as she started her car and drove away.

She dropped her girls off at the apartment that they shared. The car ride there was filled with silence and tension.

"We're going to make that money, so don't think this is over. It's us versus them, Mia. He's the enemy," Robyn stated before she got out of the car, slamming the door behind her.

Aries looked back at her friend, who was staring straight ahead, looking at the road. "Do you love him, Mia?"

"No," she quickly answered. Her heart fluttered when the word left her lips, letting her know that her body knew better. She closed her eyes, and Anisa's face popped into her mind. She slowly opened them and breathed deep. "I'm gonna kill him and everybody he loves."

Aries stepped out of the car and watched Miamor as she drove away. She looked up at Robyn, who was standing on the stairs to their building.

"Did you have to be so fucking rude? Give she a break, Robyn. Damn! You know she's in a fucked-up situation," Aries stated. "You lucky I not she, 'cuz I woulda beat your ass first and made up with you later."

Aries and Robyn walked into their building arguing, both knowing that there would never be any real beef between them.

Miamor drove around the city for two hours trying to make sense out of her dilemma. Instinctively she found herself driving toward the cemetery. She had to talk to her sister. When she made it there, she saw the same crowd of people that she had seen at Money's funeral. She knew that they were there to bury his body next to his father's, the infamous Carter Diamond, founder of The Cartel. She didn't care though. She still parked her car and walked over to her sister's grave. She knelt down and cried.

"Anisa, he's Mecca's brother," she said as she touched her sister's headstone. She closed her eyes. "He's the brother of the man who killed you. I miss you so much. I promise you that I'm not going to forget what he did to you. I'm gonna kill him. I swear on everything I love." Thoughts of Carter filled her head, but she quickly replaced them with her sister's face. "Why is this so hard?"

"It just is," a voice behind her said.

Startled, she stood to her feet and turned around.

Carter stood there in a black Sean John suit, his hands tucked away in his pockets, and his muscular physique hung his linens well. His eyes were red as they gazed down at her tear-stained face. "It's always hard when you lose someone you love," he said.

Miamor didn't respond. She had so much hate for him and his family in her heart. Her sister was underneath her feet at this very moment because of what Carter stood for.

He reached for her, but she pulled away slightly. "Don't," she whispered.

He didn't listen and stepped closer to her.

She wanted to run from him. He was the only person she had ever encountered who intimidated her, and she despised him because of it. *He's a part of The Cartel. I slept with this man. I kissed him and let him explore me. I opened up my mind and body to him. I was willing to give him my heart, and he's Mecca's brother,* she thought painfully.

He put his arms around her waist and pulled her near, even though she still tried to resist. "I wish I could've met her," he said as he pulled out a handkerchief and wiped away her tears.

His touch was so gentle, so loving. He was so perfect.

"You love her so much. I can see it in your eyes that you're hurting."

"Don't talk about her," she replied in a whisper. She didn't want him to speak Anisa's name. He had no right to.

"I want to be here for you, Mia. I want you to be here for me. I didn't know how I was going to make it through today, until I saw you at the church. Seeing your face did more for me than you know."

Miamor looked up at him, and his words played funny tricks with her heart. Loving him would be wrong. Being with him would be wrong, but playing on his feelings toward her to inflict her revenge would be so right. *Can I be around this man and not love him though? Can I do this?* she asked herself. *Yes, I'll do it. It's never been hard for me to murk a nigga before. I'm going to finish what I started.*

"I'm sorry about your family," she said sincerely as she

reached up and wrapped her arms around his neck. "I'm so sorry, Carter."

Carter thought that she was apologizing out of respect for Monroe. What he didn't know was that she was apologizing for the death and pain that she was about to cause his family. She was going to become his only weakness and then use it against him. He didn't know it yet, but he was going to contribute to his family's demise.

Chapter Fourteen

"God, please forgive me for I have sinned. Money,
Poppa, I'm coming to join you."

—Mecca Diamond

Leena's eyes shifted back and forth frantically as her blurred vision became clearer by the second. She didn't recognize where she was. Tubes were coming from her nose, and the steady beep of the heart monitor echoed through the room. The last thing she remembered was Mecca pointing the gun at her and hearing a loud blast.

Instinctively, she began calling for her man. "Mon-Monroe," she whispered as she blinked her eyes rapidly, trying to regain clear vision. She tried to sit up, but an excruciating pain shot through her body. She felt the tenderness in her arm and then realized that was where the bullet struck her.

She immediately began to think about the unborn child that she was carrying. She nervously began to feel on her belly and wondered, was her child okay. That was when she heard the unfamiliar sound of a man's voice, and she instantly grew terrified.

She saw a tall, older man with a beer belly. He had on an expensive silk shirt with the first three buttons unbuttoned, typical gangster attire for older Florida natives. An unlit cigar hung from his mouth as he stood up and walked toward her. The man was of Dominican descent and had slick hair that was neatly brushed to the back.

Leena tried to scream, but she was too weak to project her voice. She immediately tried to reach for the emergency call button next to her bed, but she was unable to move her arm.

The man loomed over her and gently tapped her, whispering, "It's okay, it's okay."

Leena quickly smacked his hand off her, and tears formed in her eyes. She knew one of Mecca's goons was there to finish what he had started.

"Don't worry. I'm not going to hurt you, Leena," the man said as he sat at the edge of her bed.

"Who are you, and how do you know my name?" Leena scooted to the opposite side of the bed, trying to get as far away from him as she could. She grimaced as she felt the pain in her arm. She clenched her stomach, all the while keeping her eyes on the man in front of her.

"My name is Emilio Estes. Monroe was my grandson," he said as he dropped his head, noticeably saddened.

"Was? What do you mean, was? Where is Money?!" Leena's face frowned up.

"He didn't make it. He's gone."

Estes stood up and wiped the tear that threatened to fall. The thought of Monroe's death made him weak. He quickly regained his composure and stared into the eyes of the woman who would birth his great grandchild. He had been with her throughout the whole time she was in a coma.

When he got to Leena's house on the night of shooting, he was the first to discover that the Haitians had left Leena alive and that she was carrying a child. He'd arranged for Leena's status to be kept a secret and got her moved to the top floor of the hospital, where they usually admitted celebrities and people of prestige. The doctor told him that the baby would be fine, and he was determined to make sure Leena would be taken care of until she delivered his first great grandchild.

Leena stared aimlessly in complete shock. The words that left Estes' mouth sent a dart straight to her heart.

"He's gone? No, he can't be," Leena said as her voice began to shake. Her whole world had just crumbled, knowing that the only man she ever loved was gone.

"His funeral was a couple of days ago. Sorry, sweetheart," Estes said as he stepped closer to the bed.

Heartbroken, Leena broke down in tears and cried like a child.

Estes put his hand on her hair, slowly stroking it to comfort her.

She gripped her stomach, remembering that she was carrying Monroe's child. Fear sunk in as she wondered if her baby was okay; it was the only piece of Monroe she had left.

Estes noticed the sudden look of worry in her face. "The baby is fine, Leena," he said.

Leena took a deep breath and buried her face into her hands. "Thank God. Thank God, my child is safe," she whispered as she continued to cry a river.

Estes wanted to be supportive of Leena, but revenge was the main thing on his mind. He wanted to affirm that Ma'tee's Haitian mob was responsible for the killing.

"I know you are going through a lot right now, but I have to ask you a question. Who killed my grandson?"

"Your grandson," she repeated as she briefly stared him in his eyes.

Estes took the cigar out of his mouth and slightly frowned, "What did you say?' he asked in a heavy Dominican accent.

"Mecca killed Monroe. Mecca did it."

Estes was at a loss for words as he clenched his teeth and involuntarily balled up his fist. He was hurt by her words, and his anger got the better of him. He angrily grabbed Leena by her hand and squeezed it tightly. "Don't fuckin' lie to me!" he yelled.

"I'm not lying, I swear to you. Mecca shot both of us. He went crazy. Monroe and I were fooling around and he walked in. But I wasn't serious with Mecca. Monroe was the one I loved."

Estes caught himself and released Leena's hand. He shook his head from side to side and remembered the look in Mecca's eyes at the funeral. He knew something wasn't right with his only living grandson. Estes was a firm believer in family morals and loyalty.

What Mecca had done was the ultimate betrayal, and Estes quickly disowned him. Estes was from the old school and played by the rules. If you went against the family, you weren't considered family anymore. The thought of vengeance was the only thing he could fathom. He motioned to the man that was in the corner of the room to come to him.

Leena was startled. She didn't even realize that they weren't alone.

A Dominican man emerged from the shadows of the darkened room, and Estes whispered something in his ear. The man quickly exited the room, and Estes sat next to Leena and instructed her that he would look after her, and everything would be okay. Unbeknownst to Leena, Estes had ordered the death of his only remaining grandson, Mecca.

Mecca sniffed the long line of cocaine, using his nostrils like a Hoover vacuum. His hair was unbraided and wild all over his head, giving him the look of a crazed man. He quickly jerked his head back so that his nose wouldn't run. He stared at the items on the table—a bottle of Rémy Martin, two Desert Eagle handguns, and a bowl of pure coke. He had already sniffed two grams and was high out of his mind.

He reached over to his end table to grab the picture of himself, Money, and their father. It was a picture that was taken when they were little boys, both of them sitting shirtless on their father's lap. He remembered that day and smiled. That smile quickly turned into a saddened expression, which was then followed by tears. He was deeply remorseful for his actions and continued to shed silent tears as he picked up the bottle and took a big gulp of liquor then another line of blow.

"I'm sorry, Money, I am so sorry, bro," he said as he broke down crying hysterically. "I love you, man," he whispered as he stood up, almost falling back down. He looked around his tri-level condominium that overlooked the sands of Miami's coastline. He staggered over to his balcony with the bottle in one hand and the picture in the other. He forcefully pushed open the door and stumbled out. He looked into the sky as the moonlight shined down on him. He felt worthless, like he was the scum of the earth.

He took another swig of the drink and threw the bottle off the balcony and watched it land in the Olympic-size swimming pool below. His condo was three stories above ground, and as he glanced down, the mixture of liquor, height, and cocaine caused him to become disoriented. He looked at the picture again and kissed it. He remembered back when he was innocent and untainted by life's ills. He wished he could start back over and have his life back with his father and brother. But now both of them were gone.

Mecca took off his Timberland boots and carefully climbed on top of the railing. He took off his shirt, exposing his definitive tattoo that covered chest and arms. He closed his eyes and spread his arms out like an eagle soaring in free air.

"God, please forgive me for I have sinned. Money, Poppa, I'm coming to join you," he said as he prepared to jump to his death.

Before he took the leap, he heard a stampede of feet coming from beneath him. He opened his eyes and glanced down and couldn't believe his eyes. *Am I drunk*? he asked himself as he saw at least fifteen men of Dominican descent creeping into his first floor patio door, all of them carrying assault rifles or handguns.

Mecca knew who'd sent them, his own grandfather. He had seen those same goons wipe out other crews while growing up. Mecca instantly grew enraged. His pride was still intact, and he figured, if he was going out, it would be with a bang.

Mecca hopped off the rails and stepped back into the house. He walked over to the table and grabbed both of his guns. He then dipped his entire face into the cocaine bowl and took a deep sniff. Cocaine was all over his face as he rose up with bloodshot-red eyes. He walked over to the radio, and the sounds of Tupac blared out of the speakers. He turned the volume up as high as he could, so the intruders didn't have to guess what part of the house he was in.

"Come on, mu'fuckas!" Mecca yelled. He pounded his chest just before breaking the bulbs in the big lamp that lit the room up. He wanted to kill every single man who came for him. He was about to set that mu'fucka off.

Mecca ran to the corner of the spacious room and kneeled behind the couch and cocked both of his guns. "Y'all trying to come in my home and get me? Do y'all know who the fuck I am? Huh!" he yelled over the couch, as four men ran into the room and positioned themselves.

Mecca's body was sweating profusely because of the drugs and his anxiousness. He was ready to get it popping. He rose up blasting, shooting anything that was moving.

The sound of Estes' henchmen's assault rifles filled the air as they tried their best to take Mecca's head off.

Mecca, even though he was high as a kite, aimed with a marksman's precision, picking them off one by one. He ducked behind the couch briefly for cover and then emerged blasting. Busting his gun was like second nature to him, and he began to kill the men in the room. Before he knew it, he was the only one left standing.

When he heard the sounds of feet coming up the stairs, he realized that he had no chance against the army. A man ran through the door, and Mecca rolled across the floor and fired his gun at him, but nothing came out. He was out of bullets.

Mecca rushed for him, but the man popped him in the shoulder. But that didn't stop Mecca. He ran and struck the man across the face, causing him to drop his gun. Mecca then began to beat the man to a pulp. Swollen to twice its normal size, the man's face became like a bloody stew as Mecca pounded the man with his gun. That's when the others came up the stairs, and Mecca caught another bullet to the mid-section.

"Ahhh!" he screamed as the burning-hot bullet ripped through his torso. Mecca fell on his back in pain and saw another man coming for him.

The room was dim, so the man couldn't see Mecca clearly and began firing aimlessly.

Mecca grabbed the dead man's gun and fired a bullet through the man's head, dropping him on contact, and the rest of the goons came in blasting.

Mecca then struggled to his feet and ran full speed toward the balcony. With bullets whizzing by his head and body he thought he had no choice, so he leaped.

"Everything is going to be okay," Young Carter said as he consoled Taryn. "I'm going to find him."

Taryn had been worried all night about her only remaining son. She had gotten the news from her father that he would be killed. She knew the rules to the game, but as a mother, there was no way she could accept the contract on her son. She tried her best to convince her father to call it off, but he wasn't budging.

She had been calling Mecca all night to tell him to flee. She just couldn't believe what Estes was telling her. She didn't want to believe that Mecca had killed Monroe.

Estes had decided not to tell Taryn about the baby, and he moved Leena in with him, so he could protect her. Potentially she could have been carrying a boy, and that would be another opportunity for a male heir to bear his last name. By Taryn being past her biological time frame to have babies, he wanted to shield Leena until the baby was born.

"I know Mecca didn't do what they saying he did. I went over there this morning, and his place was empty and riddled with bullet holes. I have to find my baby." Taryn cried hysterically on her stepson's shoulder.

"I will find him for you. Mecca is a soldier. I know he is still alive, okay. You know Mecca. He's probably laid up somewhere with a female right now. Them goons just came over and trashed the place, trying to intimidate him." Carter was selling Taryn a dream. He knew in his heart that if Estes put a contract on Mecca then most likely he wouldn't half-step. "Look, I'm going to check around and see what I come up with, okay."

"Okay, Carter. Thank you so much. Please bring my

baby home. I can't lose another son." Taryn grabbed his face gently. She looked into his eyes and was amazed at the resemblance he held with his father. At that moment, she had faith that he would make things right.

She then looked over at Breeze, who was on the couch crying, and went to soothe her.

"I will. I'm going to find him. Just don't worry," Carter said just before he exited the house. He hopped into his car and grabbed his phone from his waist so he could call Ace and Zyir to roll with him. He picked up his phone, but dropped it when he felt someone grab him from his back-seat.

"Yo, Carter, it's me!" Mecca said as he released Carter.

"Man, what the fuck are you doing?" Carter asked as he turned around to look at Mecca. He saw that he was shirt-less and bloody. The atrocious smell of liquor and blood invaded Carter's nostrils.

"Don't look! Stay turned around! They watching," he said as he lowered his voice and stayed crouched down out of sight. "Yo, fam, pull off so we can talk."

Carter pulled off, and once they were clear of the house, Mecca sat up and looked around nervously. "Man, they trying to kill me."

"I know. Taryn told me what was going on. Man, tell me you didn't do what they say you did."

"Hell nah, I didn't kill Money. I told you I saw them mu'-fuckin' dreads running out when I came. I didn't have my banger on me, so I couldn't get at them." Mecca kept his eyes moving.

Carter immediately had skepticism, because as long as he knew Mecca, he was always strapped. It didn't sound right, but he was going to give him the benefit of the doubt. "I knew it couldn't be true, man. You know we have to get at them niggas, right? We have to go to war."

"Most definitely, but I can't, with my grandfather on my

ass. I have to lay low for a minute." Mecca's voice began to break as he explained to Carter how he jumped off his balcony to get away from Estes' goons and landed in his pool. He needed medical attention for his wounds and was losing blood rapidly.

Carter looked at Mecca's bloody shoulder. "We have to get you to the hospital, man."

"Nah, I can't go to the hospital. Estes will find out. He has the whole city in his pocket. I need to holler at Doc," Mecca said, referring to one of his father's old friends that happened to be a surgeon. "Then after that I am going to have to lay low, feel me?"

"I got you. I'm gon' hold you down. I have an idea," Carter said as he jumped on the highway. He had to make Mecca disappear for a while and only knew one place where Estes would never look for him.

Chapter Fifteen

"This ain't Flint town, baby. Money flows like water
in Miami, and I got a crazy connect. I'm getting the
birds straight off the boat . . ."

—Carter Jones

Taryn looked directly into Mecca's eyes. A part of her
was relieved that he was safe and sound, but another
part of her ached at the fact that he could possibly be responsible for Money's demise. She could never imagine
him committing such an act of sin. Certainly the hands
that had shed her son's blood were not those of his
brother. It couldn't be.

"Mecca, I need to ask you a question. I will only ask you
once, and I need to you to be honest," she stated. Her
voice cracked from emotion. She was losing everything
that she and Carter had worked so hard to maintain. She
composed herself, and once Mecca's eyes met hers, she
asked, "Is it true? Did you harm Monroe?"

Mecca fixed his lips to answer honestly. He wanted to
be truthful with his mother, but the look in her eyes revealed her inability to forgive. Killing Monroe wasn't a
trespass that she could dismiss, and he loved his mother
too much to give her a reason to hate him. He couldn't
change the fact Money was gone, but he was still breath-

ing and needed his mother's love like a newborn that hadn't yet been removed from the womb, so he lied.

"No."

The lie ripped through his heart like a hollow-point, and he couldn't contain his emotions. He held onto his mother, trying to feel her heartbeat through their embrace while he wept on her shoulder, mourning the death of his brother and the loss of his sanity. Ever since he had killed Monroe, his head wasn't the same.

"Everything is going to be all right, son. I love you. No matter what your grandfather says, I know in my heart that you would never do what you've been accused of. Monroe was your other half, and you are too selfish to hurt a part of yourself." Taryn held Mecca's face in both hands. The sight of him so weak and exposed reminded her of his childhood years, and she wished that she could turn back the hands of time. She wanted to go back to the days when her husband was their protector, but those days were lost, and now it was up to her to salvage what was left of her family.

Mecca had tears in his eyes as he sniffed loudly. He knew that his mother was unaware that he was responsible for Monroe's murder, and the secret was eating out his insides.

"Now you are the only son I have left. Walk through these doors and you man the fuck up, do you hear me?"

Mecca knew that she was serious because swearing was something that his mother rarely did. He nodded his head in understanding.

"Your father isn't here, Mecca. My baby Money is gone. I'm not losing you too."

He hugged his mother tightly, and Breeze stepped up and wrapped her arms around him as well.

"Mecca, I love you," Breeze whispered as they all embraced tenderly.

"I love you too, *B*," he answered, holding on to her as if it were the last time he'd ever see her. He looked up at Carter, who stood next to his Uncle Polo, both hands tucked away in his Cavalli slacks. "Take care of them for me, man," Mecca said in an almost pleading tone.

"You know it, fam. Get your head right, baby boy. I don't know what's going on inside you, fam, but we need you healthy, nah mean? Don't worry about anything. I'm-a take care of everything," Carter told him.

Mecca embraced Carter briefly and gave his Uncle Polo a nod before he turned around to walk through the double glass doors and into the therapeutic mental institution.

Breeze fell into Carter's arms as soon as Mecca disappeared from sight, and her tears flowed freely down her golden face. "I don't want to lose you, Carter. Everyone's leaving me. All of my brothers are gone except you," she whispered in a broken voice.

Polo and Taryn stood silently as they watched the youngest member of the Diamond family break down. They knew it had been a long time coming. Breeze was by far the most vulnerable member of their dynasty, and with nothing but misery around her, they were all waiting for her to crack.

"Shh," Carter whispered. "That's not happening, Breeze. I'm not going anywhere, and neither is Mecca. He's going to get better, I promise you that. We're going to rebuild this family, you hear me?"

She nodded and rested her head against his shoulder as he walked her to Polo's Bentley.

"Get some rest, *B*. I'll be by to check on you later, a'ight."

"Okay," she said as she stepped into the open car door. "Be careful, Carter. I don't want to bury you too."

"You won't have to," Carter replied as he closed the door. He turned to Taryn and Polo then said, "Taryn, can I speak with Polo for a second?" He rubbed his hands over his neatly trimmed goatee in frustration, the stress evident on his face.

Taryn nodded and then excused herself to the passenger seat of the car.

"Yo, what the fuck, fam? Shit is getting wild. Mecca got these mu'fuckas after him, got his mental all fucked up. My baby sis is breaking down, and Money . . ." His words broke off in his throat as he thought of his current circumstances. He had just become acquainted with his siblings, and he was already losing them. "I swear to God, fam, I'm ready to murder Ma'tee."

Polo could see Carter was hurting, and he felt his pain. He had been a part of the Diamond family from the conception of the very first seed, and he too was feeling the burdens of the war with the Haitains. "Listen, son, we've got to stay smart . . . strategic. You said it yourself. We've got to think before we move. Right now, The Cartel's taking a lot of losses. We need to be about the business, get our money up and our soldiers strong before we get back at Ma'tee. We need to sit down and promote some of our street lieutenants—"

Carter interrupted Polo, "Nah, fam, I can't rock with them mu'fuckas, man. No offense, fam, I respect what The Cartel is and all that it stands for, but I don't trust them niggas. I haven't bled with them, fam. They don't know my hustle. I need my own people down here. These Haitains is playing for keeps, and I'm gambling with my life, nah mean? I need niggas around me that I can trust."

Polo nodded. "A'ight. Put your peoples on the first flight out, and let's get this money so we can dead this beef and get back on track." Polo walked toward his car and got in, leaving Carter standing on the curb alone.

Flipping up his cell phone, Carter called his right-hand man. "Yo, Ace, what's good, baby? It's about that time. I need you, fam."

It was all that needed to be said. Ace knew what time it was. He agreed to gather Zyir and be on the next flight out to chop it up with his best friend.

The next night Carter waited patiently as he watched Ace and Zyir emerge through the airport doors. A sense of relief instantly washed over him when he saw the faces of his two most trusted associates. With his own squad in town, he could lay niggas down with no reservations because he had his right and left hand beside him. He greeted Ace first, slapping hands with the one person he had come up in the game with. They were thick as thieves and had taken over their hometown of Flint with relative ease. They were seasoned and thorough. They had been putting in work together for years, and he knew that the transition to Miami would be a smooth one.

"You good, fam? You had me worried on the phone. You ain't sound right," Ace commented as they embraced.

Carter nodded his head and greeted his protégé, "Lil' Zyir, what's good, baby? I'm glad you came down, fam."

"My nigga call, I come running, fam. That's how we do, nah mean? Besides, it's warm than a mu'fucka down here. It'll do ya boy some good getting away from that Arctic shit up north."

Carter walked toward his Range, and they all packed their bags inside before pulling away from the curb, Jay-Z's *American Gangster* CD immediately filling the leather interior.

Out of habit Ace punched in the code to Carter's hidden compartment, revealing three chrome pistols. He removed two, tossing one in the backseat to Zyir.

Carter, Ace, and Zyir were the last of a dying breed and would never be caught without their heaters. Zyir and Ace had the exact hidden compartments in their own whips. The compartments always held three guns, one for each of them in case of emergencies.

"So what's so important that we had to come all the way down here?" Ace asked, admiring the change of scenery that Miami offered. The palm trees and busy streets seemed worlds away from the dilapidated houses and potholes of his hometown. "It's nice down here, fam," he commented as he waited for Carter to reply.

"It's the same game with a different face, fam. Don't let this glamorous shit fool you. I'm-a be real honest about the shit that's going on here. My father—"

"Your father?" Ace asked in astonishment, knowing that his best friend had never known his dad.

"Yeah. That's how all this started. My father was the leader of a criminal enterprise called The Cartel. Basically they run all this shit down here. Drugs, real estate, politics, anything that happens here, The Cartel makes happen or is a part of in some way."

"Yo, so these Cartel mu'fuckas on some real organized crime type shit, huh?" Zyir asked.

"Yeah, and business was good, up until my father was murdered by Ma'tee. Ma'tee runs little Haiti, and this nigga ain't holding no punches. Since killing my father, he's murdered one of my little brothers and sparked a war that is fucking with my money."

"Your money?" Ace asked. "You a part of this Cartel shit?"

"I run The Cartel. It's mine now, which is why I need the two of you here. Y'all know how I move. I trust both of you with my life," Carter said seriously.

"You know we're with you, fam, but how is the money

down here? We were making at least a hunnid thou a month in Flint. You know how lovely the hustle was there. We had our blocks on smash," Zyir said proudly.

"A hunnid thou?" Carter raised his eyebrows and looked at Zyir in the rearview mirror.

"Each," Zyir bragged. "That's good money, nah mean? Ya boy was eating."

"Don't worry about the cash, fam. You gon' eat. You will make a hunnid thou easy," Carter guaranteed.

Zyir nodded in approval, but he lost his mind when Carter added, "A week."

"Nigga, you bullshitting!" Ace exclaimed.

Carter remained silent.

Ace looked back at Zyir and said, "Yo, this mu'fucka is really serious."

"This ain't Flint town, baby. Money flows like water in Miami, and I got a crazy connect. I'm getting the birds straight off the boat, ninety percent pure, but these Haitains is plugging up my leak, nah mean? They are taking out my soldiers, which is slowing up my money. We about to rebuild, and when we're where we need to be, we'll get rid of them mu'fuckas."

Ace and Zyir trusted Carter and was with him before he even finished what he was saying.

Carter drove them to a luxury apartment community near the Diamond household. It was a 2,500-square-foot space with three bedrooms for them to share. They walked in through the attached two-car garage, a Hummer for each of them resting inside.

Carter removed two sets of keys and tossed one to each of his friends. "Y'all are all set up. This place is close to my family's home. They live a few miles from here. I'll take you through tomorrow to meet them and introduce you to your new workers."

"A'ight, a'ight, fam. I know we down here on business

and everything, but, nigga, this is Miami, and ya boy trying to see the city tonight. Let's do it big tonight for ol' times' sake, and tomorrow we can be all about the business." Zyir anxiously unlocked his new truck and hopped inside.

Ace and Carter laughed at Zyir's excitement, but they knew that he was young. At 18 he still had the world to experience. They had seen and done so much more than him, and they both knew that he was only trying to follow in their footsteps.

"A'ight, fam. We can do it right. I'll show y'all around town."

Miamor pulled out her cell phone in the middle of the crowded club to see if Carter had called. He hadn't tried to contact her in two days, and his sudden absence from her life was starting to bother her. She usually spoke with him at least twice a day, and he always made it a point to come and check for her. Now that he was doing disappearing acts, she didn't know what to think.

Aries could see the discouraged look on her friend's face. "You okay?" she shouted over the loud music.

Miamor looked up and realized that her two friends were staring at her, so she put her emotions at bay and replied, "Yeah, I'm good. I was just wondering what time it was."

"Why hasn't he called you?" Robyn asked, not buying Miamor's lie.

"He's going through a lot right now. His brother just died, and his family is having—"

"Do you hear yourself right now?" Robyn said to her. "Miamor, he is a mark. The Cartel is our mark. He runs The Cartel now. They killed Anisa."

With each day that passed, it was becoming more difficult for Miamor to keep up the charade. Yes, it was true that she harbored ill feelings toward The Cartel and wanted to murder Mecca. But it was also true that she was falling in love with Carter. She knew it, and in a way she hated herself for it. She felt like a traitor. She wanted to be wifey, wanted to be a part of Carter's life, but she knew that what she was building with him would eventually be torn down by a plot that she herself had devised. When the time came, she was going to kill him. She didn't have a choice.

"Miamor, you have to get he to break de truce with Ma'tee. That is the only way we can get de bounty on de Cartel. Push him, Mia. Make he react," Aries urged.

Miamor nodded.

"Are you sure you can handle this?" Aries asked.

"Yes," she answered simply as she took a sip from her Long Island Iced Tea.

"Then handle it," Robyn told her.

"Look, this is going to take some time. The Cartel is not like any of the other jobs. I have to be careful. Carter isn't dumb. He'll see straight through me if I'm too pushy. I have to do this my way. I have to play wifey so that he'll trust me, but don't worry, it's gonna get done. I'm good, just trust me."

"Fuck it. That's not what we here for anyway. Let's just have a good time," Aries said.

The girls agreed, and Miamor leaned with her back against the bar as she swayed sexily to the music. She made sure that she could see every angle of the club, a habit that she had acquired over the years. She was always aware of her surroundings.

Miamor held the attention of many of the men in the club. Her black spaghetti strap Prada dress dipped low in the front, revealing her C-cup cleavage and her flat stomach, and silver Choo stilettos accented her shapely, athletic legs. Her healthy hair glistened under the strobe light and was cut in a long bob with Chinese bangs, while her

MAC cosmetics complemented her almond-colored skin.
The term "Shorty is the shit," had to be meant for her, because her features always outshined every other chick in
her vicinity, and that night was no different.

Miamor watched as most of the women in the club
flocked toward the door. She squinted to see who had entered the club that deserved so much attention.

"Speak of the devil," Robyn commented as she saw
what the commotion was all about.

Carter and two other men walked into the club clad in
Cavalli jeans and fresh kicks. Carter simply wore a gray
Lacoste sweater with a white collared shirt underneath.
He was simple, but his jewels stood apart from every
other nigga in the club. He was wearing so many karats
that he was almost hypnotic as the strobe lights played
hide-and-seek with the diamonds around his neck.

Miamor watched as Carter and his friends selected
three girls to take up to the VIP section with them.

"That's why we can't get shit poppin', Mia?" Robyn continued as if Carter didn't impress her. "The nigga is playing you, Miamor. He has your fucking head gone. You
sitting up in here turning down mad niggas, waiting on
him to call, and he out courting these busted-ass bitches."

Miamor could feel her temperature rising. She was hot
as she watched Carter place his hand on the small of the
girl's back and guided her through the crowd. *Is he for
real?*

"Just say the word and I all over that bitch," Aries
stated.

The sight before Miamor had her tight. She was so
upset that she was seeing red, which usually meant blood
was about to be shed, but she controlled herself and
saved face in front of her girls. "Fuck him. He ain't my
man. The nigga is a job, nothing more and nothing less,"
she stated coldly. *I can't believe I was feeling his lying*

ass, she thought to herself. She wanted to leave the club, because deep inside she knew that her heart was broken, but she stayed. She knew that if she left, she would be admitting that she was falling for him.

She couldn't believe what she was seeing. Carter was hers. At least, he was supposed to be, and she was jealous that his attention was focused on another woman. Carter was popping bottle after bottle of champagne and had his arm draped around the young woman as if he were proud to have her on his hip. *This is bullshit*, she thought silently as she inventoried her competition. The girl with Carter was pretty in the voice, but her twice-borrowed dress and Claire's jewels were a disgrace. *This shit is un-fucking-believable*, she thought.

Her girls looked on in shock. They could tell that Miamor was beyond upset.

Carter was having a good time. His head had been fucked up since arriving in Miami, and it felt good to have his niggas by his side again. For a long time, Ace and Zyir had been the only "brothers" he'd known, and he trusted them whole-heartedly. His love for them ran deep, and they shared an unbreakable bond.

He looked around at the random chicks that Zyir had picked out of the crowd and had to admit he hadn't been so carefree in a long time. Carter was what some women would call arrogant. He was very selective when it came to who he shared his time with, and it was very rare that he dealt with a lot of women at one time.

It was even rarer to see him in a nightclub, but Zyir and Ace had talked him into it, so he decided to let loose. He told himself that he deserved to relax after all that he had been through in the past couple of months.

Carter noticed that their drinks were getting low, so he leaned over and whispered for Zyir to go to the bar to get some more Moët. Zyir arose and made his way over to the bar. He slid into the empty space next to Robyn and placed his order.

Robyn automatically clocked his pockets when he pulled out a wad of cash. She had to admit, she was impressed, because he was working with all big faces. *I should rob his young ass*, she thought playfully to herself.

Zyir noticed her watching and smiled as he licked his full lips. "Ay, ma, why don't you and your girls come and join me in VIP?" he stated.

His boyish charm was cute, and Robyn could tell that he was young from his approach. "What's your name?" she asked.

"Zyir," he replied.

When the bartender brought his drinks, he grabbed the three bottles. "You coming, or you gon' hug the bar and wait for one of these broke-ass niggas to come over and waste your time?"

Robyn leaned over and whispered in Miamor's ear, "You wanna go?"

Miamor shrugged nonchalantly. "It's whatever."

"We don't have to stay. Just let that nigga see that you see him. Maybe his guilt will get shit moving a little faster." Robyn turned to Zyir and said, "Lead the way."

Miamor took a deep breath and followed behind her girls as they approached Carter's table. Her stomach was in knots as she continued to watch him closely. It seemed like the closer she got to him, the more her eyes began to fail her. Tears built up, and she was forced to blink them away before they could fall.

"Yo, my friend and her girls are going to join us," Zyir stated as he sat the bottles of Moët down on the table.

The girl had Carter's face turned toward hers, and she had his full attention as she whispered something in his ear, so he didn't even notice Miamor.

"Yo, I didn't get y'all names," Zyir stated.

"I'm Robyn."

"Aries."

"Miamor."

As soon as her voice blessed Carter's ears, he turned his face and looked up at her in surprise. He could tell from the hurtful expression on her face that she had been there for a while, and he instantly knew that he had fucked up. He withdrew his arm from around the groupie and stood up.

"No, please don't let us break up y'all little thing," Robyn protested sarcastically to Carter.

Carter tried to make eye contact with Miamor, but she refused to look at him. She just shook her head in disgust before beginning to walk away.

Robyn turned to Zyir. "Thanks for inviting us over, but it looks like you all have enough company as it is. It's a shame too, 'cuz you had potential, young'un," she said sweetly as she lightly kissed his cheek, and they walked away from the table.

Carter excused himself and followed behind Miamor. Grabbing her arm gently, he stopped her from leaving as he tried to explain. "Miamor, it's not what it looks like," he began.

Miamor snatched her arm from his grasp and shook her head in disbelief. She was pissed and hurt. She hated herself for caring so much when the man before her was simply supposed to be a means to an end. *What is it about him?* she asked herself silently.

"Come on, ma, say something."

Miamor wanted to forget what she had just witnessed. A part of her wanted to leave the club with him, but she had never been a silly broad who believed lame excuses, and she wasn't about to become one that night. *I know what the fuck I saw. He was all in the bitch face a minute ago. If I hadn't walked up, he would probably be taking the bitch home tonight. Fuck him.*

"You know what, Carter? It doesn't even matter. Now I know who you really are. You are just like every other nigga—a liar."

Her words hit him like darts to the heart. When she turned to walk away, he reached for her hand. "Miamor."

Just then the girl he had been with in VIP eased up behind him and wrapped her arms around him as she stared Miamor down. It was obvious she was trying to make her presence felt and stake her claim. Miamor shook her head and backpedaled toward the door.

Carter removed the girl's arms from his body.

"You just made this so much easier for me. He's all yours," she said as she stormed away, her stilettos stabbing the floor to death with each step before she disappeared through the exit of the club.

The pain that was etched on her face was the last thing that Carter saw before she left. "Fuck," he whispered.

"What's wrong, daddy?" the girl asked.

Carter looked down at the girl, and all of a sudden she had become a nuisance. "Look, ma, I need some air," he said. "I'm not trying to play you or nothing, but ain't shit poppin' off tonight, a'ight." Then he walked away, leaving her dumbfounded in the middle of the dance floor.

Chapter Sixteen

"Just do your job and be my fucking bulletproof.
That's what being a rich, spoiled, dumb little bitch
gets you—a mu'fucka like you to take bullets for me."

—Breeze

"*Hi, you've reached Miamor. Unfortunately I'm un-available right now. Leave me a message, and I'll return your call.*"

Carter hung up his phone and sighed deeply from frustration. Miamor refused to take any of his calls. Each time he attempted to contact her, she gave him the fuck-you button and sent him straight to voice mail. He knew that his mind needed to be on his paper chase, but the feelings that he had begun to develop for her was unlike anything he'd ever experienced with a woman. He had never found any one who held his interest in the way that she did, and now he was kicking himself for being so stupid. He knew what it must have looked like, but he never intended on taking the girl from the club home with him. She was just someone to entertain him and his boys for the time being. He knew that it didn't make his actions any less hurtful in Miamor's eyes, and he hoped that she gave him the chance to make things right with her before she decided to write him off completely.

Carter maneuvered his car in front of Ace and Zyir's

building then called upstairs to let them know he was outside. It was time for him to get focused. With his own team in town, money was sure to flow. The sooner he got paid, the sooner he could avenge his brother's murder and move on with his life. He was on a three-year hustle plan for Miami. He wanted to flip and re-flip his money into the hundred-million-dollar range, and he knew that it was entirely possible, considering Miami's lucrative drug trade, and his father's real estate company, to which he was now the acting CEO.

Ace and Zyir hopped into Carter's truck, and he pulled away from the curb.

"Yo, fam, what was that shit that happened with you and that chick in the club last night?" Ace asked. He had noticed his friend's demeanor change drastically, but was too wrapped up in his female acquaintance to address it.

"Man, some ol' crazy shit. The chick Miamor that Zyir brought over to the table, I been kicking it with her since I've been down here. I didn't know she was in the building. My actions would've been a whole lot different, nah mean?" he stated with a smirk.

Zyir laughed from the backseat. "Shorty was tight. I could see that shit all on her face. I ain't mean to throw salt in your game, fam."

"It's all good," Carter said. "I'm about to introduce the two of you to my family. This is serious, and all jokes aside, whenever they are around, it has to be about protecting them. I'm not trying to see anything else happen to them. They've been through enough, and I'm all they have left right now, at least until Mecca comes home."

Carter pulled up to the gated home and greeted some of the security he had hired to post up around the premises. He parked his truck directly in front of the magnificent house.

"Damn, yo' people's paid, fam." Zyir got out and admired the massive estate.

Carter walked into the house and was immediately greeted by Taryn.

"Carter, it's so good to see you, sweetheart," she said as she hugged him. "Have you eaten? I can fix you something if you'd like."

"No, I'm fine, Taryn. Thanks. I came by to introduce you to my friends from Up Top. They are in town because of everything that's been going on with this war."

"Well, if they can help, then I am certainly pleased to meet them."

Ace stepped up first and held out his hand. "Hello, ma'am. I'm Ace," he said politely.

Taryn smiled graciously and accepted his hand. "It's very nice to meet you, Ace, but please call me Taryn."

"And this is Zyir," Carter said, making the introduction for his second partner.

"I'm glad to have you both here," Taryn said with a grateful smile.

Carter detected the melancholy tone in her voice and knew that she was at her breaking point.

Breeze glided into the room with the accurate style of a supermodel. Her long hair was in its natural curly state and was held back by a silver headband. She wore black leggings with an H & M silver mini dress and silver Hollister flats. Her face lit up when she saw her brother.

"Carter! I didn't know you were here," she stated as she ran to hug him.

"Breeze, I want you to meet my best friend, Ace, and my little nigga, Zyir. They are like brothers to me. They are the only people besides me and Polo that are allowed to enter this house. No one else has my permission. They are the only ones I trust with your lives. We have to keep you both safe, okay." He spoke sternly but gently as he tried to stress the importance of his rule to his hard-headed little sister.

"Okay, I understand. I'm about to go, but I'll call you later on."

"Hold up. Where you going?" Carter asked.

"To the beach and out to meet with an event planner. Poppa used to always throw a white party for the Fourth of July, so I'm throwing my own this year, you know, to get my mind off of everything."

"That's cool, *B*, but I want you to do me a favor and take Zyir with you," he said.

Breeze looked past Carter toward Zyir. His chocolate skin and medium build attracted her slightly. The tattoos that adorned his arms and neck appealed to her. *He may not be too bad*, she thought.

Carter smirked at his sister's blatant interest in his friend, but knew that Zyir would never be interested in a girl like Breeze. They were from two different worlds.

"Okay, I'll take him," she answered as she walked out of the door.

Zyir didn't know that he was going to be babysitting, but he agreed just because his man asked him to.

Breeze pulled her two-seater BMW-Z series from the garage and pulled up in front of Zyir.

"You coming or not?" she asked sweetly as she put on oversized Chloe glasses.

As Zyir reached for her door, she pressed her gas slightly, making the car move forward without him.

"You playing, shorty? I ain't gon' chase you, ma," he said, his vernacular smooth and low.

Breeze laughed. "I'm sorry. Come on, get in."

Zyir shook his head as he entered the car, and they rolled off.

Breeze was silent as she cruised through the Miami streets. She didn't know what to say to Zyir and felt awkward around him. It was clear to see that they were extremely different, but he was sexy, and she loved his dark skin. His serious demeanor reminded her of her father.

"You don't talk?" Breeze asked innocently, once she had grown uncomfortable with the silence between them.

Zyir smirked as he let his seat back and sat down low in the car.

"What, you don't want to be seen with me or something?" she asked, frowning.

Zyir looked at her. "Breeze? Is that your name?"

She nodded.

"Breeze, I talk. I just don't like to talk when there ain't nothing to talk about. I don't talk about shopping or gossip or gay shit like that. My conversations revolve around one thing."

"Oh yeah, and what's that?"

"Money."

"Money ain't everything."

"What you know about getting money, girl? You've been spoonfed your whole life." Zyir wasn't trying to be rude, but he wasn't one to hold his tongue.

"So what? You judging me? Yeah, I grew up with money, but don't act like you're the only one who's struggled. My father died trying to give me the best of everything, so you damn right, I'm gon' take advantage of everything that he left me. Ain't that what you trying to do? Provide for your family? Or are you only worried about pushing new whips and bullshit like that?"

"I'm just doing me, shorty, that's it. I don't got no kids to think about, and bitches ain't worth the headache. So, right now, I'm about stacking my chips, nah mean?"

When she didn't reply, he answered for her, "Nah, you don't know what I mean."

"Why are you so rude? Is that how you niggas in Flint get down? You act just like Carter."

"Carter basically raised me. He's the only father figure I know. I met him four years ago when I was only fourteen. He took me in and taught me everything I know. And I'm not trying to be rude, ma, so if I offended you, I apologize. You're just a little spoiled, that's all."

"You don't even know me." Breeze couldn't believe his nerve. No one had ever talked to her that way. Most were afraid to overstep their boundaries because of her affiliation with The Cartel, but Zyir didn't care. He said what he wanted to say, and she found it attractive.

"I don't have to know you. I know your type."

"So what? Because you came from the bottom, you hate everybody that's at the top? I guess you like them ol' raggedy Reebok-wearing bitches, huh? If a chick ain't from the ghetto, then you ain't interested."

"I like smart chicks. It doesn't matter where they're from." Zyir turned to face her.

"And I'm not that?"

"I don't know. You tell me. I mean, I'll admit I don't really know you, but it seems to me that you are a little naïve, self-centered." Zyir smiled. He could see that his words were bothering her. He had to admit, she was a gorgeous young woman, but her head wasn't in the right place.

"Self-centered?" Breeze repeated, her face frowned in disagreement.

"Check it, ma—After everything your family has been through, you out here trying to throw parties and shit. Trying to keep up your perception and be the center of attention while mu'fuckas is running up in your people's funerals and killing the ones you love. You're in the middle of a war and you making yourself accessible. You're the type of target a nigga would love to touch. If I was working for the other side, you would be the first one I would gun for. You're easy to get to." Zyir looked toward her and noticed the solemn expression that crossed her face. The girl was fighting back tears, and he instantly regretted bringing up the death of her loved ones.

"Yo, ma, I'm sorry—"

"You know what? Just don't say shit to me. I get it. You think I'm stupid and spoiled, so there ain't no need for us to be social, but don't ever say anything about my family. You just got here. You don't know us. Just do your job and be my fucking bulletproof. That's what being a rich, spoiled, dumb little bitch gets you—a mu'fucka like you to take bullets for me," she said arrogantly.

Breeze pulled in front of the event planner's office and slammed her door as she got out of the car. She stopped on the sidewalk in front of the building and thought about what Zyir had said to her. She couldn't help it that she was spoiled. Her father had always provided for her, but she had never been called selfish before. Zyir's words had been like a mirror that showed Breeze her true reflection. She was her family's weak spot, and it hurt.

"Damn it!" she yelled as she kept walking past the party planning spot and onto the sandy beach across the street.

Zyir watched her from the car and put his hand over his face when he saw her storm off. "Fuck, man! I should've just shut the fuck up. All this dramatic shit ain't for the kid," he mumbled to himself. He reluctantly climbed out of the car and walked down the street behind her. "Getting my mu'fuckin' kicks dirty and shit," he complained as he walked through the sand near the edge of the water in his crispy white Force One's.

He walked up behind her. "Breeze."

"You're right," she said.

"Nah, ma, I was out of line. You're right. I haven't been here. I don't know shit, just forget about it, a'ight," he said attempting to make her feel better. He wasn't used to

being sentimental, and he had never apologized for anything in his life, so he felt awkward changing his persona
for her.

"I remember my father used to bring me here when I
was little. We would come to the beach, and he would let
me run around all day. I would shop up and down these
boulevards for hours. I was the only little girl rocking
Chanel and Ferragamo." She laughed at the distant mem-
ory and then looked Zyir in his eyes. "You see, I've always
had everything I've ever wanted, ever since I can remember. Every year he threw a white party for all of our
friends and family. Everybody came out to show The Cartel love. I miss him so much. I just want things to be how
they were before all this happened. They are taking everything from me. My father, Money, Mecca's half-crazy. All I
have left are my memories and the money that my father
left me. I'm not trying to put my family in jeopardy, but I
don't want to stop living my life while I wait around to die.
Eventually they are going to get me too," Breeze whispered, as tears burned her eyes.

"No, they not, ma," Zyir said confidently. Seeing her so
weak hit a soft spot with him.

"How can you be so sure?"

"I'm your bulletproof, remember?" He nudged her
shoulder gently, trying to make her smile.

She wiped her face and smirked slightly. "Sorry about
that comment."

"It's nothing, shorty, but for real, if you want to make it
through this war, you got to be just as smart as the mu'-
fuckas gunnin' for you. Don't be the weak link, ma. If you
wanna go somewhere, all you got to do is call. I'll take
you, 'cuz, believe me, a nigga ain't murking me."

"Thank you, Zyir," she said graciously as her curly hair
blew with the ocean-misted wind.

"You're welcome, beautiful."

"Oh, so you think I'm beautiful?" Breeze grinned as she put her sunglasses back over her eyes.

Zyir shook his head and grabbed her hand to lead her back to the car. "You still trying to throw this party, or you gon' be smart and play it safe?"

"I trust you. I don't want to put my family in danger."

"Well, let me put you up on some new shit, something that will occupy your time." He hopped into the passenger seat and said, "Take me to the nearest bookstore."

Breeze and Zyir spent the entire day together. He took her to Borders and introduced her to reading, which was a pastime that she never had.

The most that Breeze ever did was flip through the pages of fashion magazines, but Zyir spoke about African American literature as if she were missing out on something. His obvious passion for reading was intriguing. He piqued her interest as he spoke fervently about authors such as James Baldwin, Langston Hughes, and Alice Walker. He even put her up on street fiction, starting her out on Donald Goines and then suggesting street writers like Ashley JaQuavis, Keisha Ervin, and Sister Souljah. Breeze had never met anyone like Zyir. He was intelligent, honest, and most importantly, she felt safe when they were together. She trusted him with her life, and she had just met him.

"What am I going to do with all these books? I can't read them all today. Maybe I should come back for some later," Breeze said, almost intimidated by the stack of books that were piling up in her hands.

"I'm-a tell you like Carter told me. Start at the beginning and work your way through until you've read them all. You've got to feed your brain, ma. Don't let these crackers hide shit from you within these pages. That's how they keep our minds imprisoned. That's why I said there is nothing more unattractive than a dumb chick," he said. "I'm surprised Carter ain't gave you that speech yet. The nigga stay grilling me and I ain't even his family."

Breeze laughed. "Well, that's a conversation that I can avoid having because you've already taught me. I guess I'll take them all then."

Zyir purchased all of the books for Breeze, and when it was time for her to go, she was reluctant to go back home. "I had a good time today," she said.

"Me too, ma, me too."

"I just feel like I finally have someone I can talk to, you know? My brothers are all about this war, and I sort of get lost in the sauce. This was nice."

"I better get you back."

Breeze shook her head in protest and smiled. "You bought me all these books and now you gon' leave me hanging? You know I might need you there to help me get through some of these big words, you know, since you think I'm dumb and all."

"First impressions are sometimes wrong. I misjudged you."

"So tonight is not over yet?" she asked as she stepped into her car.

"Nah, shorty, it ain't over. We can kick it at my place."

Zyir told her his address, and twenty minutes later, they were pulling up in front of the building.

Carter pulled up to Miamor's place and saw her as she walked across the parking lot with ten shopping bags in her hands. He smirked when he noticed that the bags were all from high-end designers. *She is definitely high-class. She can hurt a nigga's pockets for real.*

He admired her runway strut before approaching her. "You need some help?"

"What are you doing here?" she asked quietly as she stopped dead in her tracks.

"We need to talk."

"There's nothing to say," she answered quickly and sternly.

Her tone was short, and he knew that she was still upset. The way her jaw clinched was an indication as to how mad she really was. Her jealousy told him more than her words could ever say. He knew that she had feelings for him that ran deeper than she wanted to admit, and that she was stubborn, and it would take some effort for him to get back in her good graces.

He pulled the bags from her hands and motioned his head for her to walk ahead of him. She hesitated, but didn't protest as she began to walk into her building. The natural sway of her hips commanded his attention as he followed behind her.

The smell of vanilla filled Carter's senses as soon as he stepped foot inside her home. Her place was spotless, and that was one of the things he loved most about her. She was clean. She was sensitive. She was a real woman.

"Thank you for carrying my bags up. You can leave now," she said as she opened the door for him and folded her arms across her chest.

"Can we talk?"

"I told you ain't nothing to talk about," Miamor stated. "Go talk to your little girlfriend from the other night." She knew that she was being childish, but she didn't care.

"She was nobody," Carter stated as he stepped into her. He put one hand on the side of her face and swept her hair from in front of her eyes. "She was just some little bitch I met at the club. You don't have to worry."

Miamor laughed arrogantly. "Worry? Look at me, Carter—Do I look like the type of bitch that needs to worry over a nigga? No! I have a million in line that were waiting for you to fuck up. They didn't have to wait very long now, did they?"

Carter nodded his head, and for the first time she saw him get angry. His nose flared slightly, but he kept his composure.

"Okay. I'm-a let that slick shit you popping slide, because I fucked up. I hurt you."

"Whatever. Please do not give yourself that much credit," Miamor replied quickly. She knew that she had to keep the smart comments rolling off her tongue to stop herself from crying. "You know what? I don't even know why you are here. You don't have to explain anything to me. I'm not your girl, and I don't really give a fuck about what you do. I'm just glad that I found out how you are before I . . ." She stopped speaking abruptly before she said too much. *Don't let this nigga control the situation. Keep your emotions in check and use them to your advantage.*

"Before you what?"

She was silent as she tried to keep her composure.

"Tell me," he demanded.

"Before I gave you a chance to break my heart."

Carter closed his eyes and rested his forehead against hers as he released a deep sigh. She could see the regret on his face, and it was then that she knew he never meant to hurt her.

It was too late for her to care though. She had let him into her heart, and he had showed her shade, no matter how small it may have been. He was her enemy. *Yep, nigga fall right into my trap, lying-ass mu'fucka. You should feel bad*, she thought angrily.

"I'm sorry, ma. I was stupid. I shouldn't have even been in a club, especially with a bitch. I've got a lot on me right now. She didn't mean shit, and she ain't shit to me. I don't even know the girl's name. I apologize for hurting you," he whispered.

"You didn't," she said, her words stubborn and cold.

"I did. I can see it in your eyes, Miamor, and I am sincerely sorry, ma. I'm caught up in some shit with my family right now, and I wasn't thinking. I don't want you to doubt the way that I feel about you."

His words were making her weak, and she felt a single tear escape her eyes. "Just leave me alone," she whispered. Miamor wanted to kill Carter so badly that she could taste his blood in her mouth. *I hate this nigga, but I love his ass too*, she thought.

How could she love a man whose organization took her sister away from her? She was so torn and confused that she didn't know what to do. Her girls were wrong, Carter didn't have her head, but he was slowly capturing her heart.

It's too bad, I'm-a have to murder this nigga, she thought sadly.

Carter pulled her away from the front door and closed it. With her back against the wall, he kissed her neck gently. Her nipples hardened, and he removed her shirt and unclasped her bra in one motion. His hands were experienced, and he'd perfected the art of seduction like a ball player perfected his jump shot.

His full lips found their way to her breasts, sucking them gently before making his way further south. He removed her jeans, slipped her panties to the side, and licked her pussy so good that she automatically forgave him. His warm tongue wiggled in and out of her honey slit with skill. She felt the throbbing sensation in her swollen clitoris, and his lips circled around the tender spot as he sucked on it slowly, gently, passionately, French-kissing it with skill.

He slipped two of his thick fingers inside of her as his tongue continued to work its magic on her clit. His fingers felt like a hard dick as he caused her to squirm from his touch.

"You forgive me?"

"No," she moaned as she rotated her pussy in his face. She looked down, and the sight of her juices all over his face aroused her even more. She grinded furiously on his fingers as her pussy squirted multiple orgasms. She never knew getting her pussy ate could feel so good. Either the niggas she was fucking with before were amateurs, or Carter was blessed, but either way she was in heaven.

He stood back to his feet, leaving his jeans on the floor beneath him. His dick already rock-hard from the pleasing sounds erupting from Miamor. His fingers were still inside her, and she was pleading for him to continue. His manhood grew another inch, just from the seductive look on Miamor's face.

"Please put it in," she moaned. "Carter, I need you. My pussy needs you."

Carter lifted one of her legs around his waist and rubbed the head of his dick up and down her wetness. His head resembled a flower in bloom, and the width of it was mesmerizing. The heat radiating from him caused her to tremble as he teased her by rubbing it slowly against her puddle of wetness.

"Please, baby, put it in!"

He pressed the tip against her clitoris repeatedly, causing her to hump nothing but air. She was fiending for the dick, she wanted him so badly.

"You forgive me?"

"I can't," she said.

"Yes, you can," he replied as he filled her tight space.

"Oh my God! I can't, Carter," she moaned, tears slipping down her face. "I want to kill you," she admitted through her moans.

Carter was oblivious to the fact that she meant every word.

"I hate you," she moaned over and over again.

Carter lifted her other leg and balanced her against the wall as he dug into her, going in as deep as he could go.

"Ooh shit," she called out. "Right there, daddy! Yes, right there!"

"You forgive me?" he asked as his fingertips melted into her voluptuous ass.

"Yes! Yes! Oh . . . what are you doing to me?"

"I'm fucking you, ma. Them other niggas can't do this pussy like this. You fucking with another nigga?" he asked as he clenched his ass muscles.

"No! Only you. This is your pussy, Carter. I hate you! This is yours, daddy. Oh my . . . oh shit," she moaned. "I'm about to nut, Carter. I'm cumming . . . aaah!"

Carter felt her body tense up, and when her walls contracted on his dick, he released his seed inside her, with no condom and no regrets.

Her legs gave out when he set her back on the floor, so he picked her up and carried her into her bedroom. He lay down with his arms wrapped snugly around her.

Miamor felt so right in his arms, and she hated what she was doing. She knew that she would eventually have to destroy him, but being with him right now at that very moment was the only thing that she wanted to think about.

"I'll never hurt you again, ever. On everything I love, I'm-a make you mine. I love you, Miamor."

She couldn't stop herself from responding, "I love you too."

Ring, ring!
Ring, ring!

The shrill sound of Carter's cell phone woke him and Miamor out of their peaceful sleep. He looked at her digital alarm clock, which read 3:42 a.m. He groggily reached for his phone. "Hello?" he answered as he sat up in bed.

"Carter! Thank God! It's Breeze," Taryn stated in a panic. "She hasn't come home yet."

"What?"

Miamor sat up when she heard Carter's tone of voice. "What's wrong?" she asked.

Carter held up a finger for her to hold on and returned his attention back to his phone call. "Look, if she was with Zyir, I'm sure she's fine. I'll call you when I catch up with them. Give me about an hour," he said.

Carter knew that Breeze should have been safe with Zyir, but when he called his phone and didn't receive an answer, he began to worry.

"I got to go, ma," he said as he jumped up and began slipping into his clothes.

Miamor's face expressed her disappointment, and under normal circumstances, he would've handled her later, but he had just gotten back into her good graces.

"Slip on some clothes. You're coming with me," he said.

She jumped up, and in five minutes flat they were out the door.

Carter pulled up to Ace and Zyir's apartment at 4:15 a.m. and was relieved to see Breeze's car sitting out front. He still needed to see her face to make sure she was okay. *What in the fuck is she doing over here anyway?* he thought to himself. He rushed up to apartment 8B and rang the bell.

Ace answered it. "Damn, fam! Whatever it is, it can't wait until the morning?" he asked sleepily.

"Where's Zy?"

"Fam is in his room. He's been in there all night with the door closed. Why? What up?"

Miamor stood silently as she watched anger cross Carter's face.

"Is Breeze in there with him?"

"I don't know, fam."

Carter walked to the back of the apartment and opened Zyir's room door without knocking. He took a deep breath when he saw his baby sister sleeping soundly in Zyir's bed, with Zyir sleeping in the chair next to the bed, his feet propped up. They both had *Dope Fiend*, by Donald Goines, in their hands and had fallen asleep with the book still open.

Carter laughed at himself for thinking the worst. Zyir would never put his sister in danger or disrespect him by hitting and running on her. If Breeze was interested in Zyir, it was a bridge that he would cross when they all got there, but for now, she was safe and he was satisfied.

"Everything good?" Ace asked.

Carter nodded. "Yeah, fam, everything's good. I'm tripping. We gon' crash on your couch out here until morning, a'ight."

"Yeah, bro, make yourself at home. You know where everything at."

Carter placed a call to Taryn and informed her that Breeze was just fine.

"Are you all right?" Miamor asked.

"Yeah, I'm good. Let's get some sleep," he said as he pulled her near and closed his eyes.

Chapter Seventeen

"The coke connect died with my grandson. . . .
Now get the fuck out."

—Emilio Estes

"I got you, young'un. I'm about to go and talk to Estes and try to plug you in. The game is all yours now," Polo said just before hanging up the phone with Young Carter. He was just about to have a meeting with Estes. He wanted to see if he could set up a meeting with him and Carter, so he could retire and move to LA. He was done with the seesaw game that treated him both good and bad.

He pulled up to the loading dock's parking lot and smoothly got out, wearing a straw sun hat, and a toothpick sticking from his mouth. He saw that Estes and his henchmen had already arrived before him, just like he expected. He slowly approached the Dominican men, who stood on the boardwalk that led to Estes' speedboat. He raised both of his arms without them having to instruct him. He knew the drill only too well.

After getting searched, he boarded the boat and saw Estes at the head of the bow, his back turned, smoking a Cuban cigar.

"Good evening, Estes," Polo said loudly as he stuck his hands in his white linen pants.

Estes signaled for his henchmen to pick up the anchor so that he could take off.

"Polo," Estes said, not even giving him the respect of looking him in the eyes. Estes started the boat and pulled off.

Polo sat in the seat uncomfortably and wondered where Estes was taking him. He slightly moved his hat off his head, but not all the way off. He didn't want the small .22 caliber pistol he had under the hat to fall.

After a ten-minute ride, Estes finally stopped the boat, and all they could see was water. There was no sign of anything else but the royal blue Atlantic Ocean.

Estes turned to Polo and took a deep puff of his cigar. "You wanted to talk, right? Talk," he said coldly.

"First, we need to get at the—"

"That's already taken care of. The entire Haitian mob is dead. There will be no more bloodshed. The only one left is Ma'tee, but we cut his legs from under him. He has no money or no army, and most likely Miami won't see him again."

Polo was surprised at how quickly Estes moved. Estes was two steps ahead of him, managing to wipe out the whole Haitian mob with ease. He knew that Estes was the boss of all bosses, and it was another day at the job for him.

Polo continued, "Yeah, I wanted to discuss a few things. You know, since Carter died, I've been the one you've supplied. The way I see it, I'm not getting any younger, and the game has changed. I'm trying to make an exit and give this game up for good."

"You're a smart man."

"I really have faith in Young Carter, and I was wondering—"

Estes raised his hand to stop him from talking. "Let me tell you something. I never liked you. Hell, I never liked Carter, but I gave him the connect because my daughter was in love with him, and I wanted him to be able to provide for her. So, you see, this is where it all stops. No more product for The Cartel. I want nothing to do with you people. The connect died with my grandson," Estes said as he looked past Polo.

Naturally Polo followed his eyes and saw that two boats were approaching. "Oh, so that's how you gon' play it, huh?" Polo asked in disbelief as he nodded his head repeatedly. He was ready to go for his gun, but he saw the two boats pull up, one on either side.

Estes stood up and began to unzip his pants. He unleashed his small tanned penis and began to urinate on Polo's shoes.

Polo quickly moved his feet, and it took all of his willpower for him not to go for his gun and shoot Estes in the face. He felt totally disrespected, but he knew that he would only be committing suicide if he did that.

One of the men picked up a small one-person rowboat and tossed it in the water.

"Now get the fuck out," Estes said calmly as he turned his back to Polo.

Polo clenched his jaws so tightly, it began to hurt as he realized that Estes was going to make him row all the way back to shore. Swallowing his pride, Polo stepped onto the small boat, staring a hole through Estes the whole way down.

One of the henchmen tossed Polo a paddle, and they all pulled off, leaving Polo alone in the middle of nowhere. Polo, his ego bruised beyond repair, knew at that moment it was time to leave the game alone. He was tired of everything that came with it. If that would have been five years ago, he would have gone out guns blazing for the stunt that Estes pulled. But Polo had matured and knew that he would've started a fight he could never win.

Carter would have to find his own connect and start from the ground up. In the meantime, Polo had some serious paddling to do.

Chapter Eighteen

"Ain't shit changed! You know the deal, so stop playing yourself."

—Miamor

Miamor's hands shook uncontrollably as she chopped the peppers and onions on the cutting board. She took a deep breath. *Why am I so fucking nervous?* she questioned silently as she worked swiftly, following the recipe book to a tee, trying to complete the meal she was preparing for Carter before he arrived at her house. Her eyes darted towards the clock. She didn't have much time. She needed to be dressed and finished before he knocked on her door.

She stuffed the smoked salmon with a lobster, portobello, and spice bake then put it into the oven. She prepared a special lemon sauce to drizzle over the top of it once it was done baking.

Miamor didn't know how she had gotten so deeply involved with Carter, but she was ready for it all to end. She wasn't acting like herself, and the pressure that her girls were putting on her was becoming overwhelming. She knew that she had to make a move and do it quickly, but everything was so uncertain now. Miamor's head was spinning.

Carter had thrown shit in the game by going hard at Ma'tee. The entire Haitian operation had been disabled, and, Ma'tee, a man who she had thought was so untouchable, was now on the run for his life. She was frustrated and confused all at the same time. She felt like a trader. She wanted to kill Mecca for bringing the Grim Reaper to her sister's door, but there were too many doubts. Too many variables had been added to the equation. An eye for eye did not seem as simple as it did before she met Carter. He was making her weak. With three little words, he'd changed who she was.

Ding-dong! The ringing of her doorbell startled her.

He can't be here yet. It's only eight o'clock. He's not supposed to be here until nine.

She quickly went to the mirror that was hanging near her entryway and scanned herself. She wasn't even dressed. Carter had never seen her dressed so casually. She wore a wife-beater with baggy sweatpants, and her hair was pulled up in a raggedy ponytail. She tried to run her French tips through her hair to make herself look a little decent, but that was useless.

She sighed deeply then opened the door slightly. "What are you doing here so early? I'm not even dressed yet, Carter."

"You look fine," he replied as he leaned down to kiss her on her forehead. "You don't have to dress all up. We're staying in anyway. This is your house, so be comfortable."

"Comfortable is not the same as tore down," she joked as she went back to the mirror.

Carter walked up behind her and kissed the nape of her neck as he slid his strong arms around her waist. He looked at their reflection in the mirror. "You're beautiful, ma. Stop tripping."

She smiled. Carter was considerate and always made her feel like she was worth more than she was, because in actuality, she felt like she wasn't shit. He was caring, and she wasn't. If she was, there would be no way that she could have put thallium sulfate in his dinner. She had made sure to put the odorless, tasteless powder in the lemon sauce that she planned on drizzling over his lobster. She was done bullshitting with The Cartel. She concluded that the timing would never be right for her to get at them, so tonight was just as good as any.

Unfortunately for Carter, he would be the first to go. She really needed to kill him first because then she wouldn't have him around all the time, making it difficult for her to stay focused.

"Are you hungry?" she asked sweetly as she pulled out one of her dining room chairs and motioned for him to have a seat.

"I don't know. Is the food safe to eat?" he asked.

His statement threw her off slightly.

Does he know? "W-what?" she asked, her eyes penetrating his.

"I mean, you know you ain't the world's best chef." A smile appeared on his face.

Miamor gave him a playful left jab to the chest. "You ain't funny, nigga," she said, breathing a sigh of relief. *Relax. He doesn't know anything is up. Stop acting so damn guilty.*

Her silent demands caused her nerves to settle some, and she went to the oven and pulled out the lobster then fixed two plates of food.

Her heart began to beat so loudly in her ears that she was sure that even Carter could hear it as she placed his dinner in front of him. She lit the candles on the table, poured them both a glass of wine, and then grabbed the lemon sauce. She poured it all over Carter's lobster then took a seat.

"This looks good, ma. Thank you for cooking for me. I

know you said you didn't like to cook. I appreciate you going through all of this trouble."

Miamor smiled and watched him intently as he took a sip out of his wine goblet.

"I want to talk to you about something important," Carter stated. He didn't wait for Miamor to respond. "I'm into you, Miamor, but there are some things that you don't know about me, or about my family."

I know all I need to know about your family. Miamor tried to conceal her hatred behind her eyes.

"Tomorrow is not promised to me right now, ma. My family is at war with some very dangerous people, and I don't ever want to put you in jeopardy. My father and little brother have already been murdered behind this beef. I'm willing to accept the fact that I could be next, but I would never forgive myself if something happened to you because of me. It's not safe for me to be with you, and believe me, it's so hard for me to say this to you, but right now is not a good time for this, Miamor. I can't bring you into my world right now. I would kill a nigga if he ever tried to hurt you. I love you, ma, but I'm no good for you. I have to let you go in order to keep you safe."

Miamor couldn't stop the tears from forming in her eyes. It was like his words were medicine to her ailing heart. Her conscience immediately began to turn on her. How could she hurt a man who cared so much about her? She was more than capable of taking care of herself.

Carter didn't know it, but she was the safest bitch in the city because she would pop a nigga without regret for running up, but just the simple fact that he wanted to take the burden off of her shoulders and protect her himself touched her.

Carter picked up his fork and brought it to his mouth. All she had to do was let him eat the food.

I can't, Miamor thought painfully. She stood and swept

all of the food off the table in one dramatic motion. "Aghh!" she screamed in agony as she picked up a glass and threw it at the wall in frustration. The glass shattered into tiny pieces, reminding her of how her heart felt the day that she'd held her dead sister in her arms.

"Whoa! Ma, what the fuck you doing, yo?" Carter moved toward her to restrain her temper tantrum.

"I can't do this." She shook her head from side to side. The emotional levees in her gave way, and tears built in her eyes.

"Miamor, calm down," Carter said as he took her into his arms.

"I can't do it," she cried as she breathed deeply, trying to contain herself.

Miamor wanted to get back at The Cartel for taking her sister away, but how could she, when her heart and her mind was pulling her in two different directions?

Why in the fuck did he have to tell me he loved me? Why did he have to make it so real?

Her brain felt like it was going to explode. She was playing mental chess with herself. She wanted Carter to be her opponent so desperately so that she could follow the rules of the game and defeat him. She wanted to bag his queen, not be it. She yearned to kill his family, but her heart wouldn't let her, and she was quickly beginning to realize that her only opponent, the only person standing in her way of her revenge, was herself. Her heart was following a completely different set of rules, rules that were unfamiliar to her. Her heart was begging her to open up and allow herself to feel happiness with a man. To trust a man, to believe in a man . . . her man, Carter Jones.

The emotions that she felt for him were so foreign to Miamor that they scared her and caused her to question her loyalty. In her world, hesitation never existed. There was no room for it. That was something that could get you murked in her profession. Murdering a nigga had always been simple. Some people were good at math, others good at sports, many good at singing or painting, but Miamor was good at death. When she declared war, she brought it to a nigga's doorstep without fear, without doubt, but with swagger and expertise. Now her job seemed so complex, and she didn't know what to do.

How did I let him get this close? she asked herself.

With her back to the wall, she used it for support and slid down until she felt the floor catch her. She pulled her knees into her chest, put her head down, and held herself as she cried.

Carter hadn't expected for her to take it this hard and was amazed at her reaction. He hated to see her in pain, but was oblivious to the real reason behind her outrage. *She doesn't know what the fuck she's getting herself into,* Carter thought, when in actuality he was the one in unknown territory. He was dancing with the devil by allowing himself to love her.

Carter picked her up and cradled her in his arms as she continued to cry. "Shh, it's all right, ma. I'm not going anywhere," he said.

As soon as he spoke the words he knew that he meant them. Dangerous or not, he could not stay away from Miamor. He had never felt a connection like the one he shared with the beautiful woman in his embrace. There was something about her, something that was so forbidden, it made him want her even more.

Miamor knocked on Robyn's and Aries' door early the next day. She wore Rock & Republic denims with a Lela Rose top and Christian Louboutin peep-toe pumps. Everything on her body was designer, and worth more than most people's monthly rent, yet she still felt worthless. Her usually MAC-designed face was as bare as her soul, and her hair was pulled up into a sophisticated bun. She tried to appear as if she was in control, but her red, puffy eyes revealed the truth and gave away the fact that she had cried herself to sleep in Carter's arms the night before.

Knock! Knock! Knock! Knock!

Aries opened the door.

"We need to talk," Miamor stated gravely without even offering a hello. "Is Robyn here?"

"Yeah, I think she in she room. What's wrong? You crying?" Aries asked in astonishment.

Miamor stormed past Aries and took a seat on their love seat. She placed her Gucci clutch next to her. Her cell phone rang. It was Carter calling her. She knew that he was calling to make sure she was okay. He had stayed the night at her place the night before, but as soon as daylight crept through her curtains, she got up and rushed to see her friends.

She sent him to voicemail and then looked up at Aries. "I can't do this anymore, Aries. It's over. This entire plan is done."

"What?" Aries shouted. "What do you mean, over? Why? What happened?"

"That nigga done got up in her head, that's what happened." Robyn suddenly emerged from her bedroom and leaned against the wall. "Am I right, Miamor? That is why you want to quit, ain't it?"

"I just can't do this anymore, Robyn. I can't do Carter dirty like that."

"What you mean, you can't do him like that? Oh, but you don't have a problem doing us dirty?"

"You're not the one in his face every day, Robyn. I'm fucking him! I know him, and he doesn't deserve this. I won't make him pay for his family's mistakes. I don't want to see him hurt. When does it end? I kill him or somebody in his family then they retaliate and kill another one of us. What happens after that? Huh? It doesn't bring Anisa back!"

"Miamor, he stole your sister from you."

"Don't even waste your breath, Aries. She had her mind made up who she was picking as soon as she walked through the door. We don't need her. We'll do it ourselves."

"Shut the fuck up, Robyn! You don't know shit! It's over, plain and fucking simple. Don't nothing move unless I say so! Ain't shit changed! You know the deal, so stop playing yourself. And don't pretend that you are all about the crew. You're in this for the money. This has nothing to do with my sister. Carter has already gotten to Ma'tee. There is no more beef. It's squashed. The bounty probably ain't even good anymore, so you ain't losing nothing. I'm out," Miamor yelled as she walked toward the door. She knew that she had taken it a little too far by accusing Robyn of not caring for Anisa. It was a low blow, and she knew that it wasn't entirely true, but her anger had spoken for her.

Miamor was resentful because it was always herself and Anisa that acted as the leaders. Robyn and Aries just followed suit, which meant they always played the back, while Miamor and her sister put themselves in harm's way. She wasn't trying to end up in the dirt anytime soon, so she was going to walk away . . . breathing.

"So that's it? You gon' choose him over us after all we've been through?"

"What do you want me to do, Robyn? This is it! This shit is a wrap! Aries, if you want to take it the same way, you can. It is what it is. I love you guys. You're my sisters, but I'm in love with him, Aries. I didn't mean for it to happen, and I didn't want to give him my heart, but I did. Yes, his family is responsible for Anisa's death, but how many people have we brought the same fate? We have to take responsibility for the role we played in this. We all knew it was possible. We just got caught slipping. That is something that I will regret for the rest of my life, but I won't make him pay for it."

Miamor stormed out of the house with a heavy heart. She knew that Aries would eventually forgive her, but Robyn would take it as a personal slap in the face. It was possible that their friendship may never be repaired, but it was a chance she was willing to take.

Miamor walked into her home and heard her shower running. She was glad that Carter was still there. After the morning she'd had, she needed him to prove to her that he was worth it. She walked into the bathroom. She pulled back the shower curtain and admired Carter's toned body as he washed himself. She stepped inside of the shower in her clothes and all then held on to him tightly. She hoped that he wouldn't make her regret her decision. She was taking a chance on him, trusting someone other than her immediate circle for the first time in her adult life.

"Hey, what's wrong? You're getting yourself soaked, ma," he whispered in protest, yet he never let her go.

Miamor had no regrets. She knew that he was worth the risk. She could feel his love for her even in the way that he held her. Deep inside her heart she knew that he would never hurt her. She just hoped and prayed that she could keep herself from hurting him.

"I could fucking kill her!" Robyn yelled as she paced back and forth for the twentieth time, practically burning a hole in the floor.

"What has gotten into her?" Aries asked. "Love? She's killed so many people, me didn't even know she had a heart."

"Fuck this! I'm about to call this bitch because she is

not about to just bail out on the plan. I don't care if I have to murder her little boyfriend myself—We are finishing this job! She can thank me later for getting rid of her distraction."

Robyn grabbed the cordless phone off the wall and dialed Miamor's number. The humming of a cell phone filled the room.

Aries walked over to the couch and picked up Miamor's purse. She checked inside, retrieved the phone, and threw her hands up in exasperation. "So much for that. She left she damn bag here. We have to get it together because I was depending on the money from the bounty."

A smirk came across Robyn's face as she took Miamor's phone from Aries' hand. She flipped it open and searched her address book.

"What are you doing?" Aries questioned.

"Finding Ma'tee's number. If Miamor wants out, that's fine, but we are going to get this money. It doesn't matter to me if she's with it or not. We don't need her."

Robyn located Ma'tee's number and pressed dial. She was determined to finish what they had started. By any means necessary, she was going to get paid and then get out of town.

Chapter Nineteen

"Why are you always acting like I don't matter
to you?"

—Breeze

Breeze walked beside Zyir as they headed to the
bodega where a black-owned bookstore was located.
They had grown quite fond of each other. Zyir was the
only person that Breeze really talked to. Everybody only
took her at face value, but Zyir saw through her. He knew
her and took the time to actually listen when she talked.

Zyir slowly felt himself growing closer to Breeze. He
didn't want to because he knew that it could possibly
cause conflict between him and Carter, but the more time
he spent with Breeze, the more important she became to
him. They were together twenty-four seven. Carter demanded that Zyir keep her safe, so they stayed side by
side.

At first Zyir found her annoying and immature, but once
he got to know her, he realized she was inexperienced in
the aspects of the street because her family had kept her
sheltered. She had never had to think about protecting
herself because her father and brothers had always done
it for her. Now it was Zyir's responsibility to ensure her
safety, and it was a job he took very seriously, partly be-

cause of his duty to Carter, but mostly because of his feelings for Breeze Diamond.

Day in and day out, they rocked with each other, building a solid friendship, even though they both knew they would take it to the next level if and when the time was right. They agreed to keep their friendship under wraps until they could figure out a way to tell Carter.

Since losing Monroe and sending Mecca away, Carter had been extra strict with and overprotective of Breeze. Zyir kept one hand near his waistline, the other wrapped around Breeze's shoulder, as he leaned into her.

Breeze whispered in his ear, "You need to quit fronting, acting like you don't want me to be your girl." She kissed the side of Zyir's face lightly.

Zyir smiled and rubbed his chin. Breeze wasn't as innocent as she looked, and he enjoyed her mystique. "I told you, ma, I like things like they are right now. We're cool as is. I'm not tryin'-a disrespect my man Carter by coming at you. You're his baby sister. You already know how he feels about that."

Breeze grabbed his hand that was draped around her and kissed it lightly. "I don't care how Carter feels about us. And how do you know he will trip? He will probably be glad I'm messing around with you instead of one of these other dudes out here."

"I just know, a'ight. I know Carter. I can see it in his eyes when the nigga see us together. It wouldn't be a good look for us right now," he said seriously. "You know how I feel about you, ma, but unfortunately for us, it ain't in the cards."

Breeze stopped walking and put her hands on her model-thin waist. "Zyir . . ."

"What up, *B*?" Zyir stopped walking, preparing himself to be sucked in by her charm. Zyir was usually so focused on his money, but Breeze was a constant and pleasant distraction from his everyday grind. He was constantly molding her, transforming her from a shallow little rich girl to an intelligent young woman. The beauty had always been present, and if it was up to him, he would have definitely made her wifey. If only it were up to him.

"Why are you always acting like I don't matter to you? Do you really just want us to be friends?"

That was one characteristic that Zyir couldn't change about her. She was spoiled through and through. He smiled and shook his head as he rubbed his fresh Caesar cut. "Come on, *B*, you know you matter. Stop being like that, a'ight. I'm gon' figure it out, but there's too much going on right now. We don't need to put another problem on Carter's mind. Let's wait until things die down first, a'ight."

Robyn, Aries, and Ma'tee watched closely as they sat in the BMW with tinted windows, following the young couple's every move. They had been stalking Breeze for three days straight. They needed to know when and how she moved, so constant surveillance was necessary.

Miamor had left them on stuck when she decided to grow a conscience and play wifey to their enemy, but the Murder Mamas wasn't having it. After contacting Ma'tee, they decided to kidnap the weakest member of the Diamond family and hold her for ransom. Once the ransom was paid, they planned to kill Breeze in retaliation for Anisa's murder, and then they would leave town. They hoped by then that Miamor would come to her senses. They had all been together for too long to break apart now, but with or without her, they were doing this so they could relocate to L.A. The West Coast was the only place they hadn't been yet, and they wanted to go some place where their reputation didn't precede them.

"How de fuck we suppose to grab de bitch if that nigga

always with she?" Aries screwed the silencer on her .357 Magnum. "Ah should blast he right now for being such a fucking pank, lover boy-ass nigga. How are we supposed to catch she alone if he constantly with she?"

"No," Ma'tee said. "We will stay in de shadows until de time is right, and we will get her when they least expect it. Just continue to watch. Her routine is de same each day. They come to dis same bookstore at the same time. He is her only barrier of protection, but we still have to be smart. We will get her soon enough." Ma'tee leaned back in the plush leather seat. "Soon enough."

Chapter Twenty

"... The Murder Mamas. They're ruthless. Bitches will kill they own fucking mothers without thinking twice."

—Fabian

Miamor awoke to the feel of Carter's lips on her neck. She smiled and adjusted her neck so that she could kiss him. For three days straight she had been laid up with Carter in his beachside condo. They had seen no one but each other, and being wrapped up in him kept her mind off her girls. She felt bad for switching up on them, but they didn't understand. They could never understand why she couldn't kill Carter. He was the only man who had gotten inside of her heart and made her give regard to human life. Miamor's body was exhausted from the "sexual Olympics" that Carter had taken her through. She was spent, but it was all worth it because she had pleased her man.

"What time is it?" she asked, stretching her arms above her head.

"Three o'clock. Get up and put on some clothes. I'm taking you out tonight."

No man had ever spoken to Miamor with such authority in his voice, and surprisingly she respected Carter, doing anything he asked of her.

Miamor arose, showered, and was dressed in Dolce in less than twenty minutes.

As they drove through the busy streets, Miamor's fingers intertwined with Carter's. She was silent as she watched the city fly by in a blur. *I need to contact Aries and make sure they are straight. They've been my girls for too long for me to turn my back on them now. I can help them come up on some money with a different job, but I can't go through with this one. I have to get them to understand where I'm coming from.*

Miamor was so engrossed with her thoughts that she didn't see the detour that Carter had taken until the car was parked. She frowned as she looked up at the Mercy Mental Health Hospital. She looked at Carter in confusion. "What are we doing here? I thought we were going to dinner."

Carter rubbed her hair as if she were his child. The way he soothed her made her smile. "Don't worry about it, ma, we're just making a quick stop. I need to see somebody here," he explained as he opened the car door. He walked around to her side and opened the door for her. "Come on, I don't know how long I'll be. I don't want you sitting in the car twiddling your thumbs."

Miamor got out of the car and followed him inside.

When they entered, Carter signed in and then put his hand on the small of Miamor's back as he led her down a narrow hallway into a waiting room where patients were visiting with their family and friends.

Miamor stopped walking when she saw who Carter was going to see. *So this is where the fuck this nigga been hiding,* she thought. She began to scratch the palm of her hand. Most people's hand itched when they were about to come into money, but Miamor's hand itched when she was about to commit a murder.

"Let me go holla at my brother, ma. Have a seat. I won't

be long," Carter whispered then pecked her quickly on the cheek.

It took all of her self-control not to run up on Mecca, and she stared cruelly at her sister's killer.

Carter snapped her out of her daze. "Ay, you good?"

Miamor nodded and forced herself to look away. "Yeah, I'm good. Go ahead. I'll be right over here."

Carter approached Mecca and slapped hands with him. "What's good, fam?" Mecca eyed Miamor. "That's you?"

Carter laughed. "That one's off-limit, fam. How's everything with you? You good? You need anything?"

"Nah, I'm good, bro. Have you heard anything from Estes?" Mecca asked. "I'm tired of hiding out in this mu'-fucka like a bitch. This shit in here is too calm, fam. I'm ready to come out busting at whoever standing in the way."

Carter shook his head. "That wouldn't be smart, Mecca. You barely survived the first time. I know your record. You ain't got to prove shit to me, fam, but your grandfather is operating on an entirely different level. If he wants you touched, then you will be touched. Just give things some time to settle down. You talking to the therapists about Money?"

Carter knew that Mecca didn't want to talk about Monroe's murder, but he was worried about his brother. He'd noticed the change in Mecca after Money's demise and thought it might be wise if Mecca could get whatever was bothering him off his chest.

"Fuck these crackers, man, they will never understand," Mecca replied.

Fabian emerged from his room and into the visiting room. He was eager to see his mother. She had traveled from Virginia just to come and see her only son. He sauntered out of his room with his piss bag taped to his stomach. Walking past Mecca's table, he stopped mid-step and stared in shock at Miamor. His yellow skin turned pale white as if he had seen a ghost. "Oh shit, man, oh shit!" he stated as he began to cry. He ducked down directly behind Mecca's chair.

Carter noticed the strange man and frowned. "Fuck is this crazy nigga behind your chair, fam?"

Mecca turned around and looked down at his crouching roommate. "Fuck is you doing, nigga? Is there a problem?"

"Please, man, please, man, just hide me. I don't want to die, man. Please just hide me," Fabian begged.

Mecca and Carter looked around the room. There wasn't one person in the room that seemed to be paying attention to Fabian. They didn't know that Miamor, who was calmly sitting in the corner, flipping through a magazine, had chopped off his most precious jewels.

Carter shook his head from side to side and stood from the table. All of a sudden, being inside of the hospital was becoming unbearable. *These mu'fuckas in here are loony as hell*, he thought.

Fabian was so deathly afraid of Miamor noticing him that he stayed crouched to the floor as if he were in the army, and maneuvered his way back to his room. He even missed his visit with his mother because he was afraid that Miamor would see him.

Mecca extended his hand and slapped hands with Carter.

"Stay sane in this mu'fucka, fam. Call me if you need anything, and be careful. Estes got eyes everywhere, nah mean?"

"Yeah, I hear you. Be easy, duke."

Mecca pulled up his sagging pants and strolled back to his room, where his roommate was hiding out. He looked at the nigga in disgust. He had never even held one conversation with the man. Mecca wasn't in the hospital to make friends. He simply needed to lay low for a while, so conversing and entertaining niggas that weren't on his level was pointless. He knew that, once they found out who he was, they would try to get on and would hassle him about being down with The Cartel.

"Is that bitch still out there?" Fabian asked.

"What the fuck? You running from a chick?" Mecca asked. "What, the bitch trying to stick you with child support or something?" Mecca laughed at the sight of the grown man crying before him.

Fabian shuffled to their bedroom and peeked outside in the hallway. Once he saw the coast was clear, he closed the door. "It's not just any chick," Fabian explained. "She's a Murder Mama."

"Say what?" Mecca had never heard of the group, so he wasn't impressed.

Fabian went underneath his bed and pulled out a box. Inside of it were newspaper clippings and one photo of the four girls together. "Man, I'm not in here because I'm crazy. I'm hiding from these bitches called the Murder Mamas. They're some killers, family."

"Some bitches?"

Fabian nodded as his eyes continued to roam nervously.

"Yeah, nigga! I'm telling you that bitch was here to finish me off. Look, man"—Fabian unzipped his pants and pulled them down, revealing his chopped off genitals.

Mecca turned his head and frowned. "Whoa, fam! Pull up your fucking pants, yo. You bullshitting on that faggoty shit, mu'fucka."

"I ain't on no homo shit, fam. Just look at my dick, nigga. These bitches did this to me," Fabian stated. "That bitch that was here with your visitor chopped me up."

Mecca's looked at Fabian in shock. "With my visitor?"

"Yeah, man. How did that bitch find me?"

"She did that to you?"

"Yeah, man, her and these two bitches—The Murder Mamas. They're ruthless. Bitches will kill they own fucking mothers without thinking twice." Panic-stricken, Fabian began throwing the little clothing he owned in a plastic garbage bag.

"Stop bullshitting, nigga."

Fabian shoved the pictures in Mecca's hands. "Look, nigga, that's a news article on them. They almost got caught up in some bullshit in New York. Needless to say, somebody produced some big money and made the case disappear."

Mecca's nostrils flared when he stared at the news photo. He saw four girls—Miamor, his brother's new chick, two girls he didn't recognize, and Anisa, the girl he had killed in the hotel room. He knew that Ma'tee had tried to have him hit that night and had sent the girl at him. He put two and two together. He knew that Miamor had to be sent by Ma'tee to get at Carter.

"Who do they work for?" Mecca asked, to confirm his suspicions.

"Nigga, anybody who can afford their services. I heard that this boss nigga from St. Louis paid them to do a job against some hustler he was beefing with. They fucked around and killed that same nigga two months later because somebody put that cake up to have it done. They don't have no loyalty, man. Anything is game. You see what they did with a nigga love stick, man. I got to get the fuck up out of here." Fabian peeked out in the hall once more then rushed out of the room.

Mecca's head was spinning. If it were under any other circumstances, he would have fucked Miamor. The fact that she had the balls to cut a nigga dick off amused him.

He had never seen any shit like that in real life, only in the movies.

Carter couldn't have known that this chick was affiliated with Ma'tee. From what Mecca knew, Miamor had been fucking with Carter for a little while now, so he silently wondered why she hadn't made her move yet. He didn't want to jump to conclusions. He needed to get out and back on the streets so that he could keep a watchful eye over his brother's new girlfriend, and find out more information, but he knew that if he left anytime soon, then Estes would put the dogs on his heels. Mecca decided that he would fix his problems with his grandfather first, and as soon as it was safe, he would find out more about The Murder Mamas . . . before it was too late.

Chapter Twenty-one

"I am Miami, nigga!"

—Mecca

"Zyir . . ." Breeze mumbled as she held both of her legs open for him, giving Zyir a clear pathway to her clitoris. The sand on her back and the waves washing up on the shore heightened Breeze's first sexual encounter. She had never felt the type of pleasure she was experiencing at that moment, staring into the stars and moaning constantly.

It was around midnight that Zyir had convinced Breeze to sneak out and talk with him, and what started off as a conversation ended up becoming a night of passion.

Breeze had masturbated plenty of times, but she was a virgin to a man's touch. Zyir operated on her love box like a skilled surgeon would on a patient on the sands of the small, secluded beach just five miles away from the Diamond estate. She moaned loudly as she gripped his head tightly and moved her buttocks in a circular motion, gyrating in his face.

Zyir arose from Breeze's warmth and looked into her green eyes. Never had he seen a woman so pure, so beautiful. "You are very special, ma," he said in a low tone. "I want to be inside you." He let his rock-hard pole exit his boxers.

Breeze's body squirmed as she was soaked with her own juices. She gently grabbed Zyir's face, and they began to kiss passionately.

As Zyir attempted to enter Breeze's tight virgin wound, she grabbed him by the shoulders, stopping him. "Zyir, you got a condom on?" she asked.

Damn! Zyir thought as his world came crumbling down. He wanted to feel her virgin walls without any latex. That was a dope boy's dream, and she was ruining it for him. "Come on, ma, I want you so bad right now." Zyir rubbed his tip against her clitoris, trying to persuade her to finish what they'd already started.

"No, Zyir. No glove, no love. Let's just run to that 7-Eleven around the way." Breeze moved his pole and sat up.

Zyir took a deep breath and gave in. "All right. Let's go. You drive a hard bargain, ma," Zyir said.

They both broke out into laughter and put their clothes back on.

Zyir pushed his black tinted Benz through the Miami streets like a madman. He was anxious to feel the inside of Breeze Diamond. As they approached the store, he swerved into the parking lot, almost hitting another car. "I'll be right back," he said as he threw the car in park and jumped out. His manhood was erect and pulsating, showing in his baggy jeans.

He walked into the store and headed straight to the front counter and grabbed a three-pack of Magnum condoms. "Let me get this and a box of lemon heads," he said as he tossed them on the counter to the pimple-faced Asian clerk.

That's when the bell rang, indicating someone was entering the store. Zyir's eyes immediately shot toward the door, and he saw a beautiful woman walk through. He didn't want to stare, but the Daisy Duke shorts she was wearing, not to mention her pumps, demanded his undivided attention. His soldier stood even straighter in his jeans as she strutted behind him to get in line.

"Looks like someting's happy to see me," she said in a thick accent.

Zyir looked down and saw his rod pitching a tent in his pants. He smiled as he looked back up at the girl, but he got a big surprise—A .22 semi-automatic pistol was pointed to his head.

"Getcha bitch-ass hands up," Aries said as she gripped the gun. She looked over at the clerk, who looked like he shitted on himself. "And turn your Jackie Chan ass around before ah smoke yuh."

Instantly the clerk put his hands up and turned around as ordered.

Zyir kicked himself for not having his gun on him. He was so worried about pussy, he didn't even think to grab his gun out of his glove compartment before getting out of the car. He glanced out of the store's front glass window and saw a woman stuffing Breeze into the trunk of a Dodge Charger. He immediately yelled, "Damn!" while keeping both of his hands up. He knew that the Haitians had sent for her, and watched the girl walk backwards toward the door, the gun still pointed at him.

Once she exited the door, she lowered her weapon, jumped into the Dodge, and they screeched off.

Zyir quickly ran out and went to his car, but he noticed that all four tires had been slashed. "Shit!" he yelled as he rushed to the passenger side and grabbed his gun out of the glove box. He ran to the middle of the street, busting his gun wildly, trying to hit their tires, but they were too far away. Zyir dropped to his knees in the middle of the

street with both hands on his head. He had failed to protect Breeze, and guilt consumed him. He screamed,
"Nooo!"

Ma'tee smiled as he peeked through the safe house's
blind and saw the Dodge Charger pull in. He knew that
their payday was soon to come, and the thought of his
murdered daughter came into play. He promised himself
he would make the Cartel family feel the same pain that
he had just experienced.

Aries and Robyn had been tailing Breeze and Zyir for
days and were waiting for the right moment to put their
plan into play. They noticed that they were getting careless, and Ma'tee wanted to pounce on the opportunity. As
the girls brought Breeze, a pillowcase covering her head,
Ma'tee sinisterly smiled.

Ma'tee was in dire need of money since Estes' goons
had robbed all of his safes and took all of his drugs. He
had nothing left. Not even one of his former workers
made it; they were all dead. He was lucky he wasn't at the
house when they ambushed him. Actually he wished he
was, so he could have died with his baby's mother and
only child.

Ma'tee instructed the girls to take her to the back room,
where only a mattress on the floor occupied the room.
When they got to the room, Robyn aggressively tossed
Breeze onto the floor by the mattress and locked the door
shut.

Breeze had duct tape across her mouth under the
pillowcase, so she was unable to scream. He arms were
also duct taped behind her back. Fear took over Breeze's
body as she cried and used her legs to scramble to the
corner. *Oh my God, they are going to kill me*, she thought
as she tried her hardest to escape from the duct tape.

Breeze was unlike the other members in her family and hadn't been exposed to the drugs or hands-on violence. Not built for a situation like this, panic overwhelmed her. She heard someone come in the door, and that's when her nerves got the best of her, and she vomited. The tape caused the vomit to stay in her mouth, choking her.

I can't breathe, I can't breathe, she thought as she choked on herself.

Suddenly she felt a strong hand snatch the pillowcase from her head and then the duct tape. Her throw-up flowed out of her mouth as she began to cough harshly.

Ma'tee stared at Breeze and was amazed on how beautiful she was. He was in total awe of her. Her silky black hair and olive skin tone were marvelous to Ma'tee's eyes. *Too bad I have to kill she*, he thought as he paced the room, staring at her.

After Breeze caught her breath, she looked up at Ma'tee. "What do you want from me?" she yelled.

"Ah want revenge!' Ma'tee said through his clenched teeth.

When Breeze heard the accent and saw Ma'tee's dreadlocks, she knew who he was. At that point, she knew her life was on a countdown. She began to cry her eyes out.

Ma'tee just stared at her as if she was a work of art, no remorse in his heart. He walked out of the room and couldn't wait until he could get the fiasco over with so he could return to his homeland, where he would stay for good.

Taryn was on the floor praying and crying, a scene that was becoming too familiar. She had been through more than any woman could handle the past year.

Carter pounded his fist against the wall as Zyir, Ace,

Polo, and Mecca stood in the Diamond kitchen. "Fuck!!" he yelled as he read the ransom note that was left on the doorstep the previous night.

They had been out all night looking for Breeze after Zyir rushed and told everyone what had happened, leaving out the part about them about to have sex. He told them that she wanted to go for a midnight stroll to clear her head and that he forgot to bring his gun. Zyir was dying inside from guilt.

"I'm-a kill that nigga!" Mecca roared as tears fell down his cheek. He looked at Zyir, who was across the counter from him, with deadly eyes, not comfortable with the fact that he was with her when she got grabbed and didn't protect her. "And yo' bitch ass probably working for the dreads!" Mecca made his way around the counter to put his hands on Zyir.

Zyir smoothly slid his hand down to his pistol. He'd already told himself that he would put a hollow-tip through Mecca's forehead if he ran up on him.

Carter quickly put his hand on Mecca's chest and almost in a whisper said, "Mecca, you don't want to do that." Carter knew his young'un wouldn't hesitate to rock Mecca to sleep if he ran up. He'd taught Zyir himself to shoot first, ask questions last.

Mecca stopped dead in his tracks and looked Carter directly in the eye.

Carter prepared for Mecca to spazz out, but he did the complete opposite. Then there was a brief moment of silence before Mecca broke down in tears and lost his balance, falling into Carter's arms.

Carter embraced his half-brother. "It's okay, fam. We're going to get her back," he tried to assure him, even though he didn't know that for a fact.

"They want a million. We have to give it to them." Polo

shook his head, knowing that his goddaughter was somewhere suffering.

"Yeah, I will go to the safe deposit box now," Carter affirmed.

"No, fuck that!" Mecca straightened up and wiped his teary eyes. "I'm-a beat whoever picks up the money until he tell me where Breeze is at. I'm tired of mu'fuckas underestimating our family. We're still strong. We still run Miami! I am Miami, nigga!"

"No, Mecca, we have to give them what they want if we want to see Breeze again." Polo looked at the note that told them the time for the drop-off and the location.

"He's right, bruh. We have to play their game and see if they give her up first. But you have to stay levelheaded and chill with that wild shit. You have to think and play chess with that Haitian mu'fucka. If we outthink him, we will always win, trust me," Carter said, sounding just like his father.

Mecca could do nothing but respect it. He just wanted his sister back.

Zyir and Carter sat in his Range Rover and waited for the man that was supposed to pick up the ransom money to arrive. They were behind a closed-down steel factory and seemed to be alone, but that wasn't the case. Carter had arranged for his goons to circle the building, and Ace and Polo were on top of the factory with telescoped semi-automatic rifles, to make sure everything ran smooth.

Carter's plan was to do the switch and have one of his henchmen tail the money, hoping that it would lead them to Breeze. He decided to make Mecca stay home with Taryn. He told him that his mother needed him, but the reality was, Carter didn't want Mecca to do anything hotheaded and stupid.

"Yo, you ready, Zyir?" Carter pulled the duffle bag from the backseat.

"Yeah, I'm good," Zyir said without enthusiasm, still feeling badly for falling off his square.

Carter could sense that Zyir was taking it hard, because he knew Zyir loved to bust his gun and lived for moments like this one.

"Listen, that could've happened to any one of us, young'un. We're going to get her back though. Watch what I tell you," Carter said as he saw a tinted Hummer pull up. He watched as the man rolled down the window, exposing himself.

A dreadhead who didn't look over a day over 16 years old appeared. He was dark as tar, with wild, nappy dreadlocks all over his head. "Yuh got de money?" he asked as he looked down into Carter's car.

"Where's Breeze, lil' nigga?" Carter yelled as he gripped the gun that was placed on his left.

"Yuh will get de girl after we get money, after I make call to me boss, feel me?"

Before Carter could even answer, he saw Mecca swiftly come out of nowhere on a motorcycle and pull up next to the driver. Before the young dread could even react, Mecca had him by his collar, and put a shiny chrome .380 to his head. "Where is my fucking sister?! Huh?!" he yelled while getting off his bike. Mecca pulled the boy out of the window and had him on ground.

"What the fuck is this nigga doing?" Carter said in frustration as he got out of the car.

He rushed over to Mecca and screamed for him to fall back, but Mecca was zoned out. He only wanted to know where Breeze was at.

"I'm-a ask you one more time—Where . . . is . . . my . . .

sister?" Mecca gripped the gun even tighter and dug it into the boy's neck.

The boy remained silent.

Mecca, tired of playing, pointed the gun at the boy's thigh and let off a round.

"Aghhh!" the boy yelled as he squirmed like a fish out of the water.

"Where is she?" Mecca yelled again.

The young dread was full of loyalty and honor, and he knew that if he told Mecca where the safe house was, he was going to die. He also knew that if he didn't, he was still going to die. So he did what would make Ma'tee proud. He spat in Mecca's face. Blood splattered over Mecca's bottom half of his face. The young dread followed by these words," Bitch, she's dead. Chu' sister is dead bitch. Me see you in hell!"

Mecca lost it. He put five bullets into the boy's head at close range, rocking him to sleep forever, and sealing his own sister's fate.

Carter screamed, "Noooo!"

Robyn and Aries had already packed up their things. Word got back that Ma'tee's worker got killed, and they knew at that point that they had to kill Breeze. They were finished with Miami. Finished with Miamor. In their eyes, she had gone soft, which was against their creed.

As they boarded the plane, Aries asked Robyn, "Yuh ready to leave Miami for good?"

"Fuck Miami. L.A. is our next playground. They never saw bitches like us. Murder Mamas 'bout to takeover a new city, that's for damn sure. We could never eat in Miami. We've done too much dirt here. It's time to go," Robyn said as they got on the plane, leaving Ma'tee to kill Breeze. They were leaving and never looking back.

Ma'tee stared at Breeze with a shotgun in his hand. He hated that he had to kill someone so beautiful, but they didn't play the game fair. He would settle the score with The Cartel forever. As Breeze cried and pleaded for her life, he blocked the remorse in his heart. He pointed the shotgun at her head and whispered, "Say good night."

Chapter Twenty-two

"You my lady forever."

—Carter Jones

Six Months Later

A giant projector screen covered the back wall as old home-videos of Breeze as a little girl played, while people held wine glasses and mingled amongst each other, and the ballroom was decorated with balloons of Breeze's favorite colors, turquoise and cream. A live band serenaded the small crowd and created a soothing ambience.

Of course, Taryn, personal friends of the family, and "The New Cartel" were in attendance. One hour before, they'd held a memorial service in honor of Breeze's life. They'd all put personal notes and gifts from Breeze in a casket before it was buried.

Mecca didn't even show up. In fact, no one had seen him since the day they were supposed to drop off the ransom money for Breeze, and he hadn't surfaced since. After hearing the man say that his sister was dead, something inside of him snapped.

Taryn sat at the front table along with Carter, Miamor,

and Polo, trying her best to keep from breaking down and crying.

Carter noticed her agony and placed his hand on top of hers and gently gave it a squeeze. He leaned over and whispered to Taryn, "Are you sure that you can do this?"

A tear slid down Taryn's face as she returned the squeeze and looked into Carter's eyes. She was grateful for his presence. Even though he was her husband's illegitimate child, she loved him for being there in such trying times. She had planned a celebration for Breeze after grasping the fact that her only daughter was dead.

Taryn waited every day for Breeze to walk through the front door. False hopes and worry were driving her insane. It hurt her every day, knowing that Breeze's body was somewhere in a river or rotting somewhere. As a matter of fact, it took months before Taryn was willing to accept Breeze's fate, and for the family to come to the realization that the youngest member of the Diamond family wasn't coming home.

Taryn had lost a husband, a son, and now a daughter to drug wars and revenge. She was done. She had decided to move West with Polo to start a new life. She hadn't seen Mecca, her only living son, since everything had gone down, which was months ago, and she missed him tremendously. She knew it was time to leave Miami for good.

"Yes, I'm sure. I can't have any more funerals. I'm tired of burying the people I love. That's why I wanted to celebrate Breeze's life," she said as she broke down crying. She looked at the video of her husband pushing a five-year-old Breeze. She would trade anything to go back to that time.

"I understand." Carter nodded his head slowly. He looked at the video along with her and felt the pain of losing Breeze. He felt that he was partially to blame for her getting kidnapped.

He looked across the room and noticed Zyir in the middle, being very solitaire and observant. Carter could tell Zyir was taking it hard also and wondered why he was feeling so much grief when he barely knew Breeze. Little did Carter know that Zyir knew Breeze very well and was the last one to be with her before she was abducted.

Zyir felt so guilty and felt it was his fault that Breeze was dead. He'd never told Carter that he was about to have sex with her and left her side to pick up condoms, which was how she got kidnapped.

Carter looked over at Miamor, who sat beside him, and leaned over to kiss her on the cheek. "Hey, baby. I have something very important to tell you later on." He grinned slightly.

Miamor smiled back and nodded her head. She couldn't help but feel guilty at the celebration. She was sitting in the midst of Breeze's family, when she knew her two best friends were responsible for the murder. She hadn't talked to Robyn and Aries in months, and the only thing she knew was that they'd moved West, and to her knowledge, they were still up to their same ways.

I can't wait for this shit to be over, she thought as she tried her best not to look at the projection on the wall.

She was itching to see Mecca as she scanned the room. No one knew where he was. She was ready to leave her past life alone and spend the rest of her life with Carter, but not before she got even with Mecca. That was one itch that she just had to scratch. She couldn't let go of the fact that he had taken her sister from her. Revenge was still fresh in her heart, and she wanted him dead.

"Excuse me, ladies." Carter stood up so that he could go and talk to Ace, who was standing guard by the door, making sure only invited guests entered. Carter approached Ace and slapped hands with him.

"Yo, what's good? How you holding up?" Ace asked.

"I'm good. Just can't wait until this shit is over. I can't look at Breeze's pictures without wanting to break down, feel me?" Carter shook his head from side to side.

"Yeah, it was fucked up how everything went down. Zyir taking the shit hard too. I think he was feeling shorty," Ace said, talking too much.

"Is that right?' Carter didn't like what he heard, but he didn't want to ask Zyir about it, not now at least. "Yo, how is that money in Liberty City? Did they come to see you yet?" he asked, referring to Liberty City's hustlers. He wanted to know if they had re-upped yet.

"Yeah, they got ten yesterday. Them Overtown niggas, they copping heavy too. We're going to need another shipment in soon."

Carter began to rub his hands together and nodded slowly, knowing that Ace was talking big money. Ever since Carter had put his coke on the streets, he'd been making a killing. He saw more money in six months in Miami than he had seen his entire life back home. Carter had expanded his operation outside of Florida, hitting major cities like Atlanta, Houston, and New Orleans as well, and labeled his organization "The New Cartel."

The New Cartel was run completely differently from The Cartel. Carter recruited young hungry cats from all over Dade County and pushed out the old heads. He had a clique of goons trying to make a name for themselves, which made them ruthless. Miami was definitely treating him good.

"Cool, I will put in an order later this week. The way shit going, we're going to be able to retire in a couple of months, feel me?" Carter said.

"No doubt," Ace added.

Carter walked over to Zyir, who seemed like he was in a daze. He had to nudge him to snap him out of his mental hiatus. "Zyir, you good?"

"Yeah, I'm okay. Just got a lot of shit on my mind."

"We all do right now. You holding down them blocks I gave you, right?"

"Yeah, everything gravy. But yo' man been acting kind of funny lately. I don't know what's up with the nigga."

"Who you talking about, Ace?"

"Yeah. He be taking all day when I call him so I can re-up. My young'uns be running through that shit. So when he takes all day to call me back, we losing money. He never picks up my call. Shit gets frustrating, feel me? Nigga acting like a fed o' something," Zyir stated seriously, as he ice-grilled Ace.

Although he and Ace lived together, Zyir had noticed a lot of things that didn't sit right with him. Since being in Miami, Ace had changed, and it definitely wasn't for the better.

"I'll talk to him about it. Don't worry about Ace. I've known him since we were in the sandbox, fam. He ain't no mu'fuckin fed, believe that."

Carter smiled, admiring Zyir's boldness. He reminded Carter of himself at his age. Zyir was only 18, but moved through life like it was a big chess game. *That nigga don't trust anybody.*

Carter felt a hand on his back. It was Miamor.

"Hey, can I have this dance?" she asked sexily as the reggae band began to play a number.

Carter smiled as he took Miamor's hand and slowly began to dance with her. He pulled her slowly to him, and the delightful scent of her perfume made him smile. Though the mood in the dancehall was sad, Carter planned to brighten it up later that night by asking Miamor to marry him.

"You my lady forever," Carter whispered in Miamor's ear as he smoothly spun her around. *I love this woman with all my heart, and I want her to be my wife.* He closed his eyes and swayed back and forth to a rendition of Bob Marley's "No Woman, No Cry."

Miamor closed her eyes and enjoyed her man's embrace, swaying back and forth with him as she rested her head on his chest. "I love this song," she whispered, snapping her fingers that rested on Carter's upper back.

Just as Miamor opened her eyes, her heart nearly skipped a beat as she saw the crazed eyes of Mecca staring at her from across the room. The way he was looking at her would've sent chills through the toughest man's body. She regained her composure and stopped dancing.

Carter felt her body tense up. "What's wrong?"

"Your brother just walked in," Miamor said, trying to not seem startled. She immediately thought about her deceased sister and instantaneously wanted to get at Mecca. *When the time is right, when the time is right,* she repeated in her head as she imagined herself putting a hole through Mecca's neck.

Mecca viewed the whole room. He rubbed his neatly cut hair, trying to get used to not having his natural long-flowing mane. He had been dead to the world for six long months for three reasons: to stay away from Estes, to grieve his sister's death, and also to plot. He walked in and noticed that all eyes were on him. He ignored the staring and made his way to his mother, who was so busy sobbing into a handkerchief at the front table, she didn't see her son approaching.

"Hello, mama," he said as he stood before her.

She didn't respond, so he reached over the table to try to hug and comfort her.

"It's okay, mama. I'm here now," Mecca said in a soft voice. The guilt of killing the man that picked up the ransom for Breeze burdened him. Every day he regretted that he let his anger get the better of him.

Taryn looked up and saw that her baby boy was holding

her; she hugged him tightly and placed her hands on his cheeks. "Baby, I was worried about you. I didn't know where you were," she said as she hugged him again tightly, squeezing him as if he might disappear before her eyes.

"I know, I know, but I'm home now, mama, and I'm not going nowhere," Mecca assured his mother as he rubbed her back.

Mecca then looked over at Carter and Miamor and decided to go have a chat with Carter. He wanted to tell him about his woman. He was about to put Miamor on blast. He knew that Carter didn't know who she really was.

During his brief absence, he began to do research on the Murder Mamas and confirmed that they were allies with Ma'tee. Fabian had known a lot of people that the Murder Mamas had done jobs for. That immediately threw up a red flag with Mecca. Miamor was a cold-blooded killer, and he knew she had an ulterior motive with Carter, who was sleeping with the enemy.

Mecca poured a glass of wine and headed across the room to talk to Carter.

Carter continued to dance with Miamor, but he knew that her mood had suddenly changed since Mecca entered the building. "Is everything all right?" he asked concerned and confused.

"Yeah, I'm good. Just got a light headache, that's all," Miamor responded distractedly.

As soon as she finished her sentence, Mecca came over with a wine glass in his hand. He came over with a smile and greeted his half-brother with a light hug. "What's up, bro?" Mecca yelled.

"What's good, Mecca? Glad to you could make it," Carter answered.

Mecca looked at Miamor and put on a fake smile. "Hello. It's Miamor, right?"

"Yes, it is. Hello to you," she answered coldly as she stared into his eyes.

Mecca quickly picked up Miamor's hand and kissed it like a gentleman would do. He then gave her the glass of wine and said, "May I borrow your fella for a minute? We have to discuss business."

"Sure." Miamor grabbed the wine and walked over to talk to Taryn. Her blood boiled as she itched to kill Mecca. She had to just wait for the perfect timing to do it. *He's going to get his*, she thought as she sat next to Taryn to comfort her.

In the meantime, Carter and Mecca began to converse.

"It's good to see you, Mecca. How is that place that I set you up in?" Carter asked, referring to the low-key apartment that he had for Mecca in Atlanta, far out of the reach of Estes and his goons.

"It's cool. But, look, I have to tell you some shit about your girl. She's not who she seems to be." Mecca rubbed his goatee.

"What?" Carter asked, totally taken aback by Mecca's comment.

"Look, man, the bitch is foul!" Mecca said under his breath as he looked in Carter's eyes.

"Watch yo' mouth, fam," Carter said through clenched teeth. He put one hand in his pocket and raised a wine glass to his lips with the other. He eyed Mecca and could see the larceny in his heart. It took everything in him not to smack the shit out of him for even having Miamor's name in his mouth.

Before Mecca could respond, Miamor walked up to them. She had watched their entire conversation and couldn't tell what they were saying, but Carter's body language told her that he was upset. She gently kissed him on the cheek, calming him down, and then she grabbed Mecca's hand.

"I never got a chance to get acquainted with you. Can I have this dance?" she asked sweetly.

Carter looked at her like she was crazy and thought about what Mecca had just told him. He was totally confused. *What the fuck is she doing?* He stepped back and watched them begin to dance. Miamor wasn't being disrespectful since there was distance between them while dancing, but Carter was still heated.

"So I guess we finally get to talk, huh?" Miamor asked as she danced with Mecca.

They both squeezed one another's hand tightly, obviously both of them trying to hurt the other.

"Yeah, bitch! Finally!" Mecca said as he kept a fake smile on his face as a front.

At that moment Miamor knew that Mecca knew her past and her connection with Ma'tee and the woman that killed Breeze.

"You knew about Breeze getting kidnapped, didn't you? You were how they got so close and told them how to get her, didn't you?" Mecca asked.

Miamor's nails were dug so deep into Mecca's hand, blood began to trickle. "No, I had nothing to do with that, but I am going to have something to do with your murder. You killed my sister, and you're going to pay," she said between clenched teeth.

They continued to dance as if they weren't having a murderous conversation.

"Let me tell you something—You won't get the chance to kill me. I'm a mu'fuckin' Diamond, and Diamonds are forever. I got a surprise for you, Murder Mama," Mecca said sarcastically with a scowl on his face.

"And what's that?" Miamor never showed an ounce of intimidation. She was indeed a bad bitch and had tangoed with the best in her field, always coming out victoriously.

This dance she was doing with Mecca was nothing new. She was going to kill him, even if it meant she had to die in the process.

"You know, that glass of wine you just drank, it was full of sodium hydroxide, a poison that first invades your respiratory system and makes you feel like you're drowning right before your heart bursts and kills you. That shit is killing you right now. I say you have about thirty more seconds until you drop dead. You're dying, bitch," Mecca said smugly.

"Is that it?" Miamor asked. "Now, I have a surprise for you, Mecca Diamond." Miamor stopped dancing and then leaned over to whisper in Mecca's ear, "I would never drink anything you give me. I'm a Murder Mama for a reason, nigga. I gave the drink to your mama. She's dying, bitch," she muttered just before gently kissing Mecca on the cheek.

Mecca instantly looked over at Taryn, who grabbed her neck as if she was choking, her face turned bloodshot red. A small crowd began to form around her. He took off to try to help his dying mother, but just before he reached her, dozens of FBI agents burst through the door with guns drawn.

Mecca crawled over to his mother as she fell on the floor. Tears were in his eyes as he witnessed his mother struggle for air. She clawed at Mecca, as her body shook rapidly. Her eyes began to roll in the back of her head, and Mecca tried to shake his mother out of it, but nothing could save her. He saw the empty wine glass next to her and knew that there was no saving her. He had put enough poison in the glass to kill ten people, but it wasn't meant for his mother.

"Help!!" Mecca cried like a baby as tears flowed down his eyes. He watched as Taryn took her last breath and fell limply into his arms. He closed his mother's eyelids and kissed her on the forehead. Murder was the only thing on his mind.

"Everybody on the ground now!" the sergeant yelled. He went straight for Carter and handcuffed him. He began to read Carter his rights.

Miamor was in shock. "Carter, what's going on? What's going? Why are they arresting you?" Miamor watched them escort her man out.

"Don't worry about it. Come bond me out!" Carter yelled as he got guided out with his hands handcuffed behind his back. He glanced across the room at Mecca, who was lying on the floor with Taryn, and he didn't know what had happened. Carter watched as Zyir and Ace were also handcuffed, and at that point he knew that someone had been snitching. They went straight for the heads of his operation, so they knew about The Cartel and its chain of command.

Mecca went for his gun on his waist but stopped himself, because he knew that he could not retaliate at that moment with all the feds in the room. With shaking hands and a broken heart he snuck out of the back without being seen.

Carter's leather Mezlan shoes clicked and echoed through the cell as he paced back and forth. He kept wondering what they were arresting him for exactly. He figured it was in connection with his drug empire, but he was hoping otherwise. But when he saw the federal agents bring some of his workers out of Overtown in, along with bags and bags of cocaine, he knew the deal. They had seized the drugs from his stash spot.

"Damn!" He knew he was in deep shit. *How the fuck did they find out where my spots were?* Carter thought as he continued to pace the room. He ran his business very precisely, and his operation was built for perfection. They only thing that could bring turmoil was snitching. That's how he knew there was a snake amongst him. He wished he could talk to Ace and Zyir, but they were all put in different cells. The Cartel was about to go down, and the police had enough coke to put Carter away forever.

Ace sat in the interrogation room sweating bullets. He hated himself for what he had done. Two months back, he had gotten pulled over with two kilos in his trunk. The cops found it and immediately cut him a deal. As soon as he mentioned The Cartel, they knew that they had snagged the big fish. He had ratted on his own team and their leader, and for the past month, they had been putting Zyir and Carter on wiretaps, recording their conversations.

Miamor's hands shook as she guided Carter's Range Rover out of the parking lot as she headed for the police station. She had already contacted Carter's lawyer, instructing him to meet her at the precinct.

After the feds searched everyone and took everyone's names, they let the people at the party go. Miamor kept visualizing the look in Mecca's face when she told him that he'd poisoned his own flesh and blood.

As she pulled up to a red light, without warning, a strong hand covered her mouth. She could smell an intoxicant on the rag that was suffocating her, and knew it was only a matter of time before her body lost its strength. She got a glimpse of the man's face when she looked in her rearview. It was Mecca.

She was getting weaker by the second. The smell of the strong substance burned her nostrils as she began to slip in and out of consciousness. Trying to struggle against Mecca, she mistakenly put her feet on the gas, and the car began to swerve wildly.

"Aghh!" she screamed as she scratched at his arms, forgetting she was driving.

Miamor's eyes widened when she felt the car go out of control, spinning wildly and crashing violently against the brick wall on the side of the street. She couldn't help but think that this was the day she was going to die.

Chapter Twenty-three

"Yuh a long way from Miami."

—Ma'tee

Ma'tee moved around the kitchen swiftly as he prepared a meal for his new companion. He looked at
the security monitors that he had installed in each room
of his immaculate home in his native land of Haiti. He had
become extra cautious, some would even say paranoid,
since the invasion of his home at the hands of Estes. It
was the same day that fate had robbed him of his beautiful little girl.

The fresh Caribbean wind tickled Ma'tee's neck and his
paranoia kicked in full throttle, causing him to turn
around with a butcher knife clasped tightly in his hand.
He sliced at an imaginary enemy, and his breathing was la-
bored as his eyes bucked wide open. He looked around in
panic, but calmed himself down when he realized that
there was no one else in the room.

Although he loved his homeland and its majestic tropical setting, he hated been forced out of the States by The
Cartel. His entire organization had been dismantled. His
most loyal soldiers were now casualties of a drug war that
he himself had initiated. He was like a pariah on the

streets of Miami, and to show his face right then would've been like committing suicide. So he didn't have a choice but to stay low.

No one knew Haiti like Ma'tee knew it, and in order to stay alive, he needed to be in his own neck of the woods.

In fear of his life, he retreated to the Black Mountains. No one knew of his home there, and he was confident that he would be safe and could live without the intrusion of his adversaries. There were no neighbors. His 5,000-square foot home sat atop a plateau that went on for miles and miles. It was 4,000 feet above the town below, too high for sight or sound to be captured by the towns-people. He was in complete seclusion and planned to stay there until he could rebuild his empire.

He would get his revenge for the undeserving murder of his daughter. His daughter had been innocent, but she was forced to pay with her life when the Dominican mob annihilated his men. The Dominicans had taken no pris-oners and felt sympathy for no one, not even his only child. When she was murdered in cold blood, Ma'tee's world came crashing down around him because he knew that he only had himself to blame. *If they can do this to me beautiful princess, what do they have planned for me?* His body shuddered at the thought and he knew that he didn't want to find out what cruelty lie in store for him.

The only time he intended to leave his fortress was when he planned to make the trip to the market for food and supplies, and his only human contact would be that of his new queen. The woman that he knew was meant for him. The voyeur in him watched her in the monitors as she slept, and a wicked smile crept across his face. He couldn't tear his eyes away from the monitor.

Since the death of his daughter, he hadn't been the same. Something in his head, or rather his heart, was bro-ken, and he no longer respected the social limits of right and wrong. He was no longer the composed, self-respecting man that he once was. He was now a predator, and he was staring at his prey on the monitor. His dick hardened at the sight of her. She was beautiful, and he was well aware of his growing obsession.

He was supposed to kill her, that was the plan, but once their kidnapping scheme had gone wrong, he and the Murder Mamas decided it was time for Breeze to go. When it was time to pull the trigger, he couldn't will himself to complete the task. He was drawn to her beauty, which was just as addictive as the cocaine he sold. So instead of killing her, he drugged her and then retreated with her, taking her across the U.S. border on a private boat.

Ma'tee fixated and fantasized over his new island beauty. He admired her slim frame, her long flexible legs, and her naturally curly hair. He was positive that he loved her, or maybe he needed someone to love him, since his daughter no longer could, but either way, he needed her and was determined to keep her.

Her body curled up in a fetal position, and her hands tucked between her legs, she hadn't awakened since they'd made the trip across the seas. The vicious beating that the Murder Mamas had inflicted upon her had left her badly injured, and right at death's doorstep.

For six long months Ma'tee had taken great care of his young princess, nursing her back to health. Now he anxiously awaited her arousal. Her body was ripe, and ready to be plucked. He knew she was made just for him from the first moment he saw her.

He finished squeezing the juice from the fresh oranges and placed a glassful onto the tray then made his way downstairs to awaken his sleeping beauty.

She heard the heavy thud of footsteps as they descended the stairs. She played possum, not wanting to wake up and face her captors. She didn't know how long it had been since she had been taken. The last thing she remembered was taking blows to her head with a gun.

"Diamond Princess, my princess, wake up." Ma'tee placed the tray of food on the nightstand beside the luxury queen-sized bed.

Startled, Breeze jumped up and scrambled away from him. Her body shook as she put as much distance as possible between herself and Ma'tee. Her arms and legs were weak from being in bed for so long, but she was determined to get away. Her back hit the wall and she pulled her knees close to her body as she huddled on the bed. She surveyed her surroundings. There were no windows, only a pale light bulb illuminated the room.

It was far from a dungeon, however. Ma'tee had made sure that anything she could ever need was inside the room. The plush red carpet, imported French furniture, and marble bathroom made the space look like a studio apartment.

Breeze was instantly confused. She remembered being kidnapped, and she had heard the girls that had taken her say that they were going to kill her. *What happened? Why am I here?* Quivering and crying, she looked around frantically. "W-where am I?" she asked. "You can't keep me here. My family will come for me," she stated, her words breaking in her throat.

Ma'tee sat on the bed and crawled over toward Breeze. He felt his manhood harden. She was so beautiful, so young, and her body so tight, and now she was his and his alone. He ran his fingers through her hair, his eyes focusing on her as if he were staring at a piece of historical art.

She cringed as his fingertips touched her face and smacked his hand away. "Don't," she whispered weakly.

"You don't have to be afraid of me, princess. I won't hurt you. Just let me touch you," he whispered lustfully.

"No! Help me! Please, somebody help!" Breeze screamed at the top of her lungs as she fought Ma'tee off.

Ma'tee was relentless in his pursuit. He was like a dog in heat. He just had to discover the treasure that Breeze was hiding between her legs. He didn't care that she screamed in protest. No one could hear her. And even if she did run, there was nowhere for her to go. She would never be able to navigate her way through the Black Mountains and the Noire Forest that accompanied them.

He groped her and ripped at her clothes, as he forced his tongue into her mouth.

Breeze did the only thing she could think of and bit down as hard as she could on his tongue.

"Aghh!" Ma'tee screamed. He smacked Breeze across the face, causing her to hit her head against the night-stand hard enough to leave her disoriented.

A river the color of crimson flowed onto the white sheets, and she felt the pressure of Ma'tee's weight as he climbed on top of her.

"Ah didn't mean to hurt you. Ah just want to love you. Stop fighting me, my princess. Yuh belong to me now."

Those were the last words she heard before her vision became blurry, and her entire world went black.

When Breeze awoke, her entire body ached, and Ma'tee was by her bedside, watching her. She could see insanity in his eyes. *What does he want from me?* She felt a pounding underneath her skull and reached up to find a bandage across her forehead.

"So yuh finally decided to awaken?" he asked. "I tasted you while you were asleep. Me never tasted pussy as sweet as yours. Me will be with you forever."

The way he said the word *forever* caused a shiver to travel down Breeze's spine. Forever wouldn't be very long, if she had anything to do with it. She refused to live as his prisoner, even if the cell she'd been confined to was a luxury one. She'd die first. *At least then, I'd be with Poppa and Money.*

Tears came to Breeze's eyes, and her hands shakily found their way to the space between her legs. It was wet, and when she examined her fingers, she noticed the blood on her fingertips. She immediately knew that Ma'tee had been inside of her. He had touched her, invaded her, and taken her against her will. Her once virgin pussy no longer existed, thanks to Ma'tee.

"Why the fuck are you doing this to me?!" she screamed, her hatred and fear evident in each word. "My family is going to come for me, and when they find me, they are going to kill you!"

Ma'tee remained calm, because he didn't entertain idle threats. "Yuh dead to yuh family. Yuh been missing for six months. They haven't come for yuh yet, and they will never come for yuh. Nobody knows yuh alive," Ma'tee said, a smug expression on his face. "Me brought yuh hear to make yuh me princess. The longer yuh resist me, the harder it will be on yuh. Yuh can scream, fight, yell all yuh want, no one will hear. There are no windows for yuh to escape from. The doors are double bolted and chained. Yuh a long way from Miami. This is yuh new home. Welcome to Haiti."

Breeze's hopes began to die as Ma'tee's words penetrated her brain. She knew that no one would be coming for her, if what he was speaking was indeed true. She jumped up from the bed and ran up the flight of steps. "Help! Please somebody help me!" she yelled. She looked back at Ma'tee in fear as he approached her. Her screams became frantic. "Please!" Tears burned her eyes, and her hands hit the wooden door so hard that her skin began to bleed.

In her heart she knew that it was true. She had felt the sway of the boat and heard the waves of the ocean as she was being brought over to the island. She thought that it was just a dream, a hallucination of some sort, but it was her reality. She felt like a slave and that Ma'tee was her master, the man who killed her father and brother.

"Right now yuh fear me, but yuh will grow to love me with time," Ma'tee stated with a crazed look in his eyes. "Ah will never let yuh go. Haiti is yuh new home. When yuh ready, me will let yuh out of this dungeon, but not until yuh ready to accept your new life here as my queen. Forget who yuh were, and accept who yuh are now. No one is coming, ever. Me will kill yuh before me let yuh go."

Breeze fell to her knees and sobbed desperately at the feet of Ma'tee. "Please don't do this," she begged. "I just want to go home."

"This is home."

Breeze reverted to her childhood ways as anger began to simmer inside of her heart. She began to demolish the room. "This is not my home!" she screamed forcefully as she threw lamps and overturned tables and chairs. "This is not my home! Let me go!"

She broke any and everything in her path as Ma'tee watched her without giving her a reaction. Once she ran out of energy and things to break, she collapsed on the floor and bawled in defeat.

"Yuh can destroy as much as yuh want and scream all day and night. It won't change the fact that yuh here. Nothing can change that. Yuh belong to me."

Ma'tee walked over and removed the tray of food that he'd brought her. He walked past her and made his exit. Before he left, he said, "Yuh will see food when yuh show me yuh deserve to eat. The longer yuh deny me, the longer yuh will starve."

When he closed the door, Breeze heard the clicking of

multiple locks, and all of a sudden, the entire room went black. She thought of the ones that she loved. Her mother's face flashed before her eyes. Then she saw her brothers, Carter and Mecca. Last but not least, Zyir's face appeared.

Please help me, Zyir. Please don't stop looking for me, she thought as she tried to send a message from her heart, hoping that she was as connected to him as she thought she was. Even though their love was new, she hoped that it was strong enough for him to feel her presence. She needed him to believe she was alive. She needed him to get her family to come for her.

After she wrecked her body with exhaustion from crying, Breeze did the only thing that she could do. She prayed.

Chapter Twenty-four

"Who you praying to, bitch? I *am* God."

—Mecca

"Hmm," Miamor moaned as she drowsily opened her eyes and became aware of what was going on around her. "Hmm." She tried to speak, but something muffled her sounds. She jerked against the chair that she was sitting in but couldn't move. She shook the fuzzy haze from her mind and forced herself to become focused. *Okay, Mia, okay, stay calm. You can get out of this*, she thought.

Gagged and bound to a chair, her head was pounding from the impact of the crash, and she had no idea where Mecca had taken her. The odds were against her, no doubt, and she feared for her life. She knew that she was dealing with a man whose murderous abilities matched her own. Her senses were heightened, causing her anxiety to skyrocket.

She bucked against the chair quietly, trying to keep her noise to a minimum. She didn't want Mecca to realize she was awake. She needed to level the playing field and free herself from her constraints before facing him. She tried to see through the darkness that had enveloped the room. *Where the fuck am I?*

Her body ached all over, and she shook uncontrollably as the cold crept through her skin. She smelled the scent of weed burning somewhere in the room and realized she wasn't alone. She froze instantly. Unable to see, her other senses worked overtime as they helped her locate who she assumed to be Mecca. She forced the towel out of her lips with her tongue and coughed uncontrollably as the pressure eased from her choking chest.

"What the fuck you hiding for, you bitch mu'fucka?" she asked, her teeth chattering. *Why the fuck am I so cold?* She couldn't get control of her reflexes, as her body shivered involuntarily.

"You talk a lot of shit for a bitch that's tied to a fucking chair," Mecca stated as he stood. He had sat silently in the dark for hours, waiting patiently for her to wake up. He was itching to kill her since she was responsible for the murder of both his mother and sister.

As Mecca flipped the light switch, he appeared before Miamor's eyes. Her vision was blurry, and all she saw was a shadow standing in front of her. "What the fuck? I can't see," she whispered, shaking her head from side to side, trying to clear her vision.

"That's the bleach eating at your eyes, bitch. I'm gon' love killing you. I'm-a torture you slow, so get comfortable."

Miamor's eyes fell to her thighs. She was naked. Her clothes had been stripped, and she had a lot of tiny cuts all over her body. "What the fuck did you do to me?" she yelled.

Mecca didn't respond but instead circled her as if he was preparing to attack. He carried a long, thick chain in his hands. It scratched the floor as he walked, making Miamor's skin crawl from the eerie sound. He brought the chain up and swung it with as much force as he could over Miamor's body, cutting her skin almost to the bone.

Miamor cringed in agony as her eyes ran with continuous tears. She was in tremendous pain. She could see the blurry hue of blood on her legs.

Mecca brought the chain down on her again, this time using more force.

"Aghh! Fuck!! You!!" she screamed. She refused to give Mecca the pleasure of crying or begging for her life.

For years she had dished out the same cruel and unusual death sentences, so if it was her time, she wasn't going to cry like a little bitch, but be a woman about her shit and go out like the killer she was.

The chain whipped her again, this time hitting her bare breasts and stomach.

"Aghh!"

"You're not gon' beg like your sister, bitch? Huh?" Mecca asked through clenched teeth as he hit Miamor repeatedly. and he found pleasure in bringing so much pain to the person responsible for his sister's and mother's death.

"Fuck you, pussy! Faggot-ass nigga! Fuck—Aghhh!—you!" Miamor yelled. Her mind told her to stay strong, but her body rebelled against her.

"Suck my dick, you dirty bitch," Mecca stated. "I'm-a put your ass in the dirt just like I did your sister."

Mecca had beaten Miamor for so long that he was out of breath and sweating profusely. He threw the chain to the ground and retrieved the bottle of ammonia from the corner. He knew that the liquid fire would eat through her skin like acid as soon as it doused her open wounds. He unscrewed the top and splashed the poisonous liquid all over Miamor's bloody body, which now resembled that of a runaway slave.

"Aghhhhhhh!"

Her blood-curdling scream was enough to make the average man cringe in regret, but Mecca continued his relentless assault on her without mercy.

Miamor felt like she was burning alive. Her eyes, legs, arms, hell, even her hair hurt. She knew that she would never make it out of the basement alive. Mecca had too much to prove.

"Our Father, who art in Heaven, hallowed be Thy name—"

"Who you praying to, bitch?" Mecca asked, taunting her, as he slapped the words from Miamor's mouth. "I *am* God."

Miamor could hear the insanity and hate in his voice. She knew that he wasn't going to stop beating her until there was nothing left to beat. She couldn't change that fact. This was her fate. She felt herself growing faint and continued, "Thy kingdom come, thy will be done, on Earth as it is in Heaven."

The chain seared through her skin once more, but this time she didn't scream. She was past the point of pain. She was near death. She felt the walls closing in on her. She could see the shadow of the devil standing behind Mecca. She knew she wasn't destined for Heaven. She had too much blood on her hands. She had sinned beyond reproach, and the devil was waiting to snatch her soul and damn her to hell. She knew it. She embraced it. She was a bad bitch, and she was going to die like one.

As Mecca's fist collided with her face one more time, she slowly turned her head toward him. She spat blood. "Fuck you, Mecca! I hope you enjoy watching me die just like I enjoyed watching your mother and sister die, mu'-fucka!"

"Shut the fuck up!" Mecca grabbed the ammonia, pinched the sides of her mouth harshly, and poured the chemical down her throat and on her face.

Miamor struggled against his grasp, desperately trying to close her eyes and mouth. It burnt her lips and nose. She saw the Grim Reaper stepping closer to her.

"I got something for you, bitch. I'm not gon' kill you. I'm-a let my man handle you."

Miamor watched as Mecca walked out of the room and the devil stepped closer to her, her heart jumping with every step the devil took. His face came into view, and when it became fully visible, her eyes grew wide in shock. *Fabian!*

The shadow in her peripheral vision wasn't the devil, but a part of her wished that it was. Surely, death would have been better than what Fabian had in store for her. He had a score to settle. She closed her eyes to finish talking with God. "Give us this day, our daily bread and forgive us our trespasses as we forgive those who trespass against us." Her voice broke, and tears filled her eyes.

Fabian leaned into her, his hot breath blowing against her burning skin. "It's too late for prayers, bitch. You're gonna die tonight," he stated with no emotion.

Miamor couldn't believe that her past had come back to haunt her. This scary mu'fucka was the same one begging her for his life just months ago. Now he was standing before her getting ready to take her own.

"I should have cut off your fucking balls when I took your dick, mu'fucka. Do what you got to do, nigga. Fuck you!"

Fabian punched Miamor with so much force that her jaw collapsed on the right side.

Miamor felt the weight of her face as her jaw caved in. She cringed, absorbed the pain, recited the Lord's Prayer in her mind, and then spat teeth and blood onto the floor. She sat up straight and prepared herself for what was in store. She hoped for a quick death, but she knew that it wasn't going to happen, so she breathed deep, squared her shoulders, and forced herself to open her eyes, ignoring the agonizing pain from the chemicals in her eyes.

She stared Fabian directly in the eyes and smirked. *This nigga ain't a killer. He'll never be like me. Fuck it, if I'm-a go out, it ain't gon' be on my knees.* "Fuck you!"

The Cartel 2 . . . COMING SOON